THE BONE READER

MAGIC IN THE IMPERIUM, BOOK TWO

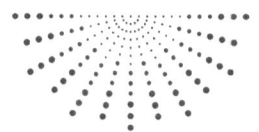

JORDAN R. MURRAY

TABLE OF CONTENTS

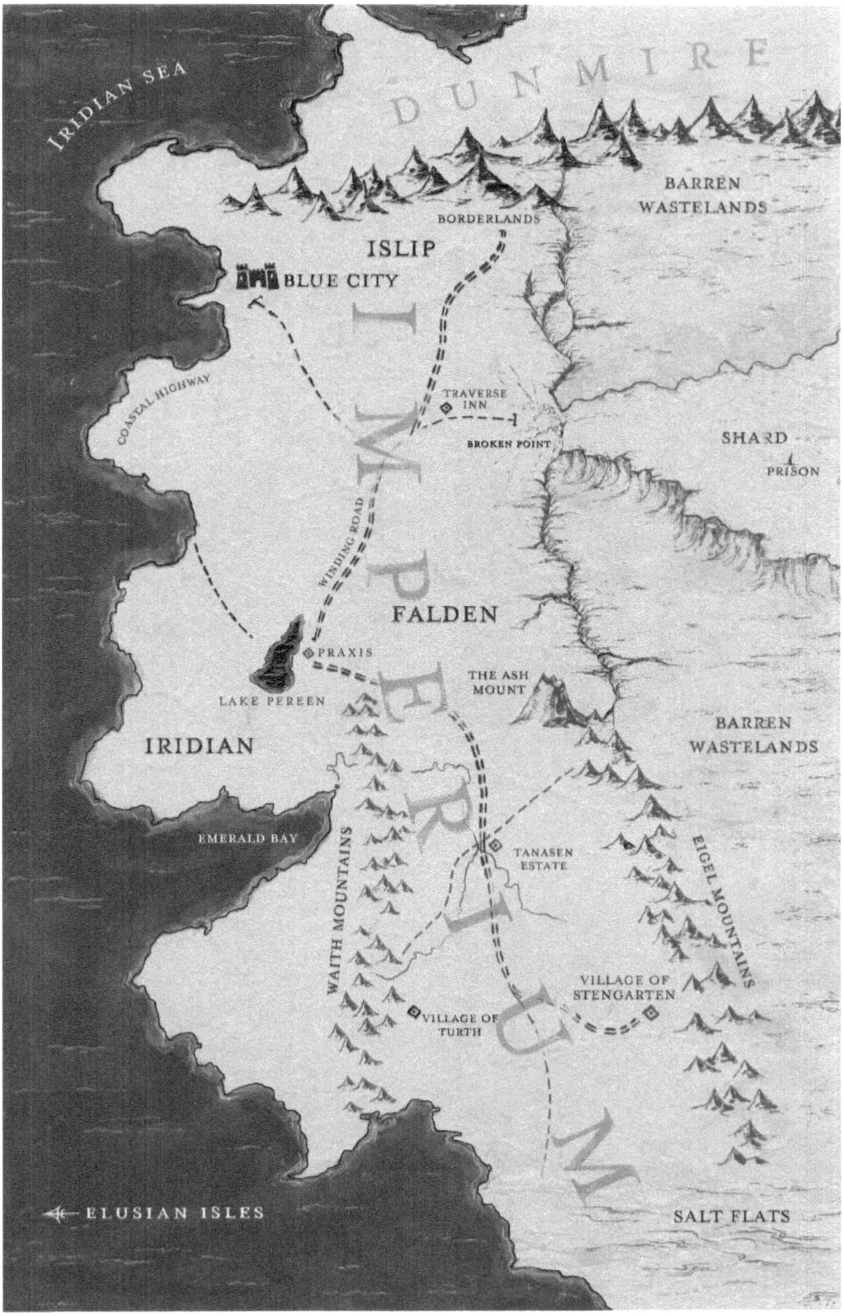
IRIDIAN SEA
DUNMIRE
BARREN WASTELANDS
BORDERLANDS
ISLIP
BLUE CITY
IMPERIUM
COASTAL HIGHWAY
TRAVERSE INN
BROKEN POINT
SHARD
PRISON
WINDING ROAD
FALDEN
PRAXIS
LAKE PEREEN
THE ASH MOUNT
BARREN WASTELANDS
IRIDIAN
EMERALD BAY
WAITH MOUNTAINS
TANASEN ESTATE
EIGEL MOUNTAINS
VILLAGE OF STENGARTEN
VILLAGE OF TURTH
ELUSIAN ISLES
SALT FLATS

Call to me bone reader,
Speak to me in the darkness.
Come to me bone shaker,
Secret keeper,
Illumine my path as you share, in grief,
My pain.
Honor me with your choosing and
We will bond in memories
Bright and sharp.
Call to the bones,
I will tell you
My end.

~ Chant from the Predestine Book of the Dead

WHISPERS FROM BONE

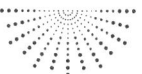

Tebral fought to contain her excitement at the heady danger of being outside and alone. A moment to calm her thoughts, a deep breath to steady her nerves. The night wind prickled and froze her skin.

She squinted at the brightness of both moons. The light was a gift she did not intend to waste, for this rare full bloom illuminated even the darkest corners of the desert. Flexing her hands, she ran her fingers along the smooth and polished hilts of her throwing knives, sheathed in her armguard. *Breathe*, she told herself. *Stay calm. Focus.*

There were as many ways to die in the desert as there were grains of sand. Tonight, she hunted darkwings, the subtle and swift killers whose victims were called *tannai pazan*, or death by surprise. Unlike sandspitters, they had no paralyzing venom or sharp spines. The low humming call of the giant birds would freeze creatures in their tracks, or force them from their dens in a panic.

Any warrior who killed a darkwing would be thrown feasts and celebrations for days. The full moons were an opportunity to prove herself. Tebral, the darkwing hunter. She liked the sound of that.

Tebral left the shelter of the rocks, trying to move without drawing attention to her position. She made good progress but risked a glance behind her at a sudden hissing. Baby snakes scattered in every direction not five paces behind her. She cursed under her breath for not seeing the nest, and ran.

There it was. A low vibration, humming in her chest. She had been marked. Where was the darkwing hiding on this cloudless night?

The sand dunes were slowing her down. As the vibration grew unbearable, she threw herself into the sand like a burrowing den lizard. A rush of air pressed against her neck.

Tebral shivered at the near miss. Spitting out sand, she dragged herself the last few feet to take cover under a thorny bramble. She looked up to see not one, but two of the birds, brilliant and sharp points of inky blackness illuminated in the night sky.

Darkwings hunted in pairs? She could not believe it. Never had such a story been told. Or, no one had lived to tell of it. Her spirits sank.

The birds climbed higher and circled her position. Hands shaking, Tebral crouched beside a needle tree and freed her heaviest throwing dagger. One of the darkwings dove.

She flicked her wrist in a practiced motion. The blade sliced into the right wing of the bird. It swerved sluggishly and, with a keening sound that chilled her blood, tried to gain altitude. Then it circled back toward its companion. The pair were moving to attack together.

This was happening too fast. Tebral unsheathed two more daggers as she tried to judge their weight against the distance between her and her targets.

There was no time. The injured darkwing turned and folded its wings as it hurtled toward her with a cry. Its injured wing slowed it little and the second bird followed closely behind.

Blinking back tears, Tebral threw her next dagger. The injured darkwing died instantly and crumpled to drop at her feet.

She had just enough time to throw her last dagger before the second darkwing closed in with a louder call. The sound shot pain through her body. She recoiled. Her dagger passed harmlessly by the second darkwing without changing its path.

There was no time left to run.

~

LAVINIA TROUG'S mouth twisted open in a silent scream as she gripped her chest. Another death witnessed; it hurt all the more when they were young. She placed the small leg bone of the girl called Tebral on a pile beside her bed.

Bones lay around her in scattered heaps. Bones, bleached by the sun. Bones, blackened by smoke and flame. Bones, cracked and splintered and stained by unmistakable signs of battle. They were her treasure trove of memories. Windows she could open with her magic for glimpses into the long-forgotten past. It was a priceless gift with a heavy cost.

For borrowed time was unforgiving. Magic burrowed inside her with agonizing precision, yet as each bone took away a sliver of identity, it brought her closer to memories of the Relic Wars, when magic was at its height. Magic as unique as the sacrifice it claimed.

Lavinia had become a shadow of her former self. Her wrinkles sank into scars, curving and cutting patterns across her whole body to strip away plump, healthy flesh. She had never been a beauty but her hair, once lustrous and soft, was now brittle to the touch and fell in wisps of white across her gaunt face. Her eyes were hollow orbs, sunken as she lost both sleep and the sharp edge of her intellect.

Surrounded as she was, by bones of an ancient battle and life beyond the Imperium, she was unable to resist such a bounty. They pulled her in, these bones. They melted her confidence into terror with their stories of loss.

The past could not lie to her and here it was, surrounding her with tantalizing first-hand knowledge. Truth, raw and unbound. Hers to unlock.

Memories of a hundred lives ran through her head. So many met a tragic end. This latest one broke through the others and overwhelmed her senses and, for a moment, she forgot who she was entirely.

A tear rolled down her cheek and fell to the sandstone. Bones were memories and memories were truth. Pure, exquisite truth.

TRAVERSE INN

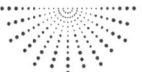

Grease lanterns spat on the downcast faces at Traverse Inn, the last stopping point before the border of Falden Province lost itself in the Barren Wastelands. The inn was a reflection of the landscape that surrounded it; tired and worn and left behind to be forgotten by the rest of the world. It was built and furnished with pieces of travelers' lives, with mismatched and broken tables and chairs that sank into unevenly worn patches in the dirt floor.

It was a pity, thought Teguin Dorst as he shifted his drink from one hand to the other. A thousand cycles ago this land was fertile and prosperous, but from what he had found in Master Lingermort's archives at Praxis, the Relic Wars had stripped the landscape until nothing of its former glory was left. Over time, the lifeless ground shifted to form broken hills, complaining by way of a constant, scouring tempest of dust and sand.

The only thing that clung to these hills was sweetgrass; a kind of thin dry leaf that was tough and prickling sharp. The inn, the furniture, everything here was made from the overgrown stalks.

Teguin could see at a glance that there was scant else to do other than eat, drink, and toil in the sweetgrass fields. It was necessity alone that made him pause at such a place, for both the history and future of the town was written in the small collection of shacks which had sprung up around the sweetgrass hills. Traveling east, those hills collapsed into fields, laboriously tended to produce the closest thing to survival that could be found.

The lost and destitute were the only ones who remained here, though it felt cruel to think so lowly of this place and its people. A grim determination to survive left little time for anything else, but it brought those that lived here together in a stubborn kind of pride which he admired. Even now, a dozen locals were bent over bowls of a sticky sweetgrass mash that resembled brown sludge. It was thin and sour but potent all the same. Despite its name, sweetgrass was far from palatable.

He was the only traveler drinking at the inn. The field hands and farmers who filled the place gave his well-made boots and fine cloak a wide berth with covetous glances. When he asked for the owner of the sweetgrass fields they kept their eyes and ears open in a way that made him all the more eager to leave.

Desperation lingered in the air like the smell of sour gruel.

"If ye value yer life, leave the Wastelands be, Teguin." The man sitting across from him sloshed sweetgrass spirits down his front in drunken enthusiasm. "Only dark terrors livin' there—"

He broke into a cough that whistled through his crooked teeth. Somewhere outside, a dog howled. Reaching their table, the innkeeper gave the man a sharp slap on the back with one hand, and a new drink joined the other cups, emptied to the last.

"Easy, Samson." The innkeeper peeled his hand away from rotting strips of snakeskin on Samson's vest and wiped it on a muddy rag at his waist. When he left without clearing the table, Teguin winced.

Distracted by the filth of the place, he tried not to guess when the rag had last been washed. When the man was out of earshot, he continued his questions, leaning forward. "But...you've been there? Into the Barren Wastelands?"

His eyes searched Samson's face, and he twisted a black ring on his right hand, pulling the sleeve of his shirt down to keep the scars on his arm hidden from sight.

"Wastelands?" The man clutched his new cup with sweaty hands and swayed back and forth. His brow furrowed as he tried to focus.

With a slow breath, Teguin forced himself to take a drink, feeling the grit of the sweetgrass on his teeth while he waited for an answer to trickle through the man's drunken fog.

"Sure have," Samson finally managed to say. "Been loads of times I, er, used t'be tradin' with the desert folk. Earned coin t'buy me my sweetgrass farm, ye ken. We're our own spot, ye see. Got the inn. Name and all, we're lookin' fer a spot on the Imperial map soon as they make it out here t'be findin' it."

Samson grinned at the accomplishment, but did not elaborate on who "they" were, and Teguin did not ask. Taking a large gulp, the cup slipped out of the man's hand and a thick liquid that resembled slime poured down his front onto the table.

Teguin leaned back in his seat to avoid the spill but the innkeeper only threw his rag down as he passed, not bothering to stop. They watched the spill pool around the towel. Before he could help himself Teguin wiped up the worst of it. The smell of the rag made his stomach protest. When he was done, he thought better of wiping his hand off on his cloak, wiping it on his boot instead.

Samson was lying. This man was no Imperial trader. It was a careless attempt to try and fool him, but Teguin was more interested in learning what the man knew than in calling the bluff.

His drinking companion had a shifty look about him and didn't use any of the words or phrases that were as familiar to a merchant as coin. He could have been a thief or scavenger, even a bandit—Teguin would have believed that without question. It was more likely that Samson took part in raids that attacked supply runs to the prison.

From what Teguin knew, the supply runs held only common goods, but in such deserted areas as these it would mean a fortune. The convoys weren't about to lose their skins for a few barrels of grain or the contents of their pockets. There was coin to be made for those desperate enough to try and escape the consequences, but if they were caught they would go with the convoy as prisoners. Maybe the gruel they served in prison was better than sweetgrass porridge.

policy, though his uncle would have scolded him for making himself such an obvious target of interest. He was tired, but that was a bad excuse and he knew it.

Distracted by the thought, he wrestled with the door which scraped and stuck on the dirt floor until he dislodged it with a hard shove. The inn was built from so many scraps that he suspected it would not stand for more than a season or two before it collapsed. If the beds were also made of sweetgrass, the dirt floor might be kinder to his back.

A black pouch was tucked in one of Teguin's deeper vest pockets. Its red powder disappeared between his fingers and, with a light touch, he traced a few lines across the door. Focusing his thoughts on the familiar feeling unique to the stone caverns of Praxis, a faint buzzing entered his mind. The nature of the door transformed until its edges hardened into stone.

There were so many unknowns surrounding the origin and use of magic, and it was no small burden to live with its consequences. Teguin grimaced at the answering stab of pain that shot up his right arm, which could glow red and crush rock and bone with little effort.

A loud snore made Teguin smile. He turned to find his friend, Herbert Tanasen, sprawled across a sagging mattress stuffed with sharp sweetgrass leaves. A heavy sleeper, Herbert was still in his traveling clothes with his long legs and boots spilling onto the floor.

The snores were impressive. Teguin hesitated to wake him, but then he remembered which of them had kept Samson talking all afternoon while the other slept. He nudged Herbert's boot. "Wake up, we need to talk."

Herbert woke with a groan, wiping at a damp corner of his mouth. "Rotten sod, this bed tastes somethin' awful."

Teguin's worries about the door relaxed at the sound of Herbert's lilting Falden accent. It amused him that his friend's farming past crept more heavily into his speech when he was tired. Twisting to fit onto the other cot shoved into the room, he reached into his cloak for the piece of glass Samson had given him, which joined a forgotten loaf of sweetbread he had bought earlier that day, but hadn't the courage to try. He sat down on the lumpy mattress with a groan.

Herbert ripped off a piece of bread, pulling at his dirty, rumpled clothing. "I'd give a whole field of green-wheat fer a bath."

"And I would trade a silver for some dried boar meat. Unfortunately, the innkeeper said it's another ten leagues down the road before we find water worth bathing in, unless you want to pay a silver to share the trough with their horses. He said that's what a lot of folk do to clean up for supper."

Herbert made a face. "Course he did. Olivia would say that a man's worth is shaped by what he gives, but have ye not seen, the faces here have a hungry look. It's the takin' part that's on their minds."

Olivia again. Ever since the woman's death, Herbert had refused to let go and move on. Her name was always on his lips, and at times it felt as though her wandering spirit traveled with them, given shape and form by Herbert's grief.

"Hand me our map, would you?"

Herbert shoved the bread into his mouth and flicked away a few leaves to pull a thin slip of parchment from his own lumpy travel sack. He tossed it over his shoulder.

Teguin caught it with a frown. "Fragile, remember?" It bothered him how little Herbert respected parchment.

At least their time studying magic at Praxis had allowed him to teach Herbert to read passably well—as few others but nobles in the Imperium could. Herbert lost no opportunity to remind him that written words were useless and archaic, while Teguin held them as priceless beyond measure.

They hunched over the faded ink that streaked the oil-stained parchment.

Teguin held up the piece of glass. "I've been with a sweetgrass farmer, Samson, for the better part of the evening. That trader back in Thestel was right, the man does know how to get into the desert without going through the Imperial checkpoints. He won't take us but he gave me this to mark the way."

Picking up the glass from the table and blinking sleep from his eyes, Herbert gave it a curious look. "That's an odd piece. So this is it, then?"

Teguin nodded. His knee protested when he knelt to search the map for where Samson's markings would coincide. Not well explored, the Barren Wastelands were an indiscriminate puddle on the map, spreading from the south-eastern border of Dunmire to the eastern part of the Eigel mountains in the Imperium. He could only guess if it stretched all the way south to the Dark Seas.

Traveling to avoid Imperial soldiers was one kind of foolishness, but entering the desert without a guide would mean a swift death. The shifting of the unstable sweetgrass fields was nothing compared to the sinking sands known to swallow a person in seconds without a trace. They needed a guide who stepped lightly and would keep them alive.

There were rumors of sandstone which cut through the heart of the desert like veins, but the scrolls kept at Praxis held as many false accounts as truthful ones, if the Masters who kept them were honest. Master Lingermort in particular loved to make his students, or prens, guess which were the most reliable before admitting he had no idea himself.

Now that he was planning on walking the desert, Teguin was determined to find as much information as he could about his destination, real or exaggerated. A less useful and particularly nasty note written along the bottom of this map cautioned: *If the sinking sands and heat do not kill you, the creatures of the desert will gladly finish the job.*

That was enough to give anyone pause. Teguin had found the map amidst piles of rotten tombs and bleached parchment in the archives. Legible notes added a kind of authenticity that other options lacked. Warnings like this hinted at experience, and surviving long enough to write them was also a good sign.

Herbert gave up the piece of glass in order to wrap the remains of their bread, tossing it toward the pile of empty bottles and labels which had spilled out of his travel sack. He grimaced, rubbed a finger over his teeth, and scratched his beard and scalp until his own personal cloud of dust hung around his head to form a shadowed halo in the light.

"Strange, this sweetgrass. T'give so much but be a trial all the while. Riddin' a mouth of the grit is terrible. Bitter, sour..."

Herbert barely managed to duck in time as Teguin tried to improve his friend's mood by throwing his only pillow, sending it flying over Herbert's head to fall against the wall behind them with a thud that shook the roof. Dust and sweetgrass leaves floated down from the ceiling.

"Terrible, even the pillows are full of the stuff." Teguin took a precious sip of water from the flask at his waist. For a fleeting moment he worried that all this sweetgrass might be changing his ability to taste anything at all.

"All the same it can't help it," said Herbert, suddenly defensive. "Imagine all ye grow on is dry dust and empty wind. Sad, really."

"Only you would make sweetgrass a victim."

"May not look or taste like much, but it's useful enough t'these folk. Buildin' their homes, purifyin' their food and drink that'd otherwise be poison in their mouths. Plenty useful."

Teguin couldn't argue that point. "Master Jayce will be excited with any plants you find him, even sweetgrass," he admitted.

Herbert brushed away dry breadcrumbs that trailed down his shirt. "I will be lettin' him make his own judgments on the flavor of it when we return." They both knew how much the Master Healer at Praxis enjoyed his own opinions over that of others.

"We keep hearin' that 'na'en' grows in the Wastelands," Herbert continued, "but if there's a bit of green I aim t'find it; it's the only reason Jayce let me come with ye. Olivia would have found a use for it, I'm certain she would have."

Teguin had learned that it was easier to accept and ignore Herbert's mention of Olivia. Protesting would only send Herbert into a dark mood that lasted for days. They had a long journey ahead of them.

"It would be a new level of boasting, even for Master Jayce." It was a hard truth to swallow that Herbert's master was more concerned with his own reputation than the potential for progress and discovery that inspired most at Praxis. Jayce had turned a blind eye to plenty of inconvenient truths, including the dangerous and violent nature of another pren, Jameson, who had tried to murder Herbert and nearly succeeded.

Teguin knew that Herbert had more than just hope of finding something growing in the Wastelands; the bottles and labels the man carried with him were proof enough of his confidence. Looking over the map, Herbert traced the Iridian sea with one finger, following the main route Teguin showed him used by merchants traveling the coastline. Then he went further inland to Falden province and found the University emblem of a Mulberry Tree that stood out in emerald green against the parchment.

"That is the way we came," Teguin said as Herbert found their path south from the University, and then due east along the Winding Road to a general area of blank, broken hills, where Falden Province abruptly changed into desert and ragged cliffs. "Here," Teguin tapped, "is where we go next. The locals call it Broken Point."

"D'ye reckon we'll find someone crazy enough t'go through these Wastelands with us?"

"If there is profit to be made, yes."

"In truth, Teguin, it feels odd t'be sneakin' in like this."

"Feran called me bereft of my senses, and that was before I told him you were coming as well. But it takes far too long to get Imperial permission, proper papers, an escort… we would have to go all the way to the Blue City, and then turn around and come right back the way we came, and only after getting approval, which could take months. What a waste." Teguin rolled up the map and gave the glass to Herbert for safekeeping, this time putting the map alongside the other folded papers in his vest, each of them precious.

Herbert stretched back out on his cot. "I wager yer uncle's wishin' he could go with us."

"How do you figure that?"

"Well, he's traveled every bit of the Imperium from what ye've told me, but has he set foot in the desert? That's like t'make a person itch in their boots."

"Jealous of sand storms and deadly beasts?" Teguin smiled at the thought. Feran would be the last person he could see in the desert.

The man liked his comforts far too much to make that journey. Sending an emissary, though… of course he gave plenty of hints. Like any merchant worth his silver, Teguin made no promises.

Herbert rescued Teguin's pillow from the floor and threw it on top of his own. "Fer all Merchant Dorst hears, the lack of trade is a ruse hidin' all manner of treasure. I'm here t'search fer plants, but ye've the harder task yet. Searchin' the desert fer what, cold tracks of Master Troug lost in the sands? Yer worse off than I am, that's fair and certain."

"There were rumors I could not ignore. If there is a chance she's alive, even a small one, I have to take it. To Master Frost, I am nothing but a ripe melon to squeeze; she takes my magic to make those experiments of hers but I swear she does not take the slightest interest in my own progress. I threatened to leave Praxis without completing my studies unless she let me do this, did I tell you?"

"Ye did what?" Herbert's shocked face reminded Teguin that he had kept a lot of his frustrations to himself since the attack last spring.

"I am surprised I said it aloud," he admitted. "I am not one to lose my temper, but she forgets all too often how painful it is to cut my shoulder open and drain this damned magic." Teguin clenched his hand into a fist, stretching the skin as he willed the constant discomfort to take a smaller part of his thoughts.

With powerful magic of her own, and a unique insight into his abilities, Teguin was convinced that Master Troug was the only person he had encountered so far who truly understood the unusual properties of Destructive magic. Her abduction was hard to bear. After months of keeping his ear to the ground, he finally had enough information and the opportunity to search for her in earnest.

Let Master Frost think what she wanted about his motives. She had enough of his magic to keep busy. And when she ran out, well, that would be the end of it as far as he was concerned.

Lost in thought, he started when Herbert hissed a warning. The sound of footsteps in the hallway came a moment later. They stopped outside their door. Though the floors were dirt, the walls were so poorly built that they shook right away when muffled blows and shouts erupted into a violent assault on their door.

"Empress protect us," Herbert said under his breath, looking wildly around them.

Teguin wanted to swear. He should have told Herbert that he flashed coin in such a desperate place. They should have left right away instead of assuming it was safe.

Only a small part of the door was hardened by his magic, but it would not hold for long. He threw both hands against the frame, focusing again on the cool and hardened stone that was a core of his being, impartial and strong.

Fists that pounded on the other side of the door. Shouts of anger when their efforts did not immediately break down the door.

How long before they tried the wall instead? Each blow grew more desperate than the last, sending sharp pain up Teguin's arms that brought sweat dripping down his face.

Who would care in this place if their blood was spilled? They were strangers. Samson had been right to warn him; they had no protection save their wits and the magic they swore not to reveal. So much for the benefits of skirting an Imperial escort.

"I can't hold them off much longer," Teguin said through gritted teeth. "The walls are like dry twigs in this place."

"Nearly ready." Rattling bottles and ripping cloth behind him told Teguin that Herbert was frantically pulling together their belongings. Then another sound distracted him to the point where he almost lost focus, wanting to watch Herbert in action. His own magic was destructive, while Herbert's was constructive, alive in a way that both terrified and fascinated him.

There was an inhuman gasp behind Teguin. A dry rasping. A crackle of energy that made the hair stand up on the back of his neck, mingling with something more, a groaning as if a sleeper of many ages awoke to stretch. And something was stretching, erupting, twisting, flinging pieces of sweetgrass roots against the walls. An ominous groan shook the inn.

Teguin had to focus for several heartrending seconds about how his hands were supposed to look like flesh and not stone before he managed to free himself. The door collapsed. Half the wall gave way to a tumble of bodies and cries of surprise mingled with fear at the sight of sweetgrass moving on its own. There was now a hole in the back wall of their room. It was large enough to squeeze through, and the twisting roots opened just long enough for Teguin to follow Herbert with his travel sack before they snapped back together into a dense cluster of sharpened, newly grown sweetgrass.

"So much for hiding magic," Teguin gasped as they hurried into the darkness.

Howling in frustration, bruised and bleeding hands clawed through the roots to find emptiness outside.

3

AN IMPERIAL EDICT

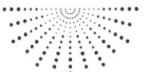

Praelor Thurst blinked as he stared out to sea. Shivering as the wind ripped through his robes, he tried to find the motion of cresting waves. He knew the waves were there, but he could not observe them. Listening to them crash against the rocks sheltering the Blue City was an empty comfort. Curse these eyes; they failed him like the rest of this rotting, feeble body.

He squinted to keep his eyes open despite the wind, but there was nothing beyond the swirling mist except for indistinct shapes in blue or grey. Coughing, he limped away like the wretched cripple he was while his escort dragged their steps to avoid trampling him. He wheezed, coughed again, and fought with each breath to reach the entrance of the Imperial palace. The palace stretched upward in defiance of wind and weather, its slim towers of deep blue stone carved into pointed spikes which erupted from the ground to reach the golden sky. Memory sharp as ever, Thurst imagined four large corner domes that connected behind the walls.

Beside the main road, the walking paths were filled with Imperial shrines. The footsteps of the many supplicants carved deep clefts in the stone, bearing witness to the many who made a pilgrimage to honor the Empress as their ruler and deity. The only prayer Thurst found on his lips that day was to not tumble into the pathways and break his neck.

A hand would reach out to steer him when he walked too far in the wrong direction. He would claw it away, intent on maintaining the ruse of independence for as long as he could. But always, the hand returned.

He stayed away from the edge of the cliffs and the road which led down to the homes of the most affluent nobles in the capital; homes which sprawled to the Iridian sea. It was once a lonely expanse of rocks and sea kelp. Now, the buildings were built so thickly across the black stone shoreline that the beach itself was hidden by layers of the mismatched shapes.

Cascades of colored domes competed with their neighbors, each lavish and fashionable and covered by a layer of sea salt. It did the eye a favor, for the garish hues were glazed and muted into a subdued radiance from the morning light. At least, that was what Thurst remembered.

A lingering chill settled in his bones as he scuttled inside. It was an unavoidable necessity to visit the Empress in person despite the worsening of his illness. He needed to keep her faith in him, especially during these unstable times. The presence of magic was growing at an alarming rate. All of Estralon was touched by its return.

With the discovery and disappearance of the Horn, Thurst feared that the Empress no longer trusted his ability to keep the magic in their Imperium under control. This summons to visit the palace marked the sixth trip in as many weeks.

With another rasping cough, he arrived at one of the more informal receiving rooms of the Imperial Palace. He stepped inside and bowed as low as his creaking back would allow. Before him sat Empress Iridinia Lealis Renulind, Sovereign of the Imperium.

Not more than fifty cycles old, she was the only surviving child of the late Emperor Theramore, who passed away when Thurst had been in the prime of his life. Any physical sign that would betray her age was cleverly disguised through the artful arrangement of her golden wig and a vast assortment of small pots she kept on her dressing table, layers of shimmering gold and creams and colors to cover spots and wrinkles. She was always waited upon by an entourage of hand-maidens who moved in a blur as she prepared to hold her daily audi-ence in the largest chamber of the palace.

Thurst felt another spasm in his back. He could almost taste the youth and beauty in the room, and it was painful for him to be reminded of how little of his own life remained. Each handmaiden was a daughter of the nobility who hoped to gain notice.

A sea of unfamiliar faces stared at him.

"Leave us," said the Empress.

Waves of perfume and embroidered cloth flowed past Thurst and out the door. He held back a sigh until they left.

It was unusual for her personal guard to wait outside. Not a cour-tesy, but an insult to him. Why would they worry about the venom of a cripple? He licked sea salt from his lips and felt the eyes of the Empress upon him. His weakness was hers as well. She needed to remember that.

"Tell me, Praelor, what progress is made?" Her voice was high and nasal. Even his failing eyes could see the shine on her lips; she liked to coat them with large flecks of gold, which matched her wig.

He swallowed hard and his throat tightened. "Radiant Majesty, there is daily progress in the collection of Artifacts. Many of them are quite old, but—"

"Are any of these discoveries your Greater Artifacts? Weapons? Powerful armor? Something of equal value to the Horn you lost?"

Thurst gave the Empress another deep bow, gasping with the effort it took. "None have been recovered so far, Majesty. But we must remember that the existence of the Horn is just as important as control-ling it. The Horn is powerful indeed, if it can collect and harness magic as it once did. What it symbolizes, however, is far more important."

"Oh?"

"That any artifact of its age could survive… I dared not hope such powerful magic still existed. We stand on the precipice of other discov-eries. I feel it."

"I would feel better, Praelor, if your words were based on more than your feelings."

He persisted. "The discovery of the Horn has changed the very nature of our search. Where one exists, there are more. We will scour the Imperium. Artifacts have gone unrecognized for so long that most may be destroyed, dismantled, or hidden well beyond our borders in the other lands of Estralon. The Imperium has traded little with neighboring kingdoms over the centuries."

"What about the Elusian Isles?"

"Well… we know little of their history, but surely such a meager collection of rocks has nothing to offer. They trade in cloth and shells, not magic."

"Do you know this? Remember this? I have no use for rumors from merchants, Praelor. If you have not seen it with your own eyes, do not waste my time by speculating."

"And what fleet would we send to investigate? There are few who would risk such a dangerous journey. Even the merchants of Emerald Bay would not risk their contracts, their livelihood, to dare spy on the Elusians."

Being alone with the Empress had its advantages. They could speak more freely. She would never have tolerated such an admission in the presence of witnesses.

When she didn't respond, he cleared his dry throat. "Praxis is at our disposal. Thanks to Master Frost's talents, and my suggestions, we have these new rings of hers ready. Even a novice can detect strong magic similar to their own."

"Good. Where are these rings now?"

"It's taken some time to coordinate, but all save for the Seeker in Dunmire shall have rings by Ferul's new moon. And our Dunmire spies are making excellent progress."

"Yes, yes." The Empress held her chin high but her tone was one of dismissal.

Thurst, who had known her since her infancy, could see that she wanted no reminder of their exploits in Dunmire. They were breaking an ancient peace treaty by sending spies and Seekers to every part of Estralon that the Imperium bordered. The discovery of such a bold move would risk a premature leap into war if they were caught at the wrong moment.

Whether their current owners would part with discovered magic or Artifacts was of no concern to Thurst. What did concern him was that his Seekers were in great danger of being discovered. It pained him to admit that he no longer had the strength to train anyone else.

While new Seekers were essential, training those who had barely scraps of magic to command would be a waste of precious time. Where were the foci, all the crystals? He would cut them from the corners of hearthstones, pry them from jeweled crowns, and rip them from the cradles of children to get what he needed.

"What of those whose paths we cannot influence?" the Empress asked. "Bandits—those nuisances the Tarnished Blades; surely, they may become stronger adversaries to our goals and the interests of the Imperium. They are after magic themselves, and you believe they may have the Horn. I want it back. Their defiance vexes me."

Thurst decided to introduce his idea with haste before they fell into an old argument. "I've had an edict written for you to look over. This should have been issued a long time ago, with how magic has faded in its potency. It would be a way to reintroduce magic as a miracle. Bring magic to your doorstep. Gather it up. Keep it close to the throne with an open, easy reason for your interest."

"An edict?"

"The first of many, if all goes well. If we were to introduce the existence of magic, but as a divine gift to the people, we would be able to act openly against those who would seek to use magic against the Imperium as blasphemers. These Blades would be seen not as bandits, but as usurpers of our very divinity."

"I see."

Thurst nodded, closing his eyes to try and calm the pounding ache in his head. "This would also be the fastest way to have access to as much magic as we can. People would rip apart their own houses in search of magical objects to bring you for your favor, or rush to learn magic for our benefit; why, we could have an army of magic wielders and even more natural-born Seekers within a matter of months!"

"I find it difficult to believe, Praelor, that once told of magic people would simply step forward. We would surely have a rush of people, but I suspect it would be just that; empty pledges with little use to my needs."

"Love and fear are powerful motivators, Majesty. We have learned what happens to people who are taught to fear magic. But what if they are told it is a thing to love, a thing to cherish?"

Thurst was not surprised by her lack of enthusiasm. He should have guessed that she would use his own past arguments against the idea. He held in a coughing fit as he instinctively squeezed the flask he kept at his side.

The Empress pulled a flake of gold from her wig and let it fall to the ground. "Without training, the revelation and use of magic would be catastrophic. It would encourage our ruin. I am surprised you would make such a dangerous suggestion."

Thurst suppressed another cough until it throttled his insides. Appealing to the Empress by way of an edict was the best way he knew to soften her. Here it was again, that same nagging problem: how could he search for powerful magic when he depended upon weak minds who did not understand.

"How would an edict help my reign?" the Empress asked again, stifling a yawn.

"I have plans," the Praelor said wearily, but he continued with more confidence than he felt. "However, I need more time. As one, the people will rise up and in time, the Horn will be ours again. We must be patient."

"And in the meanwhile, I must wait."

"I, well," he wheezed, trying to hide the shortness of his breath by clearing his throat several times. He longed to sit down but knew his weakness would only encourage her boldness. He must stay where he was while the Empress sat before him.

"Empress, our future lies in keeping those with prolific magical skills close and happy, especially nobles. That was always the goal. All who graduate from Praxis and come to court are given advantageous placements by their sponsors. Those with magic can blend in, be welcome and shown favor. It would erase so many complications to reveal magic as a natural gift, rather than conceal it."

He tried to start again, hoping to clear his own thoughts in the process. "We arrange for those with stronger magic to marry into noble families and keep them in power. Those nobles in turn will look to you for support and guidance. We must use this to our advantage, to influence and to secure a firm hold on them."

She frowned. "Declaring the existence of magic is too dangerous. It would be seen as a test, a way to lure the more powerful magic users into the open and into vulnerable positions. Those of an age with me will not have forgotten the uprising we put down just as I took the throne—or the methods used to force confessions. We put people to death for using magic!"

"Very few knew that magic was involved, Radiant Majesty. It's well known and accepted that the uprising was a threat to the Imperium. If it bothers you so, we could pardon those still alive that were involved."

"If there are any still alive."

"Their families could return to court if those involved were pardoned," continued Thurst, the appeal growing. "Those still alive would certainly have the magic to aid us in our time of need. We cannot turn away any advantage, not now."

The Empress greeted this suggestion with silence.

"Don't be too quick to dismiss a pardon as a possibility," he pleaded, annoyed at the desperate note in his voice. He was too tired to withstand his pain for much longer. "We must remember that even those imprisoned in the Wastelands by Imperial decree have magic we could use… "

"I will consider it." She turned her back to him without another word.

"I can ask for no greater pleasure, Radiant Majesty." Bowing deeply, he left her presence. It took all of his control to wait until he was out of earshot before he collapsed against the wall.

Coughing, he fought for breath and waved away the attentiveness of a nearby guard to retrieve his flask. He drank deeply until full to the point of bursting. His breathing eased.

The bout of weakness was brief. Thurst wiped away a blue trail that dribbled down his chin. He shook his head at the turn in their conversation. If she rejected the edict, how far would she be willing to go down other paths in order to keep her control, and her position as a divine ruler?

No, she would accept his advice. The bitterness in her dismissal was out of frustration. In the end she would see the wisdom of his words. She would not ignore the opportunity to put the nobility even further in her debt.

It would be foolishness itself to refuse a divine gift. He only wished that he had thought of it sooner. To bestow one would make the people adore her as they never had. *Always would*, he corrected himself with a sharp look around. Even a silent thought might reveal itself in a body of such weakness as this.

He made his way back outside. The sight of someone leaving the palace during the late morning brought a hailstorm of words upon him from the desperate and poor waiting to plead for scraps. Prayers dissolved into curses as he turned away from the outstretched hands that reached to pull him down. He was shaking by the time the palace guards handed him back into his carriage and turned the beggars away.

How quickly would blind faith and adoration turn to hatred and upheaval if the actions of the Empress were handled improperly? He should never have told her about the Horn. Not without having it in his possession.

Outside the carriage, mutters of anger broke through the prayers of religious fervor. Fearful of his own thoughts, Thurst clutched at his chest and closed his eyes. He wiped the bitter salt from his face.

4

COMPLICATIONS

Feran Dorst stepped down from a hired carriage. He strained his neck to make out the fluttering strips of fabric which marked the entrance to the Imperial Merchant's Guild Hall. It was still open for visitors. Good.

Guild halls were the only buildings allowed to carve deep into the black cliffs beneath the Imperial Palace. Storage vaults kept the most valuable goods and coin protected from the sea, while the trouble to reach the top of the stairs kept all but the most determined at bay. It also allowed the Empress to take her share of the goods without lifting a finger.

It was a fruitful alliance that encouraged a constant and nearly endless expansion. Feran paused to take in the view and prepare himself for the long climb ahead. Clamoring street urchins pressed at his pockets, promising to bear a message or climb the slippery stairs to the top and back again for a quick penny.

He pushed them aside with an eye to his purse. The most persistent begged to be taken on as an apprentice. He ignored them.

The thought of replacing his nephew, Teguin, had come to him from time to time. But he was too suspicious of strangers, and the goods he kept and traded were precious. It was better to keep them away from greedy fingers until the right amount of coin came his way.

The steps were always crowded at the street level. Feran climbed, his long strides only managing one tall step at a time, his head bowed in concentration. The noises from the street were soon drowned out by the wind.

Visiting merchants were quite safe from harm or harassment once they climbed the first few steps. Sprays of saltwater, thick with foam near high tide, brought a mist to the steps. It left many queasy at the thought of slipping. At this height, a fall would mean more than a broken limb.

Red in the face, Feran thought of all the visitors who attempted the climb only to be turned away at the top. Had he breath to spare, he would have laughed at the cruel attempt to add so many impediments to supplicants that were not members of the Guild. Only full members could send spry, young apprentices of their establishments instead of coming in person, but he had no such position.

Feran regretted letting Teguin go to Praxis every time he climbed these stairs. He had hoped to send Teguin on business with the Guild as a full member, grooming the man to stay by his side. But cycle after trading cycle his hopes were dashed against these same black saltwater rocks. Every application, bribe, and plea fell on deaf ears, curse them.

But he kept on trying. The Dorst name would be known again as one of power and influence. He would be respected and regain his nobility if it took every last breath and penny he had.

Feran stopped to regain his composure when he reached the entrance, grateful for the cool sea air at his back now that it was no longer pitted against him. He tugged his vest back into place. He made sure that the gold stitching on each shirt sleeve was intact. The sweat and salt from his brow he wiped with a damp cloth and gave a small huff of triumph.

This time, the Guild would not see him put down by their petty slights. He would come to them calm and haughty. May this be the day that they finally allowed him his due. No more disrespect, no more limitations or added taxation or sudden shifts in rules or appointments to exclude him.

Feran stepped inside. He blinked as his vision adjusted from bright outdoor sunshine to the low light of glowstone. The inside of the hall remained unchanged from when he first visited as a young man, with long benches designed to keep people waiting in hobbled and breathless discomfort until they could beg for the privilege of an audience with a scribe. At least he had paid enough to the Guild in his lifetime to avoid that insult.

He swept past the benches, past apprentices and messengers and lesser merchants than he, all waiting, half still red in the face from the climb, others frozen as statues from the cold and damp sea air. Feran stepped up to a stone oak desk and admired in the mirror polish his reflection. After waiting half a lifetime, he was ready.

The man at the desk looked up with a pinched expression. "Name," he said in a nasal tone.

This frequent annoyance now seemed like an amusing ritual and Feran laughed, his enjoyment deepening when the desk clerk started at the sound, clearly unaccustomed to anyone laughing in a place designed to diminish and demean.

"Merchant Dorst," he said. The benches behind him creaked.

"Dorst?" asked the clerk, pretending not to recognize the man in front of him that visited several times a cycle.

"Feran Dorst," he pronounced his name with added emphasis. "I'm expected." Summoned, but not welcome, he wanted to say, eager to share his victory at being invited.

The clerk disappeared. When he returned he gave Feran a short bow, his eyes wide. "The guild master will see you."

The guild master's room. At last he would have an audience. When he entered, Feran was surprised by the smile spread across the face of the old woman who rose to greet him. Her snow-white hair was pulled back into a loose bun, and she wore a loose dress of Elusian vereen whose colors bloomed and faded from dark blue to raven black, reflecting the light in the room.

"Merchant Dorst," the woman said, "good to see you."

"Good fortune to you, Guild Master," he replied. The words of respect and greeting were automatic. They helped to hide his surprise as she took his hands and squeezed them with a fondness that felt like a doting aunt rather than a pillar of trade and finance in the Imperium.

"Please, you must call me Serentina. Yes yes, I find guild master such a heavy title to bear at times. It is good to hear my name—a woman of my age needs reminding of such things, you understand. Come. Sit. I hear you favor mulberry wine. I had one of the clerks dig up a bottle from down below. Shall we try it?"

Feran watched the woman wipe off a thick layer of dust with an embroidered cloth whose golden threads gleamed. "It would be an insult to refuse such a generous offer."

"Excellent, excellent," she chuckled. "I do love an excuse to drink in the morning; give me a hand, won't you?"

Feran had to admire the woman. In a few consummate strokes she had him at a disadvantage. Yet the gestures of an old woman would not hide the brightness of her eyes or the sharpness of her gaze as she watched Feran open the bottle and pour generously into the two goblets on her desk.

They had their drinks raised in a toast when the door burst open.

A man Feran knew too well for his own liking stormed in. "This cannot be, mother! You work against me in secret to bring this, this speck of fish-bait in by special invitation? Do you wish to ruin our reputation?"

The guild master put down her glass. "Your presence tires me, Brexel. Must I have you removed bodily from my office in front of our scribes and every visitor in the hall?"

The man blanched. "You wouldn't dare."

"Either you stay but remain utterly silent, or you leave. Now."

"I—"

"Decide."

Feran smiled and looked down, swirling the syrupy liquid in his glass. What a wonderful day this was.

Brexel slammed himself down into a nearby chair. He cleared his throat several times, but shook his head violently when his mother offered him a glass of wine.

"I apologize for my son's lack of manners," she said at last to Feran, who fought a grin to see Brexel squirm out of the corner of his eye, the man's face contorted in rage.

"Patience is a valuable tool of our trade," replied Feran, "but so easily overlooked." He stopped for fear of crowing too loudly. This chastisement of Brexel was too rich a meal for him to spoil with his own lesser insults.

"Persistence, too," added the older woman. "You have always been eager to join the Guild, Feran. Your work has not gone unnoticed. When possible, you have made us both wealthy."

A slight tinge of regret colored the excellent flavor of the mulberry wine as he sipped it. Feran remembered how he squeezed the demand for Tanasen apples and cut out the Guild from trading with the valuable fruit when they refused him membership the last time he applied. It was not one of his proudest moments. He had since relinquished the ban and traded freely with them, but without full membership the taxes and limited avenues of trade substantially carved into his profits.

Brexel shifted in his chair, dragging it in grating swipes across the floor to a narrow bookcase. In a thinly veiled attempt to ignore their conversation, the man picked up several small iron ingots and dropped each onto a measurement scale to study their weight with a tiny, distracting clatter.

"I appreciate your invitation, Guild—Serentina," he corrected himself. "Such courtesies have not been extended to me before. Have you had word from the palace?" He tried to limit the smug satisfaction in his voice.

"Have you, Merchant Dorst?"

As the guild master sipped her wine, Feran was forced into an honest and direct answer that pained him to admit. "Not yet. But we have all heard the rumors. Word is spreading through the city that our Empress is considering pardoning all past crimes committed by the noble houses during the first cycles of her reign."

Brexel shifted in his chair again.

"Oh, it will happen I think," agreed the guild master. She took a long sip of the wine. "I did not know your father well, Feran. But those days were dark and too full of blood debts and executions. Not all of us were happy to see Her Imperial Majesty so harsh in her sentencing, Blessed Empress forgive me for saying so, but executing leaders of noble houses, well. It is bad for business. And then banishing her head justikar to the Wastelands as the prison warden... it was hard to watch. Noble houses are rarely stripped of their titles, especially *profitable* ones like yours."

Feran emptied his glass. "As far as I'm concerned, Warden Moonstone can stay in the Wastelands and rot for what he did to my family."

"Of course. My apologies for bringing up such a delicate subject." The guild master finished her drink and poured him another. "I asked you here as a courtesy, Feran. Do you still speak with your brother? Would Legan return to the Blue City and accept the noble title, pledging a renewed loyalty to the Empress?"

The implication of her questions left Feran speechless. After fighting for so long to be accepted despite the family's exile, he needed his brother to accept the title? This was a cruel blow. His brother wanted nothing to do with court or the Empress.

"The eldest child?" he croaked, his mouth suddenly dry.

"I took the liberty of confirming it with the Imperial justikar. It is such an unusual situation that naturally, I was curious. It seems the laws of inheritance would apply if House Dorst were to be restored. Bringing back the exiled houses would have quite an effect on trade in the Imperium. I like to know how politics will influence such things, you understand."

"Of course."

Brexel had given up all pretense of ignoring them and was following his mother's words with an intensity that made Feran's heart sink as she continued.

"If the laws of inheritance do apply in this situation then they are quite clear. Following the same path as Imperial inheritance, the eldest child in the family inherits and either accepts or denies the title when it is offered. Your elder brother left suddenly after your father's death...

no one quite knows what happened to him. Though my son informs me that you brought your nephew back to the capital as your apprentice. Do you know where Legan might be reached?"

Feran didn't know what to say. This obstacle was not one he antici-pated and now, oh the trouble it would cause. An unusual situation indeed. A complication that would throw all his plans to the wind.

Relaxing the grip on his glass, he smiled. "Legan is a quiet man who likes his privacy, you understand. I will... be in contact with my brother to work out the details, of course. He lives quite some distance away but I believe, indeed I am certain, that he would be honored to be pardoned by the Empress, Blessed Be."

"Indeed?" asked Brexel, breaking the silence by injecting a mocking curiosity, amusement and disbelief into that one word.

The guild master held up a hand. "Leave us."

"With pleasure, Guild Master."

Feran searched for any number of assurances to promise his title would be reinstated, but the prospect of convincing his estranged brother to return to the Blue City and embrace the pardon of the Empress made his blood run cold. What could possibly make Legan accept the title that caused their father's death?

As if she read Feran's thoughts, the guild master filled their glasses again. "You know, Feran, I have been watching you all these cycles. You work harder than any merchant I have ever met. You hunger for the next trade. I admire that."

Feran sipped the mulberry wine. His mind spun out endless scenarios which might convince his brother to accept and return to court.

The guild master continued, "We were not allowed to accept a disgraced noble house into the honorable Guild, despite your *very* successful history. A pity. Under these unusual circumstances, you might finally have a legitimate claim of entry."

She peered at Feran over her glass. "The question is, Feran, how far are you willing to go to bring the Dorst name back to court?"

The sweet wine was sour at the finish. The final pour held sediment that stuck in Feran's throat, but courtesy demanded he finish it. "As soon as I have an answer to that question," he managed to say, "I will let you know."

"Excellent. I would like to hear from you again soon. The pleasure of your company would be welcome, as well as the excuse to open another bottle of mulberry wine. Fortune favor you, Feran." She inclined her head and he bowed in return, remembering to leave the glass in his hand only at the last moment before he left.

Brexel waited just outside the door. He flipped an iron ingot into the air. "So. Another denial for Merchant Dorst. You must tire of disappointment. But do come back and try again, if you can bear the humiliation."

Feran whirled around and pushed the sniggering coward against the wall. Brexel recoiled, but Feran reconsidered striking the man. Instead, he looked Brexel up and down and spoke softly, "I will return soon, Brexel. And I will remember today and every day that you were rude or insulting. Count them as your count your coins."

Feran released him. The man brushed off his coat and straightened. The grimace on his face relaxed into a slow, haughty smile. "The tides are high. Watch your step, it's a long way down to the bottom."

BROKEN POINT

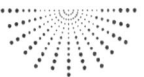

Herbert wiped streaks of muddy water from his forehead so he could see to faithfully readjust his grip, trying to keep each stake level while Teguin hammered bracing lines into the sandstone. The moment his last hammer strike landed they both ducked inside, sputtering and half-drowned by the rain.

"Nicely done, lads," said the woman named Rinzi, already inside the tent. She grinned with her feet propped up under the wide, rotting awning. "First time in a desert storm? No matter. There's not been a sand-blessed one fer a fair while."

She pointed to a stack of pans and hollow gourds. "Set out yer catchers, and quick. Fills while ye wait. It'll anger the desert if ye refuse a gift of water."

Herbert handed Teguin some of his sample jars. Their cooking pan went under the dripping tent flap. Scrambling, they looked for anything else they could use from their packs to trap the water before it disappeared. Herbert was grateful for the shelter.

There were benefits to traveling light. The only times he regretted not bringing a tent were when it meant sleeping outside during a storm such as this. "D'ye reckon a mud bath is cleaner than sand?" he asked, wiping his beard.

The smoke in the room was so thick that Teguin's head swam when he tried to stand. He sat down again and clutched the table. Winds, strong and weak in turn, blew upon the hillsides with such disinterested scorn that no one dared open a whole shutter to let the clouds of smoke escape. Any that found its way out through the cracks in the walls was quickly replaced by fresh pipesmoke.

Samson slid something heavy across what remained of the spilled drink. Teguin wiped it off as best he could and saw a piece of rounded glass. On it there were scratches and rounded shapes that suggested landmarks. An odd and crude sort of map to carry.

"Broken Point's the way," Samson explained to his empty cups. He looked up with a surprised expression. "That's what ye'll be needin'. Best place t'find a guide and be avoidin' the worst of Imperials. But there's plenty t'knife ye in the back as well; it's a wary sort that lives out in those parts."

The man lurched forward until he was almost nose-to-nose with Teguin. With a belch, he waved an arm from his rumpled travel cloak to his dirty boots. "Ye ken yer path, lad? The desert ain't a place fer a passin' fancy like yerself."

Teguin pocketed the piece of glass. He pulled his cloak around him in an attempt to keep the smoke that hovered at bay. A strange map, but it was better than nothing. He shuddered. That slimy drink. His throat was caked in the stuff, whatever it was.

"Fortune favor you," he said. It was a parting phrase merchants used with one another. Even if Teguin believed the man was not a former merchant, he still paid him the courtesy of an equal. He tossed a coin onto the table, but the sound rang out louder than he intended and cut through most of the voices in the room.

Samson scooped it up with grubby fingers. "Hope t'see yer face back here," he slurred, "but keep yer sayin'. Ye'll need it."

Teguin gave a small bow. The man's words added new weight to the many eyes that followed him as he ducked into the narrow corridor, heading to one of the only rooms at the back of the inn. Tired as he was, he would not sleep well tonight.

Feran had taught him that being overly polite was always a good

"Well, we're nothing but mud right now as it is from traveling the roads," Teguin replied. "If you stand outside in your clothes you could wash both at once."

Herbert took a few steps to leave the tent and within seconds the water soaked the rest of him to the skin. This was not a familiar rain. It was an open wall of water that pounded and pummeled. So long as he knew he could dry off afterward, it was glorious.

Taking a scoop of sand in each hand, he scrubbed everything he could reach and shook his head like a wet dog. Water was more than a gift to slake their thirst. Water brought even dried and buried seeds to life.

A promising beginning. He would have crawled into the desert on hands and knees in the rain in search of sprouting specks of life if Rinzi hadn't warned them of the snake nests. Creeping and slimy, no doubt, these wriggling things that found their way into unattended boots and dark corners.

With a shudder of disgust at the thought, Herbert tried to make out Broken Point. Beside the cliffs, each decaying shelter held together like a row of crooked teeth. Surely it was no more than fifty paces of open space.

At its end it looked less a path and more a crack which allowed passage between the cliffs. Only generous folk would call this waste of space a part of Falden Province. This place might as well have been the other edge of the world, Herbert decided. It looked nothing like his home.

The promise of rain had hung over them in swollen, dark clouds all day. Their poor horses had no trees under which to take shelter, and Herbert gave them a quick pat of apology before ducking back into the tent.

"Good fer trade, bad fer travel," said Rinzi as she rolled her one good eye. She wore a patch of scaled hide over the other eye, which matched the rest of her clothing. Herbert thought she rather resembled a snake herself, coiled in her chair and looking him over with an intensity he found unsettling.

"What d'ye mean, good fer trade?" he asked, looking away to

squeeze water from his shirt into the dirtiest of the pans, hoping to salvage something for later washing.

"Us traders," Rinzi said with a swipe of her calloused hands. "We bide our time and then the first chance we get, we strike." She smacked her hands together. "Strip the desert clean. Most folk here stay on the edges and scrape what they need. Rain makes the desert a death trap but it's all the better fer us snake hunters. We all go in the end. Little choice."

"Do you know anyone here willing to go deeper into the desert as a guide?" asked Teguin.

Rinzi gave them both a long look. "Why?"

"We're explorin'," said Herbert. "I'm lookin' fer plants, anythin' that might grow in the desert. Teguin, here—"

"We want to explore the deep desert," finished Teguin. His face kept a blank expression that he often used with strangers.

Uncommunicative, and unwilling to share the details with someone they had only just met. That was Teguin all right. Polite and blank as a stone statue until he wanted to show different.

"That so," replied Rinzi. "The only Imperial folk foolish enough t'travel freely in the Wastes are the soldiers that run supplies t'the prison. They should be the ones t'take ye but ye missed their wagons."

She gestured around them. "That's good fer us, t'have them gone save a quick stop in t'say they did as much. It takes a bribe t'stay this side of the cliffs. Last week they beat old Harn near t'death when he fell short of his due."

Half-listening, Herbert gazed out at the distant sand dunes as the rain lightened. "What a lonely place."

"Will ye pay?" she asked suddenly. "We've no use fer coin out here, but in other goods?"

Herbert would have said no to try and find another guide but to his annoyance, Teguin coughed to interrupt him, then said some of his fancy merchant-flattery to answer, which made Rinzi laugh. Far be it for him to want to negotiate for once, Herbert thought sourly.

He had a fast tongue as Teguin called it. His friend always told him he was too hot-tempered to strike a good bargain. Still, he didn't like the look of this woman for a guide.

"If ye brought heavy coin," continued Rinzi, "I would call ye both fools. But yer on a fool's errand t'be anywhere near the Wastes with no idea where yer headed."

Teguin pulled out their map. "First we are headed to the prison, but afterward we mean to travel for as long as it takes to reach the western cliffs."

Rinzi gaped at the map. She kicked around to face Teguin and her boots barely missed Herbert's face. "The prison?" she cried. "How many poor, banished souls will be with ye? New guards," she spat, "I should have known and I'll not have ye here!"

"Wait, please," said Teguin. "We are no guards and there are no prisoners."

Herbert knew he had to act fast. He dug in his pockets to pull out a wrapped strip of fine cloth. With a flick of his wrist he unrolled it and put out a hand to steady the small table in front of Rinzi.

She leapt back from them but only sweetgrass plants fell out, now tumbled together in a small green-brown pile of spikes and leaves. "What new trickery is this?"

Herbert touched his chest. "D'ye see strong, hardened soldiers here, Rinzi? Or d'ye see the simple truth: a farmer and a merchant trader seekin' a risky venture?"

Rinzi's good eye narrowed. She stepped forward to join them at the table, looking over the map and the plants. She peered out her tent at their sodden, miserable horses, and then looked from Herbert to Teguin.

"If ye are what ye say, then empty yer wares."

Herbert shrugged. He turned out the contents of his pack and scrambled to grab at the empty spools of cloth bandages that unwound. The tumble of his clothing smelled badly enough that Rinzi wrinkled her nose. With a shrug, Herbert tossed them out of the tent and into the rain.

Rinzi snorted. "Few guards would carry such a worthless pile. Best keep an eye on yer clothes in a place like this. Yer horses as well, when the rain lets up."

When she turned to Teguin he looked as though he had eaten a pile of sour grapes. "I protect my goods with my life. I will not lay out all my possessions to prove who I am. My pack is my own."

Herbert looked between Rinzi and Teguin. The woman's expression darkened. He wondered if she would throw them out, or stab them with one of the knives she kept in her belt. A low growl started in Rinzi's throat, but before Herbert could grab his staff the woman slammed a hand on her table and laughed.

"Just what I would expect a merchant t'say. Well. What have ye fer trade, then?"

Herbert decided not to watch. Trading and bartering and exaggerated interest or anger at coin was something for which he had little patience. Rinzi's warning had him worried about his clothing.

He was already wet, so it was little change to wash the rest of his clothes while he could. He slapped them against the sandstone, rubbing them with a bar of soap laced with selveth that left a light, woody scent behind. Rinzi's other words stung with more truth than he liked to admit.

The smell of the soap reminded him of the way saplings smelled when he cut his first grafts of the season, so fresh with a hint of sweet sap. How would the orchards fare without him if he failed to return by the end of spring?

His mother wanted nothing but the best of everything and now that the orchards were doing well, his family spent all their time at court in the Blue City enjoying their new status. Except for him.

Herbert could not see himself in such a place. Westerling had argued on his behalf that the orchards needed him. More orchards would increase their status. But that point had not been well received, even coming from the head of their valuable orchards. What else would convince her?

In truth, his parents saw one path before him: negotiate an advantageous marriage and have him be some kind of tool or symbol of their own success. He often thought of the day his father sent him off to

Praxis as the final negotiation with Teguin's uncle without even asking him. He was a symbol all right, but of a trade agreement.

Being away from Praxis meant little to Herbert now that Olivia was dead. The underground passages were impassable, and he dreamed of buckled caverns and those smoldering ruins which kept the happiest and darkest moments of his life buried with equal indifference.

He could not stop thinking of how close he came to being happy. Olivia would never see his home, never greet the fruit trees in the orchards, nor feel the greenwheat ripple under her hands. What was it all for, if not to share the sheer joy of greenery with someone else who appreciated it as he did?

Being far from Praxis was one thing, but leaving Tanasen Estate and Falden brought a different kind of isolation to his grief. He was lost. Adrift, and on his way to the most desolate place that existed.

How long had it been since he had seen his younger sister, Anisa? He had never been close with Nora, the eldest and heir of their House and fortune. At least that pressure was not on his shoulders.

Now that his family had a noble title, they had earned enough coin for him to buy most anything he wanted. But what he wanted was mere dust and ashes, scattered across Lake Pereen for eternal rest. All that was left was a void, a constant pang of grief as he could not forget what he had lost.

Why was he here really; to keep his friend company? To bring life to the desert? To run away from his family and the pressures of a future he did not want? Why choose only one, he reasoned.

When he shook out his clothes and brought them back into the tent to dry, Herbert saw Rinzi and Teguin both looked pleased in their own way. Rinzi pulled a line of hanging snakeskins next to her and tossed it toward Herbert, who jumped away from them with a cry of alarm.

"Yer horses will die in the desert. Ye'll need a different sort but we can fix that." She pointed at the pile of skins. "Pick it up, man, and take yer pick. It's a gift. Everyone needs a decent belt."

Herbert thought the gesture both generous and vile. Would live snakes see it and attack him? Teguin's expression was a good deal more relaxed; enough for Herbert to recognize a warning look when he saw it. He chose the first one that fit and tried not to touch it as he wound it around his waist.

The pile of half-wrapped parcels on Rinzi's battered table displayed a small fortune in goods. That was it, then. Another negotiation settled without him.

Herbert took a deep breath. Whether or not he knew which reason pulled him most away from home, they were at a point of no return. The desert sands seemed as decent a place as any to find a path forward. He would have plenty of time to think things through along the way.

He handed the line of other skins back to Rinzi and forced a smile. "When d'we leave?"

Rinzi gave a gentle tug to adjust her eyepatch. "First the rain ends, then the desert is yer home. Best get familiar while ye can. Ye heard of sandspitters?"

"Snakes?" guessed Herbert.

"When there's legs we call them lizards. Spit poison at ye that'll melt yer insides."

"Interesting," said Teguin. "What else?"

Herbert groaned. It was going to be a long night.

6

STUBBORN PRIDE

W arden Moonstone spat a mouthful of blood onto the floor of his office. He took the beating in silence and stayed down, determined not to cry out or call for guards. Better to have one broken man under his watch than a bloodbath.

He eyed the clean boots of the Imperial soldiers that stood over him. Somehow he managed to force his jaw open when they looked over at their master for orders. "My answer will not change, Jarvin. My daughter has broken no laws and is not a prisoner here."

"Ain't a difference, Moonstone," said Captain Jarvin. "If the Blessed Empress is wantin' the girl ye'll give her up without a fight."

The soldiers surrounding the two men gave snorts of laughter at the mention of a fight. The tops of the captain's boots were polished to a high gloss, but the warden could see specks of dried blood on the soles, where the stains were so bad that no cleaning would remove them.

The warden forced himself to look up at the man. "Unless this involves an Imperial decree or a letter signed by the royal justikar at the behest of the Empress, I'm under no obligation to obey your request, even in the Wastelands." He lightly touched his jaw. "I once enforced the laws of all Imperial soldiers and I remember them well, unless they are no longer in use?"

The captain gave a broad, mocking bow. "Yer lordship. So ye miss yer old life in the capital, then? It ain't been missin' ye back."

"What would the Empress want with the daughter of a prison warden?" Moonstone asked, his voice flat. He could not understand the man's unexpected request.

He caught the annoyance that flashed across the captain's reddened face, raw with sunburn. With a broad and heavily furrowed brow, Jarvin's expression froze at any question that wasn't of his own making, but the warden could hear the confusion in the man's voice as he tried to recover. "What her Holiness be wantin' with the girl is, is, secret."

"From you as well I see." That earned him another kick in the side. He cursed at his loss of control. Every word counted when it hurt this much to breathe. He needed a healer, and soon.

Clarity of mind, clarity of purpose, he reminded himself. "Your influence is over the supply runs here, that is all. Again I ask: where are your papers? The rest of my guard will return soon and they are not as respectful of the law as I am." The soldiers around him stirred at the mention of the prison guard.

Captain Jarvin's eyes narrowed, but sweat streaked his face as he shot a glance at the only door in the room. "Ye dare t'defy the Empress?"

The prison was too large to have a guard in every hallway, but Moonstone spoke the truth. He knew the patterns of the watch as he knew his own sword. The next rotation would bring them up the tower for a report. Up the tower, and right into the swords of Jarvin's men if they saw their warden bloodied.

He sat up. It wasn't easy to swallow down the nausea. He fought the urge to pass out, and the effort it took to speak cost him dearly.

"No Imperial decree, no daughter. Come back when you have my supplies."

The steadiness of his voice and the coldness of his reply made the soldiers back away. They whispered like guilty children, giving the warden mingled looks of disgust and grudging respect as Jarvin shook his head and signaled his men that they were leaving. At least they had the sense to keep their voices down as they left.

In some surprise, Moonstone managed to limp down the stairs and into the ward at the bottom level of the prison tower without collapsing in front of the watch. Bent over his work at a large table in the center of the room, their healer had just enough time to turn and pull out a slab of wood upon which the warden sat before he could fall to the floor.

"Bruised ribs," said the man, examining him. "A few could be broken. It is a wonder your nose is untouched this time, Warden. That jaw of yours may need to be wired shut."

"No need to touch the jaw if it isn't broken, Mason," he replied, touching his split lip with a shake of his head.

"I meant to prevent this from happening again," replied the young man. "I know I haven't been here long, but it never occurred to me that you would be more in need of my services than the other prisoners. I would make something for the pain if I had the herbs, but unless our dear Captain Jarvin delivered his latest supply run…?"

Moonstone shook his head. Did the captain think that a beating would break him, or was the man simply bored? Either way, he would not trade his daughter for a few supplies. Bruises would heal.

"There is not much else I can do, Warden."

"I expected as much." He reached for his shirt. "Men like Jarvin refuse to help anyone but themselves. They feed on the dry kernels of power they are given, but are never satisfied until they beat the very heart out of those around them, especially the innocent."

"And you will put an end to it by letting him beat you instead?"

He thought over the question. "I used to be the man whose justice put animals like Jarvin in chains. Even in exile, I must respect the order of the law. Yet I protect those weaker than myself, and I always will."

"Do not let your past weigh on you, Warden. Not like the rest of us. Those soldiers are spineless ants. They aren't fit to be in the same room with you. Why not use your position here? Cultivate the power to be the leader that an animal like Jarvin would never dream of challenging. Protect the weak by being strong, by fighting back!"

"You surprise me, healer. I will not use my position as permission to behave badly. Even though you came here as a prisoner, your healing skills have allowed others to look beyond your past mistakes. I thought you of all people would understand."

The warden struggled to pull on his shirt over the roughspun bandages. "There is a shared bond in this prison: we know what it is to suffer pain, and we see the darker side of our nature with clear eyes. All of us have punishments to bear. Let me choose my own."

7

DARKENING SKIES

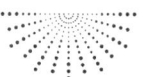

Lena Moonstone knelt in the sand. Reaching her fingers up to the sky, she enjoyed the wind as it chilled the desert. While she held the position, she took several deep breaths to calm her mind. The two moons, Iral and Ferul, hung over the rippling dunes to cast new light, one feeble, the other sharp.

On this night the moonlight was unusual. High clouds swelled. It was rare and dangerous, the threat of rain. Flooded sand dunes made drowning pits into which traveler and beast alike would perish.

When Lena rose with a groan to brush sand from her riding clothes, she turned to find the head of the prison guard waiting for her. "You look remarkably refreshed milady," he said, his mouth twitching to control a smile of amusement she knew well.

Lena flipped a braid of long hair over her shoulder. "Asleep on my feet is more like it. We have enough supplies, do we not? Admit it, Cergath, you are just as eager to be going home as I am."

The older man shook his head. "It's a good thing you do not play cards."

"It's a good thing for you then that father would never allow merchants within a hundred leagues of the prison, or I would be tempted by the chance of a few coins to spend."

Cergath's expression hardened. "If we had other means of supplying ourselves, we would be less at the mercy of our Imperial suppliers."

"To hear a bard I'd gladly do a little rule bending."

"Best not let the warden hear you say such a thing. You know how he loves his rules."

"Plenty of the guards would jump at the chance of a little entertainment. A merchant would be practical, but not half as exciting as a bard."

"A pity indeed—though, you didn't hear it from me."

"I knew it!" she cried. Laughing, Lena took the reins of her lamat from Cergath and swung easily onto the saddle, urging it forward. "Be at ease, Cergath. He will not hear of it from me."

Lamat were giant lizards. Lena was already of a height with her father, but she reckoned it would take four of her lying down to even come close to the length of her mount. The creatures moved much like their smaller venomous brethren, sandspitters, who lived in the rocky cliffs along the borders to the open desert. The prison guards kept their own lamat to breed and raise as mounts, preferring a larger, more imposing size to the smaller, more docile creatures that were native to the heat of the place.

Lamat were more reliable than horses in the desert. While it was safer to travel at night out of the blistering heat, they needed the lamat for protection as well as speed. Most creatures of the desert were awake. Awake, and hungry. Lena did not like to think about what would try to eat a lamat, which had fangs and claws as long as her forearm.

Cergath caught up with her on his own mount, nearly twice the size of hers. "If we push we could reach the prison by dawn. The rest of the hunting party are over the next rise."

"Rains could catch us in the open."

"Is it closing on us so soon?"

Lena inhaled. The moisture in the air was heavy, and it felt as though she sipped from the canteen at her side. "Can't you taste it on the wind? The clouds are building."

"We can make it home. Best not to be out in it." While it rarely rained in the desert, they both knew there was little pleasure in racing across sinking sands, hoping to survive and not stumble into a sunken pit.

They rode hard for the prison. By the time Iral faded beneath the dunes, they had their lamat safely penned in the prison stables, rolling in the sand to erase the first heavy drops of rain.

Lena decided to go and check the reservoir. Deep beneath the prison, the limestone cavern captured water from rare storms like this one. Such a wealth of water was a rare treasure.

She thought for a moment of inviting Mason to go down with her but then decided against it. It would raise too many questions. It was one thing to help Mason in the small room that he'd fashioned into a healer's ward, but quite another to be in such a secluded and romantic place alone together.

Sighing, she allowed herself a daydream where she and Mason would be together with her father's approval, living in their own quarters or even opening a small trading outpost together between the prison and the border of the Wastes. She had never been that far from home, but each time she joined a patrol she looked for possible sites where Mason would build her a place of their very own.

Her father had a high opinion of their healer since he had arrived a few months ago. He often said that 'any man who would give his time and care for those in prison deserved respect'. It was one of the reasons she loved her father so much.

But would he love Mason as a son? There was a difference between her father approving of a man who did good, and approving of a man who loved his daughter. She hoped that soon she would be able to tell him she wanted to be with Mason, and convince him of how happy they would be together. Her father was a hard man to please, and it would mean a lot to her if he approved the match.

The thought made her eager to be reunited with Mason, and Lena headed up to the healer's ward. Maybe she could convince him to sneak away with her to watch the rainfall instead. She grew giddy at the thought, but the grin slipped from her face when she ran straight into her father in the hallway.

"Father, you're hurt! What happened?"

"It's nothing. A simple misunderstanding with Captain Jarvin."

"Again?" She dropped the bundle she held and crossed her arms. The story was too familiar for her liking. "Did this misunderstanding end with your blood on his boots as well? If the Imperial soldiers think they can get away with attacking the warden inside his own prison, what will they do next?"

Her father's face was immobile as ever. "I do not need to explain myself to anyone."

She wiped blood from a small cut on his cheek. "You put too much faith in the honor of others, father. Captain Jarvin has none."

He pulled away from her touch. "The hardest part of any battle is choosing when not to fight. Anger does not justify action." Abrupt and cool as ever, he turned to go. "I must go and hear Cergath's report. Are you coming?"

Lena bit her lip. What could she say to make him understand how worried she was for his safety? The silly, stubborn man could barely walk and here he was, trying to pretend as if nothing had happened.

Clearing her throat, she picked up her bundle. "I will stay and help Mason with what we brought back."

The warden nodded and limped past her down the hall.

"Shattered stars," she muttered, entering the ward. "His stubbornness will get him killed."

With a smile that lit up his handsome face, Mason put an arm around her waist. "I know, my love. Which is why we must help when we can and keep an eye out for trouble. Now, what did you bring me?"

Lena emptied the bundle onto the table, and together they sorted the different thorns and needles by length into piles. She held up different pieces of the plant while Mason catalogued each find. "The strong and thick ones will be used for wounds and sewing," he said.

"What about the small ones?" she asked, shaking the pile into the smallest scatter pod she could find.

"Those will bring relief to aches and pains if applied in the right places. It's finding them all again once you've finished that's the trouble."

Lena shuddered. "I'll bring all you want, but don't ask me to use them. I can't stand the thought of poking someone with such things."

"You should learn. You could find yourself without a healer one day."

"Stay with me, and then I'll never have to worry about it, will I?"

He laughed. "Not if I have anything to say about it, blossom."

Blushing, Lena thought about how happy she was as they peeled strips of the harvested plants. She kept stealing kisses when she moved close to drop the spines into holders fashioned from dried plant husks. Finally, he pushed her to arm's length with a serious expression. "Your father cannot keep punishing himself for past mistakes, you know. I can't stop thinking of Captain Jarvin and how he takes advantage of the warden."

Lena tried to free herself and slid out of his grip. "What do you mean?"

"Your father is an idealist, Lena. His views are unpopular, but that is no reason for him to suffer at the hands of a pig like Captain Jarvin."

"Father believes that he deserves to be out here in the Wastes, but he wants to serve the Imperium. He has found peace here."

"It's more than that. I believe your father actually seeks out these Imperial soldiers. Provokes them. Why does he search for ways to be punished beyond his exile?"

"No," she said, "you're wrong. My father has a good reason for his words and actions. There must be something else going on here. He would never seek out a beating unless..." Her heart sank.

Mason turned at her silence. "What is it?"

"Unless he believed he was doing the noble thing by keeping their attention on him, and protecting something, or someone else." She dropped the rest of her work and ran for the stairs.

8

WHAT WAS LOST

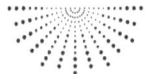

C hilled air bathed the red cliffs. A lone candle burned, melting and molding to the sandstone. The heat from the Lexicon sank into the ground where she sat, legs crossed and eyes half-closed in a light meditation that kept the candle burning and protected from the wind.

The heart-sun peeked over the horizon, and only the ripples from shifting sand rays far below betrayed signs of life, the scavengers loosening entire dunes in search of buried ticks and decaying flesh. The candle flickered.

Emerging sunlight sent sparks dancing across the Leixcon's closed eyes, and her thoughts ebbed and flowed in silent calculation. The Blades were growing in strength. With their sacrifices and her conviction, there was a path toward victory, and they would walk it without hesitation. There would be no end to the blood price paid so long as an empress sat on the throne.

"Lexicon." A woman's voice interrupted her thoughts. "The bone reader has found another sign."

Stretching stiff legs, the Lexicon released the candle from her control to watch the wax crack, and the candle tumble over the cliff. She was surprised to see Elena, and she hurried to the woman's side to catch hold of her as she reached out, limbs shaking, close to collapse.

"You know that I will be leaving you soon, Lexicon." Clouded eyes looked up at her.

"I do."

"And yet you have not come to me for guidance in two days. Are times so changed that an old woman must climb a hundred steps to seek audience with one half her age?"

The Lexicon sighed. "Times are dark, *mai-meia*. Perhaps I wish to postpone the day of your departure by not counting them at all." My mother, she called the woman.

Elena's wrinkled face stretched into a smile at the sound of the old language. "You would deny this one a chance of an honorable death? Such is the reasoning of a child, not a Predestine Lexicon. But have faith, my child. You have led us this far and the strength of the sands are beneath you."

"Shifting sands, perhaps."

The chamber they returned to was a shared space branching into a series of smaller rooms for sleeping. Deep in the cliffs, the inhabitants could take shelter from the hot sands during the day. A young man looked up when they entered and bowed low before the two women.

"You bring news from the bone reader, Daxel?" asked the Leixcon.

"She spoke of these caves," he said, "in a time when the darkwings nested but in fewer numbers. Scatter pod beds were scarce."

The Lexicon frowned. Scatter pod plants grew in the Shard, the center of the Wastelands, but that helped little with dating Troug's vision. "Does an event of significance occur?"

"Iral and Ferul were full on the same night."

"Interesting." The Lexicon turned to Elena. "I do need your help today."

"I have no memory of such an occurrence," said the woman, closing her eyes. "Yet I have heard tell of a cycle of fragrant harvest, a full season of rain across the desert. This is an ancient vision."

"We are getting closer, then. Daxel, have the bone reader focus on the bones beneath this new discovery. We must go further back. Elena, you and I must go through the archives to try and find mention of Iral and Ferul full together in the sky."

Dismissing Daxel with a wave of a crippled hand, Elena turned back to her when the boy had left. "My time to leave you will come soon. Is this how you would have us spend our last days together?"

"Do not underestimate the importance of this discovery," she said, refusing to answer such a painful question. "You are one of the only Blades left who knows the old language as I do. We will take Tamrel with us and she will continue to learn what she can before you leave."

Elena bent slowly to pick up a scatter pod husk from the floor and nodded. "Bring Tamrel, then. We will begin our work."

A wail echoed up from a lower passageway, giving the two women pause.

"You do too little to honor the bone reader's sacrifice," said Elena, changing the subject with her usual abruptness. It was one of the things the Lexicon loved about the woman.

Still, the meaning of Elena's words surprised her as though the old woman had given her a slap. "How? Her death will have the highest honor of us all."

"In death, yes," nodded Elena, "but in life she lives in a darkness so complete that joy can no longer touch her spirit. I have lived a long life and I tell you that the agonies of aging before my time would be far more painful than any torture or cruelties I suffered at the bidding of the Empress."

The Lexicon glanced at the woman's crippled hand, each finger twisted beyond use.

"Bring her what comfort you can as Lexicon, Aileen. It would be a mercy to limit her bone readings. Bring some relief to her pain."

She fought to understand the logic in Elena's request. "The bone reader is willing to hunt for the same things that we seek and works tirelessly by choice. The woman does not take notice of her surroundings. Were she with friends and loved ones at this moment she might never see nor recognize them. What comfort could I bring her?"

"Give her bones, but slowly. Have patience when she has no

restraint. We are responsible for her pain when temptation surrounds her as it does."

"I will consider it *mai-meia*. We honor our commitment to purity in death, but we must also remember that the bone reader does not know or follow our ways."

"It is an unusual confluence, is it not, to have an outsider among us who now knows more of our ways than we have forgotten?"

The Lexicon resisted the urge to dismiss Elena's request outright. "I may be too free with her readings, but the eye of the Empress will soon be upon us as she searches for the Horn."

"Why is the Horn not at your side? I know how much it means to our people, seeing proof of how we deprived the Empress of her treasure."

"It is strange, I found a connection between the Horn and my glove the moment I picked it up. There's an insistent pull, an inescapable urge which compels me to play it. When I gave in at Praxis, using it nearly tore me apart. I cannot predict with certainty what the outcome would be should it happen again. As I cannot remove my glove, I had to have the Horn taken away. The temptation of having it nearby was too much for me to bear."

"It is wise to resist temptation, Aileen. However, you must unlock the rest of its secrets."

The Lexicon nodded. "It seems time is a luxury neither of us can afford." She caught the eye of Tamrel as the young woman arrived.

Tamrel reached out to offer Elena the support of her arm. "Lexicon, *mai-meia*, you have need of me?"

"We must go to the archives, child," said Elena. "There is much to do in these last days as my time draws near."

The Lexicon allowed the two women to walk ahead of her. Elena's dragging steps filled her with a greater sense of urgency to understand the original purpose and creation of Greater Artifacts before Imperial agents did the same. The metal glove on her wrist tightened at the thought, What power these Ancient Artifacts wielded. If only she knew the true purpose behind their creation.

It was dangerous, using this older magic while they were fragmented pieces of their original whole. A Horn without a mouthpiece, a Glove without its mate; completed Greater Artifacts had once been powerful enough to defeat the Relics, ancient rulers and gods to their people.

What secrets about these Artifacts lay hidden in the memories of the dead? When she found the missing pieces, she would have a powerful enough weapons to defeat the Imperium, and bring the Empress to her knees.

9

SNAKES

The snake was long. Thicker than Herbert's neck, it stretched the length of the fire over which it cooked, twisting back and forth several times. Rinzi fed the head and scraps of the creature to their lamat.

He watched the meat cook, poking it furtively as if it might still wriggle. "Yer eatin' it like this?"

Teguin shrugged from across the fire. "Why not? We've eaten equally strange things on the road."

"Yer the one with an iron stomach. I'll try it, but there's na'en t'show it'll like me back."

"You could always… " Teguin gestured to the staff at Herbert's side. Hidden between the vines, he tended half a dozen small plants and an apple sapling at its core for the steady source of greens he craved.

He was sorely tempted. Just as he moved to take a snow pea from inside the staff, Rinzi returned. *Sod it.* He put the staff down again and rubbed his nose, savoring the smell of something fresh and green and alive. So long as they were with a stranger, they had to refrain from using their magic.

Herbert hadn't given it much thought beyond their finding a guide to travel in the desert, but now they were no longer traveling alone he had to watch his every move. It was maddening. Teguin was used to Herbert plucking a small snacking apple or delicate pea shoot from the staff along the fertile lands of Falden Province without comment. He had clearly forgotten how disconcerting it would be for his friend to be in the desert, where the sight of anything green brought the attention they swore to avoid.

Rinzi wiped her hands down the front of her pants. She gave the cooking meat a squeeze to check on its progress. "No time t'do it proper," she said to them over the fire, "but it'll do in a pinch."

She sprinkled something from her pocket over the curing snakeskin next to the fire, carefully rolling it for storing. "What this meat needs is a long soak with sweetgrass. Takes away the bitter bite and leaves the sweet behind."

Teguin managed a polite smile. Herbert couldn't look at the woman for long without spoiling his mood, and his appetite. While Teguin didn't seem to mind eating snake, Herbert couldn't get past the look and smell of this cooking fire.

A lamat sniffed near the campfire, dug into the sand, and brought up another slithering body, this one far smaller and only the length of Herbert's arm. The lamat looked over at Rinzi. The wriggling form hung from its jaws but it did not bite down. Herbert and Teguin looked at Rinzi too, but this time she made no move to take it away.

"*Zani*," she said, and waved an arm. "Let him have it."

With a rumble, the creature bit down and wandered away with its morsel as if to hide it from the others.

Rinzi moved their own meal closer to the dying fire, conserving every bit of fuel they had. "This first one'll give us more than enough meat. That scrap is small and full of holes by now. Not worth it."

Herbert flinched at the chewing and grunting over the next dune. "Like diggin' up potatoes," he said, horrified by the comparison of something he loved to do with how the lamat hunted their disgusting meals.

"Like I've been tellin' ye," said Rinzi as she stabbed at their dinner with a knife. "Out here there's little else fer a meal. Not 'til the prickly trees and scatter pods further out, and, those come with their own guardians."

She grinned. "If ye find snakes grim, wait til we cook up a sand-spitter. It's their venom that spoils the meal. But if ye kill one and keep the poison sac from burstin'... there's traders who pay fer that."

Rinzi caught Herbert reaching down to run his fingers along his staff. "Strange, ye carry a big stick like that all the way through the desert," she murmured into the fire. "Better use it fer fuel and be done with it." It wasn't the first time she questioned the way Herbert carried it around wherever he went.

He gripped it tightly. "I need it."

Teguin moved closer to Rinzi and gestured toward the staff and said under his breath. "It's from his home," he said in a low voice. "He misses his family."

Herbert didn't like the excuse, but was insulted when Rinzi snorted and said, "Right foolishness if ye ask me. If yer missin' family, ye ought find a way t'be with'em no matter the hardship."

"This from a woman who lives alone," he snapped, turning away from the fire. His staff sprouted a few thorns. Herbert muttered under his breath as he tried to pluck them off before they were noticed. He hated all this concealment. If they parted ways with Rinzi they could find their own way across this desert. How much worse could it be when staying together meant a constant belly ache?

Glancing behind him, Herbert saw Rinzi cut off the end of the turning meat. She chewed on it with great concentration, then made a face and spat it out. "Lost my brother t'the Imperial guard. Only family I had. Reckon he made time fer his family."

Before he could yell a retort she went on. "Soldiers travel this same path on their supply runs, the snatchers. If they lose a few men along the way t'this or that they take others on the road t'help them finish the job."

She sniffed. "He didn't make it."

"Your pardon, Rinzi," said Teguin, giving Herbert a hard look that made him squirm.

"Yer pardon if I've offended ye," he muttered. Hunger won out over caution and he plucked a few pea shoots from his staff, waited for Rinzi to turn away, and attacked them. Here he was, reduced to eating like a famished rabbit.

"Some of us call this place home with or without family," Rinzi said. "I wager it's not as comfortable as yer soft greenwheat fields, farmers whelp, but it's got more on offer than meets the eye."

She shoved a plate into Teguin's hands and turned back to the tent with her own portion. "Be ready t'travel. We've ground t'cover."

"Good riddance," Herbert muttered when she kicked the flaps of her tent closed.

"Are you trying to get us abandoned in the desert?" said Teguin, walking around the fire while the snake meat steamed.

"Course I am," said Herbert, his voice dripping with sarcasm. He picked shoots from his staff and willed them to regrow until a tingling sensation ran up and down his fingers. "But Teguin, d'ye reckon it wise t'be travelin' with her?"

"We need a guide."

Herbert pointed at the tent. "*Empress Above*, her brother was kidnapped by soldiers, killed by the Imperial guard, and we're headin' fer the prison!"

"And we are paying her extremely well to do it." Teguin bit into the snake meat.

Herbert picked at his teeth. "If we're already in the desert there's na'en a reason t'hide. We carry an Imperial seal if we need t'use it."

"Herbert, we need to focus on the larger task at hand," cautioned Teguin. "I can think of worse ways to buy passage in the desert than a woman who can hunt the only thing there is to eat out here."

"If what she says is true," Herbert replied. He focused on the teardrop-shaped tip of his staff where a miniature apple tree grew in concealment. After a minute he blinked a rim of green from his vision, wiping sweat from his brow. "Have ye given thought t'what we would do if she grows tired of us? Those lamat do whatever the woman says. Have ye seen their claws?"

Teguin offered him a piece of the snake. Herbert was so hungry from waiting to eat that he barely chewed before swallowing it with a shudder. It tasted of old chicken grease with... something muddy at the end.

Desperate for a change in flavor, he teased open the tip of his staff to pull out an apple and ate it in three bites so he wouldn't be caught. Each piece stuck in his throat but he was too hungry to care. Closing his eyes in appreciation, he spat out a few seeds beyond the fire.

Teguin watched the seeds vanish. "Why not save them?" he asked. "I've never seen you throw a seed away before."

"This sand could use every seed it gets. Besides, it'll mark the way back home."

"If something doesn't eat it first."

The lamat shifted nearby and he shot them a dirty look as if they were in league with Rinzi to criticize him, too. "Here now," he said, "don't ye go eatin' those."

Teguin said something under his breath, and Herbert caught the mention of how many ways in which those seeds would shrivel or blow away before they ever sprouted.

"I didn't hear ye speak up t'say how little ye visit yer own kin," he said, spitting another seed into the sand. Rinzi's had words stung his conscience. There was a pile of letters at Praxis from his mother, read but unanswered.

Teguin swallowed and coughed, choking on his last bite. "She didn't ask," he said. "I don't talk about life on the road the way you do about Tanasen Estate."

"Well, the woman makes me nervous is all. When I'm nervous I start jabberin' away. This desert makes me on edge, Teguin. There's somethin'... unnatural about havin' na'en a piece of grass fer a stretch far as the turnin' sky. We're a few hundred leagues from home but the soil is barren. Why was I so sure of finding life in this desolate place, anyway?"

Teguin dug his hands into the sand. "Be mindful of what you say to Rinzi, Herbert. I'm sure she doesn't want the reminder of how green everything is in Falden when she only looks at bare, scorched ground day in and day out. She didn't choose the place for its looks, she simply cannot afford to live anywhere else. That's no reason to rub her face in it."

A small hiss from behind them made Herbert jump. It stretched his nerves thin to think of all the creatures that crawled just beyond his sight—or beneath it. Teguin was more at home in the desert than he was, and he didn't like to admit how much that bothered him.

They had already agreed on a long journey together; he would simply have to get used to hiding his magic. And fight his aversion to snakes. He swallowed, and tried not to think of their next meal.

After concentrating again on his staff, he rolled a small apple over to rest beside Teguin. Teguin scooped it up with a furtive look at Rinzi's tent. He held onto it, turning the mottled red and yellow pattern in his hands and taking bites each the size of his knuckle. Herbert smiled, despite himself.

Fruit was a precious thing. An impossible thing in the desert and yet, here it was. Here he was.

"Apology accepted," Teguin said, spitting out a seed into his hand and putting it into his vest pocket. "In case you change your mind," he said with a smile.

"Admit it," said Herbert shaking his head as he nibbled on a delicate pea shoot. "Ye keep me travelin' with ye fer the food."

"I never denied it," Teguin said, brushing sand off his pants. "What is it Feran loves to say?"

Herbert puffed out his chest in a bad imitation of Teguin's uncle. "Damn fine apples. Now there's a fortune in fruit." And me traded along with it, he thought.

Sighing, he rubbed at his eyes. "I'm fer a quick shuteye. How long t'the prison d'ye reckon?"

"A fair number of snake meals yet, I'm afraid." Teguin spat out another seed, this time into the sand.

10

AN IMPERIAL DEMAND

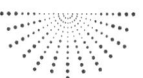

L ena slid to a stop at the entrance to the prison guard barracks, panting. "There's another company of soldiers, Cergath," she said. "They're approaching from the west to join the others."

Cergath counted on his fingers. "Ashes above, that's at least a hundred more of them."

One of the guards rubbed his jaw. "What could this mean, Captain?"

"We must plan for an assault against the prison."

"Fight our own?" muttered a guard near Lena.

"We owe loyalty t'the Empress. That's treason!"

"And when has the Empress done anythin' t'help the prison except spit on thieves and exiles?" said one of the younger guards.

"Why have our patrols not encountered them?" asked another, tugging at her lip as she looked at Lena. "You saw nothing on your last gathering?"

Lena shrugged. "We went deeper into the desert."

A few of the other guards muttered about sinking sands and risky choices.

Cergath got up from where he sat. "I do not believe that Captain

Jarvin would go so far as to attack the prison. We will find out the reason for these soldiers by speaking with him. We hear little of the Imperium in the way of news; they could be here for our own protection from some greater threat."

Lena snorted. Before she could say anything, Cergath barked out orders to the others. "Sanders, set up four-hour watches. Heran, climb the tower to take up the first position. I want a guard on that tower day and night. Gambel, take four and go down to check on the prisoners. Take a count of who we need to move to a more secure location if there is trouble on the inside."

Cergath opened a dusty locker and retrieved the formal jacket of his captain's uniform, his calloused fingers fumbling with the buttons. Lena had never seen the man wear it. "The rest of you, I want weapons sharp and your eyesight sharper. Report any unusual movements to me immediately; I will be with the warden."

Lena handed her spyglass to Heran and hurried to catch up with Cergath. "Why the sudden change in orders? The soldiers outside the prison walls kept their distance, came and went, they even let us through a few days ago. Captain Jarvin refused to deliver our supplies a month ago and they never left. What am I missing?"

"With the addition of a hundred men, that completes a pod of soldiers," said Cergath.

"A what?"

"Any Imperial worth their water waits until they have a pod unit assembled before they attack a strategic target."

"It's them that needs a thrashing. They should never have denied us those supplies in the first place," grumbled Lena.

"That's not the point. Even Jarvin would not have the clout to order such a large number of soldiers under normal circumstances." Cergath knocked on the warden's door.

"Enter," came the reply.

Lena hesitated to follow Cergath inside, but her father beckoned for her to join them. "I will not send you away when there is trouble," he said. "We learn best from hardship and challenge and—"

"—you must learn quickly in the desert," finished Lena, stepping inside. He nodded and a thrill of excitement gripped her. The warden was not generous with praise or his approval.

"Report?" he asked Cergath.

"Over a hundred new soldiers joined their ranks during the night."

Her father's expression darkened. "An Imperial pod. Did you order the guard to ready the prison for an attack?"

"Yes, but Warden, our guard will not fight the Imperial legion without damn good reason."

"I would hope that defending their own lives would be reason enough."

"What are their demands?" Lena asked her father, but he was too deep in his own train of thought to answer.

"With that many soldiers," he said to Cergath, "and knowledge of our prison, they would have a very real chance of defeating us."

"If they got inside, perhaps. But would they dare to attack?"

"That remains to be seen." He turned to Lena. "Ready two lamat. Cergath and I will ride to the encampment and see about this pod of soldiers."

THE WARDEN WATCHED his daughter leave with a heavy heart. He wanted to send her away from the danger that confronted them, but his duty kept them both at the prison. She would be at his side.

He noticed Cergath was wearing his uniform down to the formal jacket of the Imperial legion and he went to a small side chamber to pull out his own, the crimson faded, the buttons scoured by sand. It fit him like a glove.

He joined Cergath at the window. Together, they looked over the sand dunes at the Imperial encampment. New tents were popping up so close together that in some places they blocked the view of the sand.

Too much weight, he thought. *The dune could swallow a stretch of them in seconds*. It was ignorant to put them in danger where they slept. These were young soldiers, wet behind the ears and too soft for the heat and shifting sands. Were there no veterans left?

"They may no longer remember me as a General and Imperial Justikar," he remarked as he straightened the insignia on his jacket, "but at least they will be reminded of it."

"Yes sir, they will."

Their lamat carved paths into the sand with their curved claws and long tails. The creatures' legs were so wide that riding side-by-side through the encampment was impossible. At the camp, the soldiers eyed their approach.

Some stopped their work to openly stare while others drew up to attention at the sight of their uniforms. Not one soldier in sight was over thirty cycles if he was any judge. He showed all the soldiers equal respect; he was still an Imperial to the core no matter his past treatment or punishment at the hands of the Empress.

When he dismounted, Cergath was at his side in a heartbeat. A hand hovered over the hilt of the man's sword. One of the soldiers near the command tent approached them with an officer's stripe on his jacket and saluted.

"Sirs, you are welcome at the command tent," he said, his boots sinking into the sand where he stood.

"Then lead us there, Lieutenant!" ordered Cergath, his fists clenching. "Or do you enjoy making General Moonstone wait?"

Sand flew in the soldier's haste to hurry them inside. Captain Jarvin stood in conversation with a woman. The warden froze.

His heart dropped into his stomach. Jarvin was talking with Lady Jade Moonstone. His wife. He squeezed his fist so tightly the knuckles cracked.

"I would like an explanation," he said, his voice flat. "I do not care who gives it to me. You have amassed a pod of soldiers outside an Imperial prison without provocation or explanation. Why?"

Her eyes were still as blue as he remembered. Oceans of depth. Lena's eyes were brown like his, but she had her mother's smile. Lady Jade was not smiling now.

"As an Imperial Seeker, I must ask you to turn over your prisoners for inspection."

"Inspection?" the word stuck in his head. What was she up to now?

Jade looked at him with detached speculation, as if he were a small insect she might crush if she had the time. "Yes, Warden Moonstone. By the order of the Blessed Empress, may She live a thousand lives."

A breeze stirred the tent flaps behind him. Cergath wiped sweat from his brow but held his silence. A hiss came from his lamat outside when a stranger came too close.

"What will happen to them, Captain?" he asked Jarvin.

"That's far from yer concern," said the man with delight. "The prison is hereby, er, disbanded. Done with. Yer t'turn over the prisoners in the morn. The prison guard will join the Imperial soldiers on border patrol duties. Yer daughter will also submit fer inspection," he added with particular emphasis.

Dismay twisted the warden's stomach. How could his own wife turn over their daughter as if she were a prisoner? "Lena will do no such thing," he said coldly.

Lady Jade turned to Captain Jarvin and Cergath. "Give us the tent alone for a moment, please."

"Alone?" said Jarvin. His eyes narrowed as he looked at Jade, calculating the consequences of a refusal. He sighed. "Yer will, Seeker." He shot a look of naked loathing at the warden. "Ye'll find me right outside."

"I know I may rely on you for my protection."

Blood burning from her reply, the warden nodded to Cergath, who raised an eyebrow but followed Jarvin outside. Now that they were alone, he wrestled with what he could possibly say to the woman in front of him.

Fifteen cycles. A stranger before him. Beloved. No, detested. This was damn confusing.

"Are you only going to stand there and stare at me, Torven?" Her voice sounded exactly the same; melodic and sweet and full of hidden venom.

"What would you have me say? You return with no warning after saying you never wanted to see me again, wanting to take my daughter away as if she suddenly means something to you?"

"*Your* daughter? How dare you! Everything I do is for Lena, for her protection. You wouldn't understand, your head is still buried in sand even after all these cycles!"

His cool façade broke. "I never liked court intrigues and you know that!" Anger rose like bile in his throat. So much of their relationship was a haze, but the arguments returned to memory with bitter clarity.

"You are always so eager to please others, Jade. Your answers and mood change until you say the right thing to get what you want. I've had enough of those lies to last a lifetime."

"Is that... is that truly what you think, Torven?" Her eyes were pools spilling over. There were wrinkles around them now, and the hands that squeezed her arms had grown thin, though the angle of her hips revealed every curve to her advantage.

He refused to soften. "I see now how easy it must be for you to disavow your family and leave them to rot. We were simply a solution to one of your rolls of the dice and now look at you. Trying to earn back the high opinion of the Empress once again?"

A tear rolled down her cheek. "Do you not see? This is exactly why you were banished in the first place. If a poisonous snake slides into bed with you, you cannot simply kick it away. No matter how much you try to ignore it, you cannot do that either! You would ask for a snakebite rather than try to avoid it."

The silence of fifteen long cycles brought a bitterness to his lips that he had kept like soured wine. He never had the chance to speak to her of the pain of her absence. Now it was too late to talk of anything but his anger.

"What I still do not understand," he snapped, "is how you justify betrayal for the sake of your own convenience. Where is your moral compass, Jade? If you are ready to believe in everything, then you stand for nothing."

"The Imperium is changing, Torven. The Empress has pardoned

those who stood against her all those cycles ago. You can finally come home."

"Home?" the shock of such a strange word made his anger cool a measure, but it was a hollow word. Where was home except the place where he was needed, the place where he wanted to be. This place was his home.

"I asked for the Empress to send me with the message. Even if you choose not to understand what I did all those cycles ago, and no longer want anything to do with me, would you separate me forever from seeing my daughter?"

He stiffened. A gut-wrenching fear took hold of him. "Why subject her to an inspection if you care so much for her safety? Jarvin is a pig."

Jade looked to the tent entrance and lowered her voice. "I would never let anyone so much as touch her. It is me who would see her, and no one else."

The words set off a warning bell as he remembered who and what she was. That simple request held terrible meaning. "See her? Wait. You intend to look into her and find out if she could be a Seeker."

Her silence only confirmed his suspicion. "How could you wish for her to have a similar life to yours? It's one step from slavery!"

A cough from outside made them both take a step back.

"I have served the Imperium faithfully for my whole life," he said, clenching a fist and putting it over his heart. "Fulfilling a pledge of loyalty even during my banishment, but this? This is too much. You ask me to turn over our innocent daughter, sacrifice any future freedom she would have, and take her away from the only home she has ever known."

"She may not even have my skill, but if saying so could protect her—"

"*Relic bones*, Jade! Do not treat me like a fool. You would not be here if you thought she had no magic."

"Don't shout," she snapped, "or your ignorance will get us both killed."

"Ah, so the Empress forgives us, but still fears what she cannot control. You think me ignorant, Jade, but you could not be more wrong. The Empress no longer sends soldiers of honor to uphold the law, they only drag us through the mud." He looked down at his uniform and unfastened the buttons of his jacket.

"What are you doing, are you mad?"

"A crime is a crime until the rule of law is no longer valued or pursued, Jade. Look around you! There is a sickness in these people and it has nothing to do with justice."

"Madness *has* gripped you," she hissed, reaching for him, "stop this at once, Torven!"

"Do you know what a man like Jarvin will do to these prisoners? Cutting their throats before sunrise would be a mercy. Inspection," he spat the word at her as he wrenched his arm away from her outstretched hand.

He could not stand to have her touch him. "Forgiveness from the Empress? That is not justice but convenience given on a whim; it will be taken away without a second thought. Lives hang in the balance, our daughter's life given over to a savage, and here you are asking me to allow it."

"I care about what I can change," Jade said quietly. "I can save Lena if you would only let me. The rest of the prisoners, I will do what I can, but if they have no magic it is out of my hands."

Torven dropped his jacket. "I will not submit to a monster which feeds upon the fear of the ignorant."

"Torven. Torven, look at me."

He would not. "I will not allow my prisoners to be executed for something they have no control over. Any blood spilled by my actions would be a far kinder fate than mercy at Jarvin's hand."

Her betrayal lingered. To see her standing there filled him with such pain he could barely breathe. "I kept your secrets and paid the price. I would ask where your loyalties rest on this day. I would call you a Blade or a Seeker or even my wife, if I only knew it would be the truth. But if you believe all to be right then I can take no truth from your words."

"You stubborn fool. If any harm comes to Lena I will never forgive your pride in refusing my protection!"

"I am not yours to command. Good day, milady."

"On your head be it!" she shouted after him.

He stormed out of the tent and Cergath hurried to follow. "Where is your uniform?"

"It was too tight for my liking."

11

TROUBLED DREAMS

Lavinia Troug was trapped in the same dream. Night after night she reached into her robes, her rune bones smooth and cold to the touch. She shook them in both hands while murmuring. Clattered them to break the eerie stillness. She walked, turning and changing direction every few steps, but in the end she always returned to the same room.

A stone marker lay on its side. She circled it, searching the hairline fractures and dead lichen on its surface. The harder she looked, the more her vision swam.

This place felt familiar. She looked around. How many times had she found her way here, yet its meaning remained elusive as a nameless face in the shadows.

Coming to stand before the stone marker there was a change in the room. Something new. A man stood beside her, bent upon examining the standing stone.

Lavinia wanted to ask what he was doing but when he turned she recognized her pren, Teguin. Words tumbled from her and twisted the moment into a kind of lesson. "When I use my magic," she said, "I find myself in a sort of waking dream. I watch the last moments of life that each person holds onto before they die."

As she spoke of her interactions with those long dead, Teguin grew pale and immobile as if his own life were leaving him, solemn as the stone before them.

"What can you tell me of this grave?" asked Teguin, his lips barely moving.

"Grave? Oh, yes of course. It is a grave marker." Her dispassionate tone a dull reflection of the revelation.

"If you have a focus object," he said, "it would enable you to be more proactive, and less reactive."

She found herself nodding at the strange and fluid shift between who was pren and master. "Let us use your magic to discover more."

Teguin threw a hand full of stones into the air, mimicking how she threw her rune bones. "Let us discover more about him," he said.

Chills ran up and down her spine. "Him?"

Teguin said nothing in reply.

Lavinia wanted to tell Teguin of her discoveries with the Blades. So much had happened since she last saw him. But an inexplicable attraction to the stone marker in front of them forced her to push everything else aside.

Teguin caught his stones—each small as a fingertip—and rolled them around in the palm of his scarred hand. "How do I begin?"

"Remember that you are the one in control," she said. "These stones are an extension of you. Concentrate on how they feel in your hand, and, when you no longer feel a distinction between each of them focus on what you wish to know. They will become a part of your thoughts."

Teguin took a deep breath. He shut his eyes. Twisting red patterns flickered into life on the dark walls around them.

Lavinia closed her eyes at the shape of the light but it pierced through her eyelids. "Too bright," she murmured. Sweat made her palms slippery, and even her rune bones felt brittle and empty of their usual comfort.

"I am in control," said Teguin. Light twisted and danced and writhed to fill the stillness in the air. "I am in control."

A strange sensation came over Lavinia. It was as if someone

cracked an egg on her head, and the feeling ran down from her neck into her hand. She dropped her rune bones onto the floor.

"I am in control!" shouted Teguin, his eyes aglow with the bright crimson which encircled them.

Helpless, she watched Teguin absorb the red light into his skin. The stones in his hand pulsed and writhed and tried to slip out of his grasp. Fighting to keep control, Teguin moved to place his hand on the grave and instead of gently placing the stones atop the marker, he slammed his hand against it with all of his strength.

Cracks and marks of any kind were erased as the surface of the grave marker liquified. The stones from Teguin's hand sank into it and out of sight.

Lavinia fought to hold in a scream that became a moan of fear. Her eyes closed again, approaching a vast well of writhing darkness. This new depth of power Teguin displayed frightened her to the core. How could he possibly harness such destruction?

From the darkness within came a reply: *To know power, you must know pain.*

Her own horror was nothing compared to the sound of Teguin's screams. First his shoulder, then his whole arm glowed. His scars lit up as though he would be burned alive in the red flames.

His eyes met Lavinia's gaze but she had to turn away, she could not stand to look upon him. Afraid of what he had become, she knelt and cowered before him. A hissing, grinding, scraping sound filled the air as though Teguin's magic and his stones continued to burrow beneath the surface of the stone marker.

When the sound stopped, so did Teguin's screams. The red light vanished. Words appeared on the stone grave, fresh as though newly carved. Together, Lavinia and Teguin leaned in to read them.

HERE LIES
PERCIVAL VENDRICK
BELOVED SCHOLAR AND
FIRST ARCHIVIST OF THE IMPERIUM

BEFORE THEIR EYES the words shifted again, this time melting away as stones leapt from the marker like fish from a pool of water. The only word that remained untouched grew larger, until it rested, alone, in the center of the grave.

LIES

~

THE LEXICON AWOKE to a scratching sound at her chamber door. She cleared her throat. "What is it?"

Tamrel shuffled into the room. "It's the bone reader, Lexicon. Her dreams allow her no rest. After her last reading she was frantic. Daxel's been with her all night but she's raving. She calls out for Teguin "

"Teguin?" the Lexicon reached for her boots and followed the girl out into the hallway.

The Lexicon had moved Troug into quarters near her own, partially to accede to Elena's repeated requests, but also to keep an eye on the woman's condition. In her opinion the change of location had done little to improve the results of the woman's visions.

When she entered the room, Daxel tried to rise but his hand was held in a vice-like grip by Troug. "Lexicon," he said, "who is Teguin?"

A thin blanket twisted around Troug's legs as she thrashed and cried out weakly, "Lies! I will not believe it!"

Daxel tried again to free his hand.

"Don't disturb her," she cautioned. "The bone reader may have shared things of value with Teguin. Stay with her, Daxel. I want to know everything of which she speaks. Asleep, awake, or in a trance. Dreams and memory may blend together to reveal something we missed. Anything she shares could be important."

"But, Lexicon, it is nearly dawn and I must—"

"You are relieved of your other duties."

Mollified by his new freedom, the boy relaxed his hand and settled in beside Troug, biting his lower lip.

"And if she looks to you for comfort," added the Lexicon, "give it to her. Deny her nothing if it is within our means."

"What if she only wants this Teguin?"

"Then in this room, you will be Teguin."

WITH EVERY BREATH

Whispers followed Praelor Thurst as he was carried through the palace. Too weak to walk after a bad attack the day before, the necessity of a litter was a humiliation that pained him more than his agonies. Had he breath to spare, he would have laughed at his shame as they carried him in the manner of a corpse receiving final blessings before a purification ritual.

Observers bowed but whispered in confusion as the litter bearers carried an old man very much alive, wheezing and coughing. The Empress liked to keep only the beautiful and healthy around her in the palace; it reflected the perfection of her rule. The sight of him must have been upsetting for those accustomed to the uninterrupted pleasures of their surroundings.

He forced one ragged breath after another. A mind clear of this petty self-awareness was essential. He must focus on preparations for the future, on the last few tasks which bound him to this pained body. There was still work to do.

Thirty labored breaths brought him to the inner courtyard. Another twenty to the private chambers of the royal family. He blinked rapidly as his surroundings blurred. Swollen knuckles made it impossible to clutch at the seat when it wobbled, so he closed his eyes to block out the worst of the rising and falling.

When the litter came to a halt, Thurst squinted in the sunlit room. At the head of a long table sat the Empress, enjoying a late breakfast. A dozen steaming dishes rested on golden plates while her handmaidens cut fruit and mixed honey into a bowl.

A young initiate for the handmaidens sat near the Empress. Her golden curls twisted around her shoulders, and her mouth was opening and closing in curiosity and alarm at the sight of him. The girl started when a fruit bowl was thrust under her nose, then she reached in and ate several pieces, nodding her enjoyment.

The bowl was presented to the Empress. Without a glance in the girl's direction she selected a piece of fruit with a tiny golden fork. "Praelor, here you are at last."

He cleared his throat, dry as reed grass. "Majesty. A pod of Imperial soldiers surrounds the prison in the Barren Wastelands. Why was I not informed of this well in advance?"

"I did not think it wise to burden you with small matters."

His vision blurred again. His thoughts spun out of control. Small matters? What other decisions would she make without informing him? Who would she turn to for council if she thought him unable to serve?

He took a sudden and uncontrolled breath which caused an intense fit of coughing.

"Water for the Praelor," said the Empress. She speared another piece of fruit. A flicker of emotion passed across her face. Concern? Pity? The subtle difference in her bearing was beyond him.

When a goblet was offered, he took a packet of dry powder and dropped it into the water. It dissolved and the liquid turned a deep blue. He could no longer hide his weakness from the Empress. Shame burned in his cheeks as Thurst realized he had no strength to lift the drink to his lips.

He forced himself to nod. The servant held the goblet for him, spilling some of it as he coughed and gargled to swallow it down. His breathing deepened.

The coughing diminished. Slowly, faces in the room came back into focus. When the servant tried to wipe away what he had spilled Thurst waved him away; ink stains would not be so easily lifted.

Where had their conversation paused? He probed his memory all the while aware that the tickle in his throat would soon grow worse again.

"Radiant Majesty," he managed to say in a calm tone of voice, "this is a delicate time for the Imperium. The edict forgiving those involved in the uprising is a remarkable success. We have the most powerful nobility renewing pledges of loyalty and service to you in public displays that have calmed the unrest in the capital. But there is still more we need to do."

He paused to catch his breath. "Having magic in the Imperium is only the beginning; we must take steps to strengthen our influence over its creation and use among all your people."

"But that is why the prison is being emptied," said the Empress, pursing her lips. "You suggested that we put every able-bodied Imperial to use. We can hardly ignore the potential of magical uprisings in such a remote place, wouldn't you agree?"

He wanted to shout, to tear at his hair. Emptying the prison with a pod of soldiers was like using a hammer-strike when a whisper would do. If only she had confided in him; with a few careful words and a Seeker visit no one would have ever known the Empress had an interest in the prison.

A shortened sentence here or there. Transfers for the gifted. Sudden illness, perhaps. There were ways.

But now a pod of Imperial soldiers had marched through Falden, and waited outside the prison for anyone to see. It would instill fear and panic and bring others together in their resentment.

Why intimidate the most downtrodden citizenry without an example to make? It was reckless. Dangerous.

No matter the cost, the Empress must not be made to look a fool. No one feared a divine ruler who made such mistakes. Human mistakes.

"You must attack the prison," he said suddenly. There was still time for him to fix this. "Claim an uprising required Imperial discipline, or your interest was in protecting the people along the border from any kind of harm."

The Empress put down her fork. "The pod was merely for intimidation."

"How—" he started, but even in his weakened state he changed his reproach to an appeal mid-sentence. "We cannot look weak or desperate. Most importantly, we risk many questions being asked over such a display of intimidation without any cause."

She frowned at his last words. "I should not have to remind you, Praelor, that it is *my* prison. If it suits my mood I could order its existence erased from the world."

He cleared his throat, the tickle now tightening. "That may be necessary, Imperial Majesty. This prison of yours was never designed to be a resting place for our people. We should stay as far from it as possible."

She wasn't listening. "We will offer the prisoners pardons. The Imperial pod could escort them back to the Imperium. We will throw a celebration to welcome our citizens home."

That gave him pause. From only a few pardons to several hundred within a cycle. Would that convey a different kind of weakness? The ramifications could be devastating.

"Praelor?" came the voice of the Empress. "Praelor Thurst?"

The world around him whirled in shadow and color. This time, he could not hold the darkness at bay. A throbbing in his head froze his thoughts, struck into stillness as if he plunged into the ocean.

Who was he? When could he leave this place? He closed his eyes.

A WILD HOPE

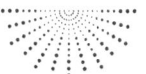

L uther paddled in his raft with swift, even strokes. Being on the water brought back memories of Breel where he lived as a boy. With cycles spent away from Iridian coast, he marveled at his luck to find a small boat. A few days of hot weather had turned melting snow from the mountains into flooding streams, carving swollen paths of frantic water coursing through the lower valley.

Dripping ice and stone drowned in churning whirlpools of mud. The current was fast and, by its grace, so was Luther's pace.

Crossing the mountains along the Borderlands had carved Luther into a new man. No coin could buy his comfort, and so he left behind the inns and their roasted meats, ripping away from him his nervous eating habits along with his larger belly. He was the happiest he had ever been in his life.

Dunmire was a desolate place. There was a raw beauty in its wilderness that took his breath away. In search of magic, he found instead a sense of peace and purpose in a simple existence.

Praelor Thurst would hate his lack of progress. What could he do? If there was no magic to be found he could not create it from nothing. The immense reach of his master had weakened in Dunmire. And where the Praelor grew weak, Luther flourished.

There was plenty of time to think about the Imperium and Dunmire while he explored. A cold silence existed between the two countries. No trade. No travel, except an occasional raid by the desperate.

Their hostility mystified him. It seemed the only thing both countries agreed upon was their mutual enmity. In the end, Luther could not see why the Imperium should be at odds with Dunmire. If the Dunmiri wanted to be left alone then why not let them?

The few people he had encountered were honest to a fault, sharing company and camp with any who passed. These were a people with the simple wish to be of help to one another when it was needed, without guise or agency. Mutual survival drew them together.

The nomadic tribes who lived here shared delight in this simple existence, content to treat outsiders with a simple meal and a refreshing lack of curiosity. To them he was simply another tribe, another traveler, perhaps stranger in his manner but when traveling alone there were many causes of strange behavior. He knew that better than most.

The daylight darkened into heavy cloud. A misting rain sent fog and dense clouds across the muddy water. It was dangerous water to steer on without clear points ahead, and Luther pulled his boat into a shelter of pine trees to settle in for the night.

Prying open a wooden box, he sparked a small fire from a pile of wood shavings. The weather in Dunmire was unpredictable, and dry wood was hard to find unless he carried some with him as he went. Almost as valuable was the covered woven basket beside the box, a gift from an old woman in the first village he found over the mountains. It took skilled hands to weave a basket that held water. With a smile, he pulled out a few swimming fish he had caught on a line and kept for later.

When he was done gutting and cleaning them, Luther washed his hands in the stream and let his dinner cook in wet leaves with a few mushrooms and a bitter herb that same woman had taught him to recognize. Under the shelter of a large tree, he pulled out his only map and made a mark along its edge to record the passing of another day. From this point he would head north to reach some kind of grasslands, a place which held some significance to the Dunmiri people, if Praelor Thurst's last report was accurate.

He scratched at his beard. Lost in thought, he plucked the wrapped fish from the edge of the fire and picked out the larger pin bones. The more he saw of their lands, the more Luther envied their unfettered way of life; it was so different than his own in the Imperium.

There was no need to enforce the worship or power of a single deity. There was no Empress here. The Dunmiri respected strength of leadership when it was earned, not imposed from what he saw in the few villages at which he stopped.

He made a bed of pine boughs, fastened a few large branches from the tree, and covered himself with a rough blanket, listening to the rain with a deep sigh. This was peace. This was wonderful.

LUTHER SAT UP, a whimper half-formed in his throat. He drew the damp blanket close around his shoulders and listened. What was it that woke him?

No longer raining, a thick fog had rolled across the swollen river. Cries from a pack of wild dogs drifted to his ears; their calls were distant but he knew little of animals and avoided those he could not eat. He looked wildly around him and checked the undisturbed ground beside where he slept. It was as if a stranger breathed down his neck.

Luther reached for a small wooden club beside the bed and rose, stomping feeling back into his stiff legs. Circling his camp, he failed to find any reason for the pricking at his skin. His boat was untouched, the area undisturbed. A flash of fur ran from the pile of fish remains beside the water.

Resting his club on the ground, he breathed on his hands to warm them and gasped at what caught his attention: vibrant and sudden, the animation of an inked tattoo across the knuckle of his first finger. It was an eye, roaming but unfocused as it glowed by way of Luther's magical sight. The piercing blue iris was moving for the first time in months.

The tattoo forged a strange connection, an unforgiving bond between Luther and the Praelor that moved of its own will. It was a presence and power which moved beyond the sending scrolls that Luther once relied upon as the sole account of his progress. Unwilling to forgive failure, the Praelor forced the eye upon Luther to keep them bound together in a way that was far beyond his understanding. To Luther's knowledge, only he could see it move when it came to life. It was such a fearsome thing that he did not dare show it to anyone else.

It took the better part of a cycle for Luther to grow accustomed to the icy blue glare. It blinked at random. When it narrowed to focus in on something Luther had passed, he flinched and waited for something to happen. Nothing ever did.

Lately, the eye was dormant and little more than a mark of ink. What did it mean that it now searched his surroundings, was he close to danger? Discovery?

Heart racing, Luther forced a few deep breaths and returned to the shelter of the trees. There was no one here. He was alone. Alone, and frozen stiff.

He added a piece of dry wood to revive the fire and breathed in the smoke to try and calm his nerves. Fighting the urge to rub at his hands again, Luther gave the eye fearful, fleeting looks as he tried to warm himself. The forceful presence behind the mark was absent.

Praelor Thurst was focused on something else. Luther cautiously waved a hand over the eye. It continued the same sightless hunt, unaffected.

Luther leaned away from the smoke, coughing. With no chance of sleep returning, he watched the fog lift to the sky while vivid patches of green and brown sunlight enlivened the ground. Flames from the fire died away again until only fingers of smoke remained.

It was only with the return of the eye's movement that Luther fully realized his fear of returning to the Imperium. The slavish nature of his work there had broken him, and yet in Dunmire he was healing in ways he did not understand. A wild, selfish hope stirred.

The Praelor was not in good health; he was dying, eaten alive from the inside by his magic. The decline was slow but relentless in its pursuit. If Praelor Thurst was finally losing control of his magic, then... it stunned him to the core. What if he remained here?

Did he have to return to the Imperium at all? No one else knew where he was. If they did somehow communicate with the Praelor, Luther's failure to return home could easily be interpreted as an unfortunate loss in an unfamiliar and hostile land.

The Praelor was a cruel master. Luther hated himself for how much he feared the man who thought him unworthy of being a Seeker. He called Luther many things. Weak. Useless. Not as much man as worm. The taunts and insults were no longer barbs but part of Luther's skin, layered down to his bones.

But what if his failures were a blessing in disguise? A sign After all, no one mourns the loss of a useless man.

It was a dream and he knew it. But it was his and he held onto it like a barb in his skin, letting it burrow deep. This place was special. For all he knew it would finally be a place to call his home.

A SIMPLE REQUEST

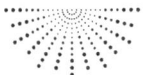

F eran settled into his brother's bearskin chair, carved and stretched and worn down to fit a set of shoulders as broad as his own. He stretched out his hands before the small fire with a sigh. It took the chill from his hands. "It is kind of you to see me after all these cycles, Iridal."

His brother's wife fixed a simple tisane, plucking herbs and dropping them into a pot over the fire. "We've no honey for you," she said, pulling away from a jumping spark. "No luxuries like you keep on your travels."

"It is no matter."

She handed him a mug. "If Legan finds you here I'll deny that I ever agreed to see you. Your letters of Teguin have only been read by me. Whatever Legan finds he destroys without a second glance." Iridal bit her lip, looking to the cabin's door and then back to Feran. "What is so important that you would come in person? Be quick."

Feran blew upon the steaming drink. "The Empress threw a ball last month for her twin daughters to celebrate their coming of age. At the ball, she pardoned any noble houses involved in the uprising and urged the need for pledging unity under her rule."

Iridal gasped. "A trick, surely."

"I assure you it is nothing of the kind." He sipped the tisane and tried to hide the intensity with which he studied her reaction to his announcement. "Come back, Iridal. You could return to the Blue City with all its luxuries and take your rightful place as part of a noble house. You gave up your name, your nobility, you sacrificed everything but it is not too late to have it back."

Footsteps shook the front steps. Feran put down his mug and cursed silently at the unwanted interruption. As always, his brother chose the worst moment to interfere.

Determined to maintain control of the situation, Feran forced a smile onto his face and stood. It was almost worth the interruption to see Legan freeze in the doorway at the sight of him.

"Greetings, brother," he said warmly. "I have excellent news! The Blessed Empress, she has issued a full pardon for any noble house involved in the uprising. You can finally drop this guise and return home."

A long, hard silence stretched between them.

"Convenient," Legan replied at last.

"How do you mean?"

"The cold, my dear," said Iridal, looking between them.

A numbing breeze swirled past Legan and into the cabin as he shoved the door closed. "Convenient, pardoning the houses when all those involved in the uprising are dead. How much did you have to pay for that favorable outcome?"

Feran's bit his tongue so hard he thought a piece might come off. "Legan, you flatter me that the Empress would take notice of a simple merchant."

"I think the Empress would sleep better at night if she could keep a closer eye on all survivors of the exiled houses, *especially* those who renounced their titles. Vengeance is a very real threat to anyone with so much blood on her hands."

This was not going well. Legan always had this effect on him, bringing out the need to exaggerate and embellish and prove that he was in the right. Feran grew more determined than ever to make his brother see the value in his reasoning.

"The Empress has kept peace in our realm for close to thirty cycles now. Our Blue City is a place of safety and prosperity, far from the bloody battleground you claim it to be. Come back with me and see for yourself. We can reclaim the honor of the Dorst name together."

His brother's laugh was harsh as it filled the cabin. "Is that it, then? The family title has to be claimed, and you need me before you can do it? What a foolish fantasy, believing that a name holds any power to change a man."

Feran's ears pounded at the sound. The blasphemy of his brother's words brought a surge of anger to his chest. "Why must you always fight me, Legan? We can finally put the past behind us!"

"I have no desire to concern myself with your petty, power-grasping schemes."

"But this changes everything, can't you see? Come out of exile. Your wife could live in comfort again, our families could carry their heads high without the fear of curses thrown in their path—"

"You dare speak to me of curses?" Legan's filthy hands clenched into fists. Cuts and bruises ran the length of his arms. "You are not welcome here and you damn well know why."

Feran refused to give up so easily. He glanced at Iridal, but the woman showed no sign of coming to his aid. "You would send me away without any word of your son? Teguin has done well at Praxis, but he has placed himself in debt and in danger by allowing others to sponsor him, and control his future. He can go no further. With a noble title he could have a limitless future. I urge you to reconsider, Legan. Even if you deny yourself, would you also deny your son his rightful place?"

Iridal slammed her mug onto the kitchen table and rose. "How dare you bring our son into this!"

Feran took out his ledger book, hiding his anger by idly leafing through it. He watched them over the gilded pages, and waited.

Legan frowned, looking at the darkening sky and back at his wife.

"It's dusk; too dangerous to travel down the mountain. You'll stay the night and leave at dawn."

"What a kind invitation—"

"I would do the same for any stray," Legan interrupted. He skewered a small fish and turned it on the fire with his back to everyone, an unlit pipe thrust in the corner of his mouth as he muttered to himself.

After a wave of compliments on the meal, Feran's one-way conversation lapsed into tense silence. In truth, the meal was poor by any standards and they all knew it. The fish was bare bones and charred flesh that stuck in the throat and refused to be washed down.

Picking small bones from his teeth, Feran snuck a glance at Iridal as he said, "I travel to Falden tomorrow to inspect what remains of the harvest. There were reports of late frost, and it is said that the snow on the mountains this winter was quite bad. One part of Falden in particular has done remarkably well despite the coldest weather, and I may just earn my place in the Imperial Merchant's Guild by renewing a very lucrative trade agreement." Feran waited, but his announcement was answered with silence.

"If I succeed, I may not be able to travel south again for several cycles." Still no response.

His voice was brimming with exasperation as he tried a third time. "There is no knowing when I will be able to return. The Empress requests—requires—a reply from every pardoned house."

"Silence will be answer enough for the Empress. We will have your mule ready at first light to speed you on your journey."

"You truly intend to remain here, no matter the cost," Feran said to them in shock. "I never thought your bitterness would lead to such poor judgement. I offer you so much; to share my wealth, to regain the honor and respect of your peers, a chance to start a new life in the capital. Has all reason left you?" The moment those last words escaped Feran knew he had slipped and let his anger take him too far.

"I will not stand here and be judged in my own house!" cried Legan. He went back out the door and slammed it behind him. Bundles of dried herbs fell from the rafters.

Feran could think of no other means of persuasion to make them change their minds. His anger cooled into a sick feeling that settled in his stomach. How could they do this to him?

"See what you have done," said Iridal as she picked up the scattered herbs. Outside came the sound of an axe splitting wood. "He will be out half the night and frozen to the bone."

"Iridal, you know what this means for all of us. Can you not speak to the man, reason with him?"

"When I married Legan, I knew what was in his heart," she replied, plucking at a hole in her skirt. "Your mother and father believed that the Empress was wrong to use magic in secret to control the people, and they were willing to give up everything to be heard. We cannot undo the past, but Legan will never forgive the Empress for killing them. Nor should you."

Iridal went to a small basket under the kitchen table. After a moment, she pulled out a tiny leather purse and dropped it onto the table in front of Feran. "Here is payment for the supplies you brought. We will not accept your bribery."

"Is it bribery to take care of my family?"

"We do not ask for your help."

Feran looked at the purse but he did not take it. "How can I change your mind?"

"It is not my decision. You cannot fight the past, Feran. It cannot be defeated or changed, only twisted into bitterness and regret if you linger on it. Be content with what you have and do not seek to control the lives of others."

"You would be happy in the Blue City, Iridal. I know it. Write to me if you change your mind, and I will do all I can for you. Family means everything to me."

She turned away from him. "Good fortune speed you on your journey."

"May fortune reach you in this bone-chilling place." He was done being polite and proper and considerate to these ants. Desperate to leave, he sat in the bearskin chair to tighten the laces of his boots. Spending the night in this rotten hovel would gain him nothing.

He could see his breath, and the smell of rotting potato made his stomach sour. Rising to his feet, he left without thanks and without seeing his brother again, shuffling with awkward steps by glowstone, stumbling and swearing as he led his mule down the mountain slopes. He would collect his wagon and continue into Falden. There was much to be done if his brother refused to return, and he had not a moment to waste.

REUNION

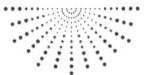

Lena watched the Imperial pod from atop the tower. Without the spyglass, she could no more make out the soldiers faces than she could their swords. Their paths wove patterns into the sand as they moved.

Contact with the Imperium had been limited for as long as she could remember. The prison was her home, and the Imperial soldiers that resupplied them had always kept their distance until Captain Jarvin had taken command a cycle ago. With his arrival, Lena had seen a new side to the prison, and to its warden.

She couldn't understand why her father accepted the increasing demands of Jarvin. Then, at the sight of Jarvin with his soldiers, Lena would be sent away with prison guards on patrols of their own. The patrols grew longer, overly complicated, more important.

They were sent to hunt and replace withheld supplies rather than lodge a protest with the Blue City. But why? When she returned from trips her father would be nursing new injuries in silence, dismissive. He was unwilling to discuss what had happened in her absence.

Whatever battle her father was fighting with Jarvin, she never expected it would cause an all-out assault on the prison. A pod of soldiers. Enough to sink this patch of desert.

She handed the guard beside her a flask. "How bad is it?"

"It's bad."

He exchanged the spyglass for the water and Lena peered through it. "I'll take your word," she said, unable to tell the differences in their formations that the guards and soldiers read with ease.

Circling the tower helped her to forget the threats beneath them. She watched the wisps of clouds that could still threaten them with rain and hoped the prison struck fear into the hearts of the soldiers below. The shape of her home was best described as forbidding. When she had been too small to leave the prison, Lena's father would bend his finger to show her its shape; a curve best seen at a distance.

Lena had overheard the older guards compare it to the tusk of a wild boar turned over. After asking what a boar was, she shrugged off their explanations. Creatures with thick fur on their skins and wild twisting masses erupting from their heads were nightmares of the imagination. The closest experience she had with forests or the creatures who lived in them were rare sightings of horse carcasses.

The prison was ancient, she knew that much. According to her father it was older than anything built in the Imperium. He had a quiet thoughtfulness when he described it, a grudging respect in his eyes. He said they owed this place. It was as if it were a fellow war-torn soldier rather than a building.

This prison was built before the existence of the Imperium; that was as far as her history lessons ever went; not even the prison warden could tell her why the place had such a strange shape to it, or why the location was so remote.

Curved to a dramatic point only a few feet wide, the top of the tower showed no sign of its age. The stairs were as unyielding as the rest of the design; and no matter the number of footfalls ground into them with each cycle the shape and pitch of steps remained, leading those who climbed to the top in a rough spiral upward and then down again to a smooth landing that allowed observers to record anything around or above them. Shallow holes and elevated blocks left spaces or raised points for a long-forgotten purpose.

Lena paced around the platform. She paused to poke at one of the holes with her foot. In times of crisis she became an outsider, the only person without a true task or obligation. The soldiers readied to attack. The guards readied their defenses. The prisoners prepared for escape or death. All Lena knew to do was keep out of the way. The guards would normally give her a certain amount of deference as the warden's daughter, though that meant nothing but a brusque dismissal when duty called.

Lena eyed the stairs. Surely no one would see a visit to Mason as suspicious, given the circumstances. "If anyone asks," she said casually, "I will be helping the healer with... bandages."

The man grunted, which was as much permission or dismissal as she wanted. As Lena turned, she heard him take a sharp breath. "Clever bastards, they've brought a rock-biter! If it gets t'the tower they'll be through our defenses, and fast. Tell yer father they've smuggled it as far as the outer wall. Go, lass!"

Eager to have a task, Lena tumbled down the stairs with reckless speed. Any faster and she might have flown without her feet touching the ground. The walls around her were smooth as glass, but for the first time they felt fragile under her trembling fingers.

She passed Cergath on the stairs. "There's a rock-biter," she called to him, then turned. "Cendrin says it won't be long now, any minute and they'll attack!"

Cergath nodded brusquely. "We've sent word to Captain Jarvin. They'll hold off; your father wants to challenge him directly for a duel to spare the prison from attack."

The shock froze her in place. "What?"

"It's done, lass. Talk to your father and wish him luck. He carries a large burden on his shoulders and will need your support."

Dazed, Lena watched Cergath continue up to the watchpoint with slow, balanced steps. She ran down to her father's study but when she approached the door, the voice of her father and a woman arguing stopped her in her tracks again.

"You know exactly what Jarvin would do to me if he knew I came here," said the woman. "Why do you refuse to let me take Lena to safety?"

"There is no safer place for her than the walls of this prison," replied her father.

"That is nonsense and you know it, Torven."

Lena gaped at the sound of her father's first name.

"No one would dare to touch her at my side," the woman's voice argued; "not even Captain Jarvin."

"You underestimate his sense of entitlement, *and* his thirst for power. Jarvin will push forward any order the Empress gives with his own twisted interpretation. He has always taken too much interest in Lena."

"We have to find another way to give him what he wants or there will be too much innocent blood spilled. Challenging him will not end this struggle."

There was a pause. "Your newfound sense of pity towards the prisoners and their fate is heartwarming."

"Pity? You think I pity them? This has nothing to do with me! I did not come here for you to attack my feelings."

The attack. Lena remembered with a jolt that she was supposed to bring her father an urgent report. Distracted, she even forgot to knock but simply walked into the room. "Cendrin reports that the Imperials have smuggled in a rock-biter, father. It has reached the outer wall and at last view they will break through easily. He urges you to—"

Lena stopped. She had never seen the look of fear on her father's face before as he watched the woman next to him. The woman started at Lena with such intensity that her jaw locked into an uncomfortable half-smile.

"Warden,' she asked her father more formally, "was Cergath right that you mean to challenge Captain Jarvin?"

"Your father has made his decision," answered the woman, biting her lip. "You cannot turn your back on the Imperial soldiers or your guards."

They looked at one another for so long that Lena wondered if they realized she was still there.

Her father went to the wall and took down his sword. "Lena, I think it is time you and your mother left."

"My mother?" A cascade of emotions rippled through Lena as she took a step back.

"I will do what must be done as warden. Jarvin will answer for his flagrant abuse of Imperial law. The winner will take command of both the soldiers and the guard."

The shock was too great. She raced forward and he enveloped her in a hug, kissing the top of her head like she was a little girl again. "Father, no!" she cried into his shoulder. "He will find a way to hurt you; worse still, he will enjoy it."

She expected him to pull away from such an unusual show of affection, but he pulled her closer. "I have been a fool. There is so much I have not told you, Lena, about the Blue City and your mother; about why we left. I never meant to put you in danger and now here we all are."

He pulled away to look at her. "You must stay away from the prison. Away from Jarvin, and even the Empress if you can."

"But why?" she asked, surprised. Tears filled her eyes. She finally had both her parents together in the same room only to see them argue and separate yet again. The unfairness of it all stung. "What has this to do with me?"

Lena jumped when her mother spoke. "I'm afraid you are more in danger than you realize, my love—"

"Don't call me that." Lena turned her anger on the woman who had been absent from her life for so long. "This is your fault. If you and those soldiers had not come, then none of this would be happening."

All her life, Lena had dreamed of her family being back together. Now she wanted to be as far away from her mother as she could. Even the sight of her father brought her pain. Why was he so eager to throw his life away?

Lena backed away from them. A buzzing rang in her ears. When she swallowed there was a bitterness on the back of her tongue, like smoke inhaled from a dying fire.

"Lena, your mother and I do not agree about many things, but I must believe now that she can protect you more than I can. Go with her."

"You always said it was just the two of us and no one else mattered. No one!"

Pain flickered in her father's eyes.

Her mother grabbed her by the shoulder. "Lena," she said, "we do not have time for this. Listen to your father."

When her mother touched Lena, the bitter taste in her mouth exploded like a bite of rotten fruit. Stars swam behind her eyes when she closed them. Something pressed against her mind like a snake burrowing into her thoughts. She dug her nails into the palms of her hands until the buzzing in her ears became a roar.

Terror replaced anger. Lena felt her hands tingle as if sand escaped them. She wished a cool breeze would carry away the weight of the noise. When she broke free, her mother's scream filled the silence.

Lena stumbled out the door. She ignored her father's calls. She would not, could not, turn around. Without thinking, she raced to the healer's ward.

She could already feel the cool touch of Mason's hands holding her. If anyone would understand her feelings it would be him. She pushed away the bitter taste that lingered, wiping her mouth on a sleeve as she ran.

Mason would give her something. He would take the pain and bitterness away. Her father wanted her to leave and she would, but not with her mother. Lena would not go with a woman who already abandoned her once before.

Did her father really want her to leave? Lena had seen the hesitation in his eyes when he asked her to go with her mother. His hand was forced, just as she had seen him forced by Jarvin into enduring terrible beatings. No one would force Lena into that kind of pain. Her mother did not deserve such blind trust.

Mason was measuring out piles of dried herbs when she arrived. "Why the hurry?" he asked, his eyes still on his work. "I could hear you running."

Lena's voice caught in her throat. Beside Mason was a cup of tisane left half-empty and forgotten. She took the cup and drank it all, her tongue heavy and useless. Mason was watching her now, frowning. "Something is wrong," he said.

"The attack," she choked out at last. "The warden wants me to leave while he fights Captain Jarvin. Mason, he will die."

"What?" Mason hesitated. "You do not know that. I suspect he has never thrown so much as a punch in Jarvin's direction. If he is finally willing to stand up to the man then that is what we always urged him to do. The warden is not trying to die, Lena, he is trying to save the guards from having to fight fellow soldiers at arms."

The sound of Mason's voice was soothing. Lena's racing heart slowed. Her mother's presence had sent her into such a spiral of panic and confusion that she could not stand still. "My mother is here," she said finally, finishing her own thoughts out loud.

"Lady Jade? Here?"

Lena was so surprised by the tone of his voice that she bit her tongue, her reply a squeak. "You know who my mother is?"

Mason dismissed the question. "No wonder you are all out of sorts, my love." He stood and joined her, tracing his fingers around the herbs on the table.

Lena leaned into him until he put his arms around her to keep her from falling. "She wants me to go with her," she explained. "Father does not trust her, not really. I could tell. And when she looked at me..."

"What did she do?"

"It was like she wanted to pull something away from me; pull me away from my father, my whole life. I cannot go with her, Mason. She scares me."

Lena had not known how deeply her mother had shaken her until she spoke of it aloud, but her words rang with such conviction that she felt an even stronger urge to leave. The thought of seeing her mother again filled her with dread. She had to get away.

"Of course not," Mason was saying, "why should you jump to obey her when she appears with no warning after all this time."

"Father insisted that I leave. I want you to come with me, Mason. Please, say that you will."

As she waited for a reply, her heart jumped to her throat. What would she do if he refused? Go alone? Would he be angry with her for even asking?

Mason left her side so suddenly she reeled from the movement. He went to his bed and dug out a worn travel pack. Layers of sand and dust fell from it as he raced around the room, filling it with reckless abandon. Then he pulled her into his arms.

With a passionate kiss that made her blush, he gave her braid a gentle tug and smiled. "When do we leave?"

THE WARDEN FELT Jade's forehead. Cold and clammy to the touch. What did that mean?

After a single haunting scream, she had collapsed onto the floor while their daughter fled. There were no visible wounds on his wife's body yet she was cold and still as death in his arms.

"Don't you scare me like this, Jade Moonstone," he said, touching her cheek, his fingers tingling as if on fire when his lips brushed her forehead. Was this part of a strange meditation? A fit? She could be dying and he would have no inkling of it.

"Answer me, damn it!"

The look on his Lena's face haunted him. He wanted to run after her, but he couldn't leave Jade behind. As he sat there, he questioned his own part in all of this.

I need a healer, he thought with sudden urgency. He moved to leave, but with a violent shudder Jade gasped. Her hands found his. Their grip was so tight that he bit the inside of his cheek.

She opened her eyes and looked at him for a moment before recognition took hold. Her grip relaxed but she still did not let go. "It is worse than I thought."

"Now is not the time for riddles or hidden meanings, Jade." He helped her lean against the wall for support.

She looked up at him with wide and fearful eyes. "You will be in danger if I tell you."

Jade always had a flare for the dramatic. Once it had held him spellbound—he even told her how charming it was when they were first in love. But now her lack of direct reasoning tried his patience. He ignored her warning. "Does she have the sight, or whatever it is that you call it?"

She responded to his question with one of her own. "Do you remember how magic can often be inside of someone, like you, where you refuse to explore it and it shrivels within you?"

It took great effort not to take offense. "Yes," he hissed, "speak plainly, Jade. Lena's still a child."

"Oh open your eyes." Jade threw her hand to the floor beside her as if she lacked the energy to keep it in her lap. "Lena does not know what she is doing, not yet. But living here she must have grown up fast. Even I can see that and I am, I am only a stranger to her."

"But this is nonsense," he said. While he did not bother to hide the skepticism in his voice, he had to admit he was shaken by how weak Jade looked propped up against the wall like a fragile blade of grass, trodden and bent to fit a new shape.

She took a deep breath. The intensity of her softly spoken words held his attention more surely than if she had shouted. "I did think she had the gift from me at first. But then... this was something else. Lena felt what I was doing. Something *twisted* it; took it away."

Jade looked up at him. "What magic is hidden in this place, Torven? My gift... it is gone."

BLOOD ON THE SAND

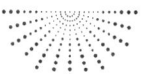

W arden Moonstone eased his mind by counting how many dunes surrounded the prison. At his back, soldiers streamed out of tents and gathered to form an open arena. The encampment held a quality of movement and energy that reminded him of a hive of bees. Those in the first few rows knelt on their jackets in the hot sand to give others behind them a view.

He noted that it was difficult for many to keep their balance when they walked along the dunes. With so many bodies moving in one space, the chance of shifting too much sand at once was a definite risk. He ground his teeth to hold back an order to hold their positions.

While Jarvin was in command, any advice or command he gave would immediately be countermanded with an order to ignore it. Jarvin had made it clear that to these men, he was only the prison warden. Had Jarvin bothered to train the newly-arrived soldiers how to survive the challenges of the Wastelands?

Doubtful. Jarvin was a man who preferred to give orders, not explanations. Only when the Imperial law was properly followed could its warden allow anyone else control of the prison.

He would step aside and give up everything once he satisfied his conscience that he had done everything in his power to ensure the soldiers held a truthful account of their orders, and not the twisted interpretation of a power-hungry man. How had it come to this, that he should have to openly challenge an Imperial decision in order to receive a clear picture of the law?

At his side, Cergath instructed the guards under his breath. "Spread out. Mix with the other soldiers rather than stay in one place. Keep an eye out for trouble."

He had to agree with such tactics. While Jarvin could count on the loyalty of a few companies of soldiers, many of the new arrivals were milling about with looks of confusion and alarm. Unusual enough that two ranking officers would openly duel, but in the Wastelands—so far from civilization—anything could happen.

The warden kept his back to the wind out of habit. He stretched and tried to force his muscles to relax; many of them were stiff and slower to respond than he liked. How long since his last patrol? He had sent Lena on many that he would have ridden himself.

While Jarvin lacked wisdom, he twisted and bent with lithe efficiency. The man threw his jacket to the ground and wiped sweat from his face. His words to the soldiers around him caused shouts of laughter, but even that sound was forced and lined with fear. What a farce.

Before Cergath could open his mouth to say anything, the warden shook his head. "I know what thoughts drift through your head, my friend. No."

"But sir, it is never too late when it comes to saving your own hide. Had I a wife and child—"

"You would think to set a good example for them, would you not? Speaking of which, where is the Lady Jade?"

"Still not feeling well, I imagine, ser."

"Or unwilling to openly choose sides." The words were like a final confirmation in his mind. When Jade was away, her actions rarely aligned with her words of support.

"Warden Moonstone!" one of the younger prison guards held out a parchment. "Urgent message from the prison." He shot a fearful look in Captain Jarvin's direction.

I'm sorry, Torven. I had no choice. Forgive me.

He folded the note and put it into his pocket. He handed the ceremonial jacket to Cergath. "Turn control over to Jarvin without delay if I am... if something happens to me."

"But sir—"

"I would not risk more violence through misunderstanding," he warned. "We must hope that Jarvin will keep this madness as a personal grudge, and nothing more." Secretly, he doubted the man's hunger for power would ever end, but what more could he do?

Sensing Cergath's restlessness at the order, he put a hand on the man's shoulder. "The measure of my character is far from what possessions and power may be taken away. I must respect the strength of my convictions, no matter the cost."

Cergath's reply was overshadowed by Jarvin, who stepped forward with a rallying cry, "Soldiers of the Blessed Empress! Warden Moonstone here has resisted Imperial orders time and time again. Now he's refusin' Imperial decrees."

"No formal decree has been presented," the warden replied. Cold anger gripped him by the throat. The man was trying to make a mockery of the reason and logic behind his actions.

Jarvin sneered and his accent grew heavier. "Yer sayin' the word of a captain ain't good enough? Followin' orders is what I'm doin'. Here's the trust I get in turn!" He raised his voice, "Fer all t'see I brought it with me, right here." Jarvin beckoned to a nearby soldier who held up a large scroll with the Imperial seal.

An Imperial scroll. It made the warden more suspicious of Jarvin's actions. His mind raced. Why make demands at all, why not hand over the scroll and take control if that was the intent of the orders? Unless the scroll held something Jarvin wanted to keep a secret.

How could he make these soldiers understand the unreasonable actions of their Jarvin? Blinded by loyalty, they would follow him into bloodshed.

Jarvin shook his head at his silence. "Ye see? Now, how can I be forgivin' such an insult t'the Blessed Empress? I feel it. Right here." He pounded on his chest as if struck by a blow. It was a disgusting performance.

The warden reached for the scroll, and in doing so braced for an attack or its withdrawal. In another surprising show of restraint, Jarvin let him have it. It seemed the captain preferred to torture his victims in private. In public, he gutted them by insisting he stood to defend the wronged, with words so quick and plain that no one stopped to remember why they were angry in the first place.

A small triumph sent the warden's heart racing as he read. Jade had told him that Lena was not a Seeker, so he was not compelled by the edict to turn her over unless Jade specifically named her as an essential asset. Captain Jarvin would only control the prisoners.

Though the wording in the decree was quite different from Jarvin's words, in essence he was correct. Labor was needed in the capital. The prison was to be emptied. Certain special skills were required of some who had the raw magical talent that a Seeker would recognize, while others would join the army as conscripts. Conscripts? Preparation?

He looked up at Jarvin and their eyes locked. The words hidden, the meaning clear: in preparation to go to war. What better place to recruit troops? Prisoners had little choice in the matter when sentences were to be pardoned for any who signed up for service. Conscripts were needed, and with the prison closing who could refuse?

The warden handed back the scroll. "This is entirely different," he said. "We will proceed to empty the prison at once. Imperial interests must be protected above all else." Those were the words he needed to ease his conscience. With preparations for war, all citizens were needed to make sacrifices for the good of survival.

Jarvin's eyebrows shot so high on his brow that for a moment they disappeared behind his hairline. "Yer turnin' them over?" he said, confused by the sudden acquiescence.

"I protested your treatment of my prisoners, my men, and even myself," said the warden, "but by this edict it is clear that *every life* is needed. Necessary." He dared not emphasize it a third time, for the man's face had turned a livid purple.

"I'll say where ye'll be taken and when," he snapped, "and ye'll be punished fer yer insults!" He drew his sword and lunged.

A line of pain raked down the warden's forearm as he stumbled to the side. It was luck the weapon was a shorter blade than most, for a deeper cut would have left his arm limp and useless. He ignored the blood that soaked his sleeve as he drew his own sword.

None of the soldiers dared to step between them. They shuffled to circle one another, wary of tripping but unable to truly dodge an attack in the shifting sand. When the warden caught sight of Cergath he managed to shake his head. Stepping away from the fight now would surely mean a cruel and more creative death sentence at a later date. He would rather know the manner of his death.

Jarvin moved forward again and aimed to cut a vicious, diagonal slice out of him. The warden managed to deflect the blade but Jarvin kept up a relentless attack against his injured arm which kept him from switching his sword to the other hand. The effort it took to block the strikes rather than dodge them drained his energy, and a madness in Jarvin's eyes changed to glee when a lucky strike cut through the shoulder clasp which held his chest plating together.

With a vicious backward swing Jarvin smashed his sword pommel into the warden's head. Bright sunlight blinded him as his head snapped to the side. He went down hard.

Jarvin pointed the tip of his blade at his chest. "Get up," he said. "Or can ye not face yer death at the hands of a true Imperial soldier?"

Blood coursed down the side of his face. He forced one eye open to look at Jarvin. "Not a soldier," he managed to say, "a butcher."

Jarvin's smiled from ear to ear, and his sword twisted to cut past the warden's armor through his side. When Jarvin sliced across his belly a scream rang in his ears, strange and unfamiliar.

"A butcher ye say." Jarvin pulled a water flask from the nearest soldier and drank, pouring the rest over his face. "Then ye've given me plenty t'practice my cuts on. Yer whole prison fer starters. Think on that while ye breathe yer last."

Blood soaked into the sand. The warden waited for death.

17

WHEN GOOD MEN DIE

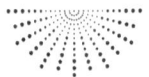

Teguin let out a slow, steady breath. In silent meditation, he listened to his lamat nearby as it clawed its way into a nest of snakes. A dozen of the smaller ones flailed against the sand to escape the long prowling nose and curved claws of their tormentor.

Rinzi had warned them of the creatures that lived within the dunes, but Teguin never seemed to have a problem knowing if he were within reach of pincers or fangs. There was a vibrant energy to the Wastelands; he sensed it the moment he had stepped from the broken, dusty ground beyond Falden and into the sand. It followed him as he traveled across the desert, remaining a constant and curious new aspect to his magic that he was eager to welcome.

Their guide worshiped what she called the "desert spirits" and spoke of their cunning at length now that they were in the heart of the Wastelands. Was there a connection between magic and the spirits Rinzi described? Teguin felt a connection to this place too; he only wished that he could speak to someone about the sensation. Master Troug would have understood.

Another breath in, another breath out. Be it lamat or snakes or the desert spirits, they were all a part of a larger whole that brought life to the Wastelands. Herbert said many times that it was a far cry from the green plants and trees of Falden Province. He was right.

It was that difference which captured his interest. He had traveled the length and breadth of the Imperium as a merchant's apprentice, and traveling in this place was nothing like those days. There was a sense of loss here, of being without, and the missing parts made it worthy of fascination.

Compared with a merchant like Feran, Rinzi was a survivalist. She kept them fed and watered as though they were the lamat that traveled with them; alive and breathing. Teguin could tell the woman was used to being on her own.

Even the thought of a luxury like spiced wine filled his head with giddy memories of feasting under the stars with a wagon of exotic goods. He resisted the temptation to make suggestions. Insulting their guide would be unwise. If this was what it meant to travel in the desert, then it would be safer to trust in Rinzi than travel on their own.

On the horizon a curved, imposing shape grew in size as they approached. Rinzi headed toward the outline of the prison with unerring concentration. Traveling this far without incident was a gift in itself.

He and Herbert were strangers in a strange land. They were not there to be entertained in comfort. Herbert decided early on in their trip that the lamat were better treated than they were. Despite Teguin's intervention, Herbert's complaints continued and Rinzi had started taking personal offense.

Teguin had to keep an eye on Herbert. The darker moods of his friend were no coincidence. It only grew worse the longer they traveled. With a distinct lack of anything fresh and green to look at, the fights between Herbert and Rinzi were an unnecessary distraction.

"Teguin? Yer peace and quiet will have t'wait."

Teguin turned his head to find Herbert approaching with a sour expression. The early hours of the morning and already, another disagreement. "Hope ye were plannin' on a fast pace," he continued. "She insists the prison is within a few leagues."

"A few leagues?" repeated Teguin.

They both looked over to a distant dune, behind which the prison stood curved and clearly defined. Its shape reminded Teguin of the Horn, an Artifact which the Lexicon had stolen from Praxis; it was wider at the base than its tip, as if the sand had been shaped when wet and then sanded smooth to a point.

"Leagues, dunes, what's a few more when yer close t'the end," said Herbert with a large wave of his arm.

"Have you eaten yet?" asked Teguin.

Herbert snorted. "Yer in fer a real treat. She's left it cold this time, seein' as we're in a hurry."

"If we are that close to the prison, then I'm sure they have a cook or table with more variety to offer guests."

Herbert's face brightened. "There's a thought. I'll get the lamat ready. If ye hear a shout it's gone after my staff again. Damn nuisance, these munchers."

Leagues were not the kind of measurement that Teguin would have used for drifts of sand that went up and back down again.

The sight of the prison as they went over each new dune kept his motivation high. They were all going strong, and Herbert had a renewed energy, urging his lamat to bound up the sand for the first time in weeks. At least it kept him too distracted to do anything but adjust his direction when Rinzi shouted a warning or pointed out an unstable path ahead.

Lagging behind, Teguin was so absorbed with the placement of each step his lamat made that he didn't notice Rinzi had stopped just shy of the latest crest and dismounted. She pulled his lamat to a halt with a hiss, and it collapsed onto its belly to flatten itself against the sand, nearly dumping him in the process.

"Get down," she scolded, "or they'll see ye." From Herbert's expression she had done the same to him.

She waved them over and spread out a blanket. Together they sat at the top of the dune and gaped at hundreds of tents and a crush of bodies, all wearing Imperial colors.

Rinzi looked mad enough to whip them both. "This here's not what we agreed on. A prison is mad enough but this, this is where I stay. No closer."

Teguin could hardly blame the woman. It was enough to make him reconsider their path as well. There were more soldiers over the rise than he'd ever seen outside of the Blue City.

"We had no idea there were this many soldiers in the desert, Rinzi," he said, swallowing a curse as he knew what this meant. "You kept your word. The prison is in sight and we can go on alone."

Rinzi pulled on her snakeskin belt until it made an ominous cracking sound. "I'll be leavin' then," she muttered. "Imperial or no, I swear t'the desert spirits I'll gut the first one that lays a hand on me."

Teguin reached into his travel pack. "The rest of your payment."

She nodded, rose, and tugged at the blanket until Teguin and Herbert moved off, Herbert cursing the heat of the sand.

Teguin had bought their lamat from Rinzi, but he grew nervous watching them snort and shift as the woman mounted and rode away. He knew now how attached they were to their own kind, and they would have to keep a sharp eye on the creatures. Herbert did not bother to conceal his smile as he watched Rinzi and her lamat slither down the dune without looking back.

"There's a happy sight," he said.

"You might not be so happy to see her go as you think," said Teguin.

Herbert shrugged off the comment. He risked another glance at the soldiers and let out a low whistle. "With cursed weather and na'en but sand, why would they be gatherin'?"

"Training of some kind?"

"Must be."

"If we went around..." Teguin suggested, but he stopped midsentence. It was a hopeless suggestion to avoid being seen by so many.

Herbert shook his head too. "Bad idea. Besides, we've just as much a right t'be here. More even, since we aim t'leave soon as we can." He looked back at Rinzi again.

Teguin didn't like Herbert's excitement, but he had to admit it seemed a better plan to approach openly rather than hide. They were bound to be seen. In fact, it seemed odd that no one marked their presence yet on the dune.

Soldiers made him nervous, it was true, but they had no real reason to avoid them. "Approaching openly makes the most sense to me," he agreed.

They moved toward the mess of red and white tents, whose frames bent and collapsed with canvas which sagged like wet rags. If Teguin had to guess, these shifting sands in the lower dunes around the prison did not take kindly to their new visitors. The soldiers were gathered in a strange crowd without any worry about the tents or in any semblance of order.

Added height from his mount gave Teguin a better view as they drew nearer. The gathering was fixated on something at its center, but what the soldiers encircled he could not say. They finally caught the attention of a few soldiers as their lamat pounded down on the sand with their enormous legs.

The first to notice them wiped at his eyes and blinked several times. "What's this, then?" he said, punching the man nearest him in the arm. They walked until they were eye-to-eye with Teguin's lamat, which bent to sniff them as they drew their short swords.

"I would not recommend that," said Teguin. "She hasn't eaten much today."

Herbert slid off his lamat and pulled out his staff. The new freedom from Rinzi showed on his friend's face as he smiled without any show of concern over the gathering in front of them. It was an admirable bluff. "We wish t'see yer commander."

The first soldier snorted. "He's a bit busy teachin' the prison warden a lesson."

Teguin's stomach sank. Imperial soldiers facing off against the prison warden? This was more serious than he realized.

"Aren't we all servin' the Blessed Empress?" said Herbert, his eyes roaming the large number of people.

"*Her Will* is law," the soldiers both replied automatically.

The second soldier shrugged and sheathed his sword. "Personal grudge or somethin'. It ain't smart t'question the captain, that's all we mind. Ye'll mind it as well if ye ken what's straight and narrow."

Shouldering their way into the crowd, the two soldiers motioned for Teguin and Herbert to follow. They led their lamat, who moved forward with grumbles of protest. The first man hadn't sheathed his sword, and now he pointed it at them both, gesturing to the tents.

"Yer makin' us miss the fun and we'll not forget it. Right then, nice and slow with yer monsters there. Ye've just earned yerselves that visit with Captain Jarvin."

"Fight's over anyways, Jerem. Heard there's a cask t'celebrate though. Let's get this over with."

Teguin didn't like the attitude of these soldiers. There was a hunger about them that had nothing to do with their last meal. He had seen that look before when he traveled the road with Feran, but it usually favored the cruel and desperate, and these soldiers certainly looked a flipped coin away from turning on someone.

His uncle liked to call them pinchers. In merchant's talk it was a person worth no more than a pinch of salt in trade, the kind quicker to rob a merchant blind and run home than honor the sword they carried. They were a law unto themselves.

Swelling with the importance of something to do, the two soldiers in front of Teguin and Herbert swaggered through their comrades and ordered the way to be cleared, though the presence of the lamat did the job for them. The groups of soldiers milled around without any structure and it struck Teguin as odd that no one appeared to be in charge. Several of them looked pale and ill at ease.

Beside him, Herbert stopped cold. He craned his neck and his jaw dropped at something Teguin could not see. A chill ran through Teguin when he saw the expression on his friend's face. "What is it?" he said.

"There's a man bleedin' t'death!"

"What?"

Before Teguin could stop him, Herbert dropped the reins of the lamat and pushed his way through the soldiers with his staff. Most gave way in surprise with a gruff hiss of protest or an elbow in the back as he passed. The protests turned to yelps of pain and Teguin saw a few large and wicked thorns had grown out from the staff. He hoped the transformation of the staff would end there.

Herbert was much better than Teguin at shaping magic to suit his needs, but when he lost his temper... Teguin pushed the reins of both lamat into the hands of one of the soldiers and hurried to follow. They quickly outdistanced their escort. Teguin could hear the two soldiers swearing and ordering others to pursue them but it was a foolish, empty gesture; they were headed further into the camp, not attempting to leave. There was no escape, and whatever mess Herbert rushed toward was not likely to be a pleasant one.

Teguin strained to see what Herbert's extra height revealed. He found a smaller dune with trailing dark stains soaking into the sand. A man, propped up and pale, clutched at his stomach as blood flowed freely from his wounds. The only thing that stunned Teguin more than the sight itself was that not one soul stopped to help him.

Herbert dropped to his knees beside the man. He fumbled with his cloak. A few of the soldiers took notice and tried to remove him.

"Damn ye lot, I'm a healer!" he swore, lashing out with his staff. "It's my oath t'the Empress, tendin' the wounded." He managed to turn over his cloak and reveal the signature light blue color that only an Imperial healer had leave to wear. "We're here at her request!"

Teguin had never seen Herbert do such a thing before. He held his breath as the soldiers backed away, wary and afraid to touch him. The rough hands pulling at Teguin also stopped, but hovered a sword's distance away.

"Murderers and monsters," Teguin muttered under his breath as he knelt beside Herbert.

"Keep yer mouth shut," snapped Herbert. "There's need fer quiet here."

Teguin bit back a protest. Once Herbert's temper was flared it was no good to point it out. He swallowed back a wave of nausea at the smell. How long had the poor man been like this? "Herbert, the man's on the path to death, even I can see it."

"There's hope yet. His breath is steady so his lungs are fair. If I stop the bleedin' he may yet recover. It's that or a painful, slow death with na'en t'mourn him." Herbert shot a disgusted look at the soldiers around them. A few had the decency to look ashamed.

"But his belly..."

"Distract them, Teguin. I've got all I need t'be fixin' it."

Teguin knew what he meant. A wound like this could only be tended with magic that would bring suspicion and violence down upon their heads if they were caught.

At Herbert's words, the eyes of the dying man opened a crack, widening to look at them with such intensity that it made Teguin's skin crawl.

"Water," said the man.

"Afraid not, ser. Ye'll need a good stitch-up first."

"No," the man insisted. "If you heal me he will only do it again."

"Again?" said Herbert. The color drained from his face.

The muscles in the man's neck bulged and tightened as he fought to speak again. "Do no more for me." He tried to push away Herbert's hands. "I served the Blessed Empress my whole life, and what has it brought me. Banishment. Betrayal. End this, please. I beg you." He lost consciousness.

Herbert looked down at the man's wounds. He took a long shuddering breath, then plucked a piece of vine with one of the larger thorns from his staff. Teguin guessed at what would happen next and quickly put a hand out. "If we interfere, it will do just what the man cautioned against and anger this Captain Jarvin against us."

Herbert pulled the thorn away from Teguin's hand. "If this were Olivia and I could not fix her, then I would do anythin' t'bring her sufferin' an end. Ye'll not stop me, Teguin." He put both hands over the stomach wound. "Peaceful rest, friend."

The man was in pain beyond understanding. Herbert appeared to plunge the thorn into his belly yet he barely twitched. Teguin felt a guilty twinge at wanting to stop Herbert. Why was this man's death less important to him than his own comfort? The body convulsed only once before it relaxed into stillness.

"Grew straight t'the heart," said Herbert quietly. His hands were covered in blood. He was true to his word; there was no sign of anything unusual. Teguin sighed with relief, but hated that they did nothing to heal the man, and that it reminded Herbert once again of losing Olivia.

Herbert rubbed sand on his hands to try and wipe away the blood. Teguin could not mistake his friend's silence for calm, he knew Herbert too well for that. Strangely the opposite of his usual calm, Teguin wanted to cry out in alarm or disgust.

In the end he had to agree with Herbert. They would have to settle for leaving this place as soon as possible. With soldiers and prison guards at odds with one another, the prison was less a waypoint than a breeding ground for chaos. With the prison warden dead, it was one small step from a war zone, and he wanted to be well away before that line could be crossed.

"Well," Herbert turned to their leery escort, "I believe we'll be seein' yer commander then?"

A nearby woman smiled with a hand resting on the hilt of her sword. "I'm certain Captain Jarvin will want to see you after that pretty scene."

Teguin's stomach dropped at the thought of meeting this captain. How could one commanding officer attack another and leave him to die in such a savage manner? This man had begged for death, and died in agony. Bitter, yes, but no one should earn such an end.

He looked around. Where was the prison guard through all this, and did they know their warden was dead? Teguin eyed the soldiers they passed with a wariness that slowed his steps. Perhaps Rinzi was right after all. Stopping at the prison was more complicated than he realized.

Ahead, the flaps of the command tent blew open and danced in the wind. Teguin and Herbert shuffled through and were finally face to face with this Captain Jarvin. The man straightened from a bucket of murky water at his side, running his fingers through damp hair. He was of average height, but every inch of him was muscular and left no doubt that he could and would enforce his authority.

Captain Jarvin looked them over. The lack of emotion on his face was singularly disturbing. Teguin's friends called his own expressions stoic, but this man was different. There was no sadness or regret in the captain's eyes, not even anger.

If Teguin had not witnessed the warden's last breath he would have assumed the captain had been training with his troops rather than gutting someone. This man looked at peace and cleansed, in the final stages of some private ecstasy. *Empress Bless*, was this a man or a monster?

It took all of Teguin's control to treat this killer with respect. He had to treat this negotiation like any other. He gave a low bow. "We apologize for our... untimely arrival to your camp, Captain. We were merely passing through, and wished to resupply at the prison." He looked over at Herbert, and said under his breath, "The Imperial seal, Herbert."

Herbert did not respond. He gripped his staff and stood still, his eyes half closed. Red in the face from the heat of the sun and the strength of his emotions, Teguin worried his friend would make their situation worse. He could no longer predict whether or not Herbert cared more for the release of his own anger than the unexpected dangers of their situation.

Herbert flinched when Teguin reached into his short jacket to pull out the small emblem of the Empress. The seal signified they were allowed passage through Imperial checkpoints. When Master Frost insisted he carry one, he thought it was excessive when it meant delaying their departure from Praxis. It was a precaution to accept and take one with them, and at the time he resented that delay.

Now, it was their only hope of safe passage through this encampment of soldiers. Captain Jarvin's thick eyebrows bristled at the mention of the prison, and they shot upward at the sight of a seal.

"Forgive me, sers, but yer awful far from home t'be travelin' yerselves without escort. Desert's a dangerous place."

Teguin had to assume they were in danger. The only impressions he had of this captain were the whispers of a dying man. He would not risk further suspicion by confiding in him.

"We had our reasons," he said. "We only wished a few words with the prison warden or someone familiar with the area, in order to get

Imperial advice on the local terrain before continuing on with our journey."

A hot prick of anger flooded Teguin's face when Captain Jarvin had the audacity to laugh. "Have ye now. Well sers, ye've traveled an awful long way fer speakin' with a corpse."

He turned to the soldier that had escorted them inside. "Or is he still alive?"

"Ye've killed the prison warden, but why?" broke in Herbert.

"It's Imperial business, but none of yers." The man's lips curled into a snarl. He held up the sigil and eyed them both. For a moment, Teguin thought he might sniff it like a dog in search of a scent.

Jarvin tossed it onto the table between them. "Bring these travelers t'the Seeker and search their packs," he said. "Is that prison guard still about? Have Steint and Harlowe take'em all back. Search the warden's quarters before the guards clean the place. If these folk ain't who they say they are, I've a knife with their names on it."

Teguin and Herbert trailed behind the soldiers until they had their new escort, who shoved them along. Teguin had little hope of finding a warm welcome at the prison itself with the warden dead. Beside them walked the only prison guard in sight, a man by the name of Cergath. Teguin watched the guard with mixed curiosity. The prison guard and these soldiers were allies and yet the man kept a hand resting on the hilt of his sword as if he expected an attack.

If a fight broke out between the two there was no telling what havoc would spread across the Wastelands. And he and Herbert would be right in the middle of it. How would they slip away from Jarvin? The man must have immense power and influence in the Imperium if he traveled with a Seeker.

Teguin was surprised to hear of a Seeker this far from home. While the Wastelands were under Imperial rule, no one truly controlled this stretch of empty desert from what he had seen. How could they?

Teguin knew that he and Herbert wouldn't be able to hide their magic from someone with a Seeker's gifts, even if they should wish to do so. They needed to think of a reason to be there and fast, or they could be in serious trouble. If only he could think of something.

The shadow of the prison tower fell across their path. Teguin shaded his eyes from the sun and craned his neck. The tip of the tower curved overhead and fired his imagination; its design was like nothing else he'd seen. At its topmost point, he might be able to see where the broken cliffs rose to meet the sky if he held a spyglass with a powerful enough lens.

Cergath hurried forward when they walked through a lower defensive wall. The man had a word with a large group gathered at the entrance. Teguin could not hear what was said, but the expressions of the other guards were grim. Saluting Cergath, they kept to themselves and moved quickly away from the new arrivals.

"This way," said Cergath. He looked at the bloodstains on Herbert's hands and turned away.

"Which way t'the warden's rooms?" asked one of Jarvin's soldiers who traveled with them.

"The warden's rooms are not to be disturbed, Lieutenant," said Cergath. He turned, and they followed him down a steep flight of steps and into a narrow hallway. "The Seeker took ill," he said to Teguin. "I believe our healer is tending her."

"Says who," another soldier interrupted. "We've orders to bring certain goods back to the captain at once."

"And your captain also commanded that these travelers be taken to the Seeker. Which is what I am doing. First."

"High and mighty—"

"Problem, ser?" A door opened, and a woman stepped out, with half a dozen prison guards at her back. She saluted Cergath.

"No, Sanders. Continue preparing the prisoners for evacuation."

"We remain low on supplies." The woman called Sanders gave Jarvin's soldiers a hard stare that made Teguin glad he was not one of them.

Cergath put an arm on her shoulder. "Once we move out, I am sure the captain will want to share the burden of transporting his supplies back to Therin Hall."

"As ye say, ser." With a nod, Sanders and the other guards crossed in front of Teguin and Herbert to enter the opposite door and disappeared.

"Let's get on with it then," snapped Jarvin's lieutenant. Cergath ignored the man.

As they went deeper underground, Teguin fought the temptation to put his hand on the walls. He knew that his magic may not react in a way that he could control if he was distracted or on edge, but the walls were nothing like the dunes and hardened sandstone he had seen in the Wastelands. They called to him.

Something in its construction reminded him of the ancient, underground passageways of Praxis. Yet this was also different. What was it? He could not put his finger on the reason. It bothered him like an itch he could not scratch.

When they entered the room at the far end of the hallway, there were empty shelves that confirmed the prison was low in medical as well as food supplies. On a large table were chaotic piles of dried plants and strange looking pods. Rinzi had described the pods as the closest thing to plant life in the desert, but they had yet to encounter them. Herbert stepped forward at once and reached out to touch the nearest spiked pod.

"Do not touch anything!" cried a voice that made them both jump. Herbert pulled away with a look of annoyance. Tucked away in the corner, the end of a long cot poked out but the speaker was hidden.

Teguin stumbled as he hurried around the table. He recognized that voice. "Lady Jade?"

18

SECRETS

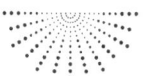

Lady Jade coughed and managed a weak smile at Teguin and his companion. "Now you're about the last familiar faces I expected to see." It was the truth. Teguin was supposed to be studying with Master Frost at Praxis.

She owed the headmistress a visit when she returned to Falden Province. As Teguin's sponsor she was entitled to know of his movements, especially when traveling to a place as remote and dangerous as this. Was it Frost who suggested it? That woman was proving to be slippery as an eel.

"You know the lady?" Cergath asked Teguin. He refused to look at Lady Jade, which sent tremors of warning through her body. Having Cergath and not Torven here was a worrying sign, and she had heard no news from anyone. The warden must have crossed swords with Captain Jarvin.

She forced herself to respond. "Thank you, Cergath. I will vouch for them."

Teguin wiped sweat from his brow. Despite the heat in the room, Jade shivered and wrapped her arms so tightly about her shoulders that she would have bruises before long, but she did not care. Her breath came in tight gasps. She was still lightheaded from her collapse earlier.

When she awoke in this strange place, she found only a prison guard as confused as she was to be there, and Jade sent him away at once with a message for the warden.

There were Imperial soldiers with Cergath and they shuffled behind them, taking up most of the small ward. "Ye heard the lady," said one of the soldiers with a nasty smile. "We're leavin', and this time there's na'en a door closed t'the captain."

Cergath stiffened as if struck. He turned without a word to Lady Jade, addressing Herbert and Teguin in a low voice. "I would speak with you, sers, when you are done here. Return to the stairs and climb until you can go no further. I will await you there."

Teguin bowed and turned back to Lady Jade. Her eyes studied his with a grave intensity. When she looked at the other man—Herbert was his name she recalled, and saw his hands, she let out a small gasp. "His blood. It is, is it not?"

Her voice dropped to a whisper without substance, dull and toneless, but Herbert was more intent on finding something in the room to clean his hands and did not notice her distress. "The prison warden? He's dead alright. Nasty business, t'see a man so—"

Jade collapsed against the cot with a low cry. She knew it, of course. She knew he would not survive. But to hear it spoken aloud made all the difference. The depth of her sorrow took her by surprise. After cycles apart, the chance to have a final farewell was lost forever.

"How do we find you here, milady?" Teguin asked with a gentle hand on her shoulder.

"You will learn soon enough. Warden Moonstone is… was, my husband." She closed her eyes and tears rolled down her cheeks.

"Yer pardon, milady. I was thoughtless."

"No, Herbert. It's better the news come from a friend. Indeed, in this wretched place you're both the closest thing I have to friends." She wiped her face with a sleeve and tried to sit up again.

Teguin found her a cup of water while Herbert hurried to wash his hands in a low basin. The stains on his hands were not entirely gone when he finished, and he refused to meet her eye as she looked down at her drink, then between them.

"This place is not safe," she said. "You must leave right away."

"But why?" asked Teguin. "Forgive me milady, but a warning so vague cannot help our avoiding trouble."

"I'm bettin' Jarvin's the cause, isn't he," said Herbert to Teguin. "Ye heard his men, they called him the red butcher."

Jade shook her head. "It is not Jarvin—though believe me when I say that he is cause enough to leave. Would that I could do so myself..." She took a sip of water and stared into the cup for a long moment.

Teguin grew restless at her words. "Our presence here is poorly timed, milady, but we must be allowed to stay and speak with the guards. You remember my old master, Lavinia Troug, and her disappearance from Praxis?"

"I remember." That was old news, and she knew more of the Blades and the attack on Praxis to steal the Horn than would ever come to light.

"She believed that there were ancient cities still intact in the Wastelands," said Teguin. "I found evidence in the archives at Praxis that the prison itself was once a part of such a city, and I hoped that if she were still alive, she might try to visit this place."

She wanted to talk with Teguin about this alone, but there were other more important things that kept her silent on the subject. Her head was spinning and she had to convince them to leave before Jarvin decided they were too much of a liability to release. The man was unpredictable, and even her authority by his side was a thin veneer that threatened to crack and dissolve at a moment's notice.

She wiped the tears from her cheeks. "Believe me when I say that this place is as dangerous as the man who now runs it. Using your magic inside these walls could be the last thing you do."

Teguin and Herbert exchanged an incredulous look.

Jade finished the water in her cup and struggled to lean forward until she could place it on the table. "I was a fool," she said, her voice bitter. "I was so preoccupied with Jarvin's vendetta that I rushed into the prison without thinking. This structure, this place has old magic as you have suspected, Teguin. Can you feel it as I can?

She fell into another silent moment as the memory of her encounter with Lena left her chilled. "It is powerful and beyond our knowledge, and we are but children poking a snake nest in the dark."

Herbert picked up his staff and took a step closer to her. "Have ye seen a healer, milady?"

Her smile was a shadow of its usual charm. She extended a palm. "If you feel you must examine me you may, but I will not hold you to your oath. I do not suffer from physical consequences the way that some do when they encounter magic. I am only tired from my ordeal. My burdens lie in other places."

"Ye've had a shock all the same." Herbert took her hand. He ran quick fingers up her arms but she could see the magic surging and pooling under his skin, where it remained. The man made a cursory check for pain or obvious discomfort and brought her more water. "Get plenty of rest."

"The rest I need can wait. Indeed, if you would do something for me first, I can guarantee I will sleep better than I have in a very long while."

"What's that, then," said Herbert, eyeing the pods on the table. Jade was a reader of people, both with and without her gifts as a Seeker. She could tell right away that Herbert had little interest in her presence at the prison. He was restless, and more interested in moving on than in vague warnings of danger. She could use that to have a word with Teguin and she intended to take advantage of the opportunity.

"My daughter, Lena, is missing. It is true that my husband and Captain Jarvin had no love for one another but I worry that Jarvin's obsession extends to the girl. He has been asking for her ever since we arrived at the prison, and I know enough about men to recognize that it is not to have a Seeker examine her." She gave a little shudder at her last words.

Teguin frowned. "Forgive me, milady, but could you not send a soldier or prison guard to find and protect your daughter?"

"Jarvin has his fingers around many throats. There is no saying whose loyalty he commands. When Lena's life and safety lies in the balance, I do not stop to trust a stranger, Teguin. Even the freedom of a Seeker has limits."

Jade's eyes never left Teguin's face, and he shrank a little under the intensity of her gaze as she watched his own magic, still concentrated around his shoulder and lining the scars that ran along his arm. To her sight they glowed stronger than any sleeve or glove could hide. What a strange and tragic bond with magic. It was fascinating to watch. She remembered why she had been so excited to meet him during her visit to Praxis.

Her fear of losing her magic was clearly premature. The cause of her attack was more complicated than she initially thought. There was another explanation for what happened, but unless she returned to Torven's study, she could not confirm her theory.

When she looked to Herbert there was no sympathy in the man's face. The Wastelands stretched for hundreds of leagues—perhaps even a thousand at its outermost edges. She could almost read his thoughts. How far in the wrong direction would a promise to rescue and return her daughter take them?

Teguin looked to his friend, and then shook his head. "I am sorry beyond measure, but we cannot help you in this, milady. We have other important work we must complete without distraction."

"May I speak with you alone, Teguin?"

Teguin hesitated, but Herbert only looked at him and shrugged. "I'll be outside, then." His staff clicked against the stone floor as he left.

Lady Jade put the cup of water back onto the table again, this time untouched. "Why do you believe that this place has the key to finding Master Troug?" she asked.

"After she was taken during the attack on Praxis, I have been following rumors that say a group of bandits calling themselves the Blades have extensive hideouts in the desert. Anyone who spends as much time patrolling the desert as the prison guard would know something of their movements. I dedicated much of my time at Praxis to the archives that no one cared to study. Everything pointed to the 'Barren Wastelands' or the 'Wasted Lands' being a place of many secrets.

Many places to hide. There were once many cities here, with wonders beyond our understanding. It was once the most fertile land and the center of culture—"

"Yes, but they were all destroyed a thousand cycles ago or more during the Relic Wars," she interrupted, trying to rise from the cot. Teguin rushed to offer her his arm but she waved him away and leaned against the table instead.

"Teguin, I have seen and read much of the chronicles kept at the Imperial Palace and I assure you, if there were cities still standing we would know of them. Sand has scoured away what little is left of such places; to seek them out is only to find another patch of desolation, not discovery. Forgive my bluntness, but why are you here? Most people would have given up hope by now."

"Without Master Troug and her guidance, I lack the clarity of purpose that I need. She understands magic, Destructive magic, in a way that no one else does. I know that beauty can be created even from magic as destructive as mine, but I need guidance from someone who sees that side of magic. I must find her."

She did not reply. Teguin clenched his scarred hand. "Milady, why did you wish to speak with me alone?" he asked.

Jade considered the question. It struck her that Teguin had little subtlety compared to his uncle. Feran was a man of great talent and ambition, but this was an honest and open question and she was within her rights to answer it any way she chose.

"You have an obligation to me, Teguin, though you do not know it. Under different circumstances you would never hear a word from me directly, not even after your Master's robes were earned. The head-mistress would be furious at me for mentioning this at all."

A breath of air escaped her in a weak attempt to laugh. "But these are strange and unusual times, are they not? If I cannot convince you to go after my daughter as a friend, then I ask you to do it as an obligation to your patron at Praxis."

The silence that filled the room made her ears pound. It was unusual to have an anonymous sponsor, and it was an unspoken rule that the identity of the sponsor be unknown. But if she revealed it to him directly it could hardly be called subversive. She no longer cared in her desperation and she waited for his response.

"It was you? But… why take such an interest in me?"

"You must listen, Teguin. Do not share this knowledge with anyone. There are many at court who would treat you badly for the connection to me after what happened to the warden. Worse indeed, than simply being a Dorst."

"Being a Dorst," he said the words with anger, though it was not directed at her.

"I owe you an explanation," she began. "My husband was a general of the Imperial guard stationed at the Blue City when your grandfather openly spoke out against the Empress. She still fears opposition—especially from noble houses—but Her Imperial Majesty was quite sensitive to criticism when she first ascended to the throne."

"A thousand blessings to the throne," Teguin responded out of polite expectation.

Jade winced, but she could not bring herself to respond in kind. She fought to swallow, and took a deep breath before she continued. "The punishments for anyone who voiced their displeasure with the Empress were harsh, and my husband enforced them. At first the court loved him for it. Imperial law without mercy. But when noble houses were stripped of power and exiled…"

"Noble houses including mine," finished Teguin.

Jade nodded. Her voice had formed a new quality in her exhaustion and sounded like a dull, rasping tone that carried no emotion. She had none left to give. "The anger of the nobility needed a scapegoat. Not the Empress, of course. Her Holiness is above reproach in all things. In the end, my husband took the blame and he bore it like the splendid, self-mutilating hero that he is. Was. Damn it all."

She rose from the cot. After taking a long drink from her cup on the table, she straightened and walked around the room. "Teguin, I serve at the pleasure of the Empress but my family has suffered greatly by her hand. So has yours. You may not realize the full extent of your exclusion—Feran may have sheltered you from the worst of it—but you are no fool."

"There were moments of exclusion I remember well as a boy. The bribes, the humiliation. Times when my uncle and I were turned away from certain noble houses or festivals at the mention of our name. Feran's vague reasons never added up."

She nodded. "Wealth alone is not enough for some."

"There are times when the Dorst name is not welcome," Teguin admitted, "but we have managed."

"And I still have my privileges as a Seeker," Jade replied. "It is the one thing that cannot be taken from me: my gifts. And yet, I stand to lose everything else. I have managed to keep my daughter safe, until now."

Turning, she was eye to eye with Teguin. "My daughter is all I have left, Teguin. Find Lena, and keep her safe until we can be reunited. Do this, and I will forgive your obligation to me at Praxis."

It was hard to give up the debt-obligation Teguin owed her, but she was desperate. Family often forgave the debt, but an outside sponsor who had no personal attachments could easily demand cycles of service, a marriage alliance, even a vast fortune in goods or coin to repay the Imperial position that came with the honor.

It was well known that Feran had chosen to sponsor Herbert Tanasen in order to win a trade deal with the family. Teguin would be a fool to refuse. It pained her to make it. She had undergone a great deal of expense and made plans to collect on that debt.

"Your offer is a tempting one, milady. How would I hold you to your word that you would release me?"

"Give me ink and parchment. I will put my name to it."

Teguin reached for his vest pocket, but he only had the map and a bit of charcoal. Still, Jade wrote a note and signed the back of it. He looked it over and nodded, adding his own name. "I will honor my promise and bring her back to you."

Her shoulders relaxed. "Excellent. My mind will be at ease. I may finally be able to rest."

"Herbert will not be pleased to learn of our new adventure," he admitted to Lady Jade as they walked together to the door.

"He will come with you all the same. As for your reasons—"

"I will keep them my own," he promised.

Opening the door, Teguin nearly tripped over his fallen friend. Herbert was curled up on the floor, twitching in fits with flecks of foam rasping through his lips. His staff lay just beyond reach as if thrown.

"Bring him quickly!" Jade cried.

Teguin dragged Herbert into the healer's ward while she took a piece of black cloth from her pocket and picked up the staff.

Teguin was able to roll his lanky friend onto the cot in the corner but could not wake Herbert, whose stiff body eerily resembled a corpse. "What new madness is this?" he asked.

"I warned you both to not use magic," she snapped. "The fool. Now, instead of leaving the prison right away you will have to come with me and face something far more dangerous. I do not have the strength to do this alone. Help me to the stairs."

Her fury blinded her to her weakness as he led her quickly down the hallway. She stopped and tightened her grip on his arm, and a pang of regret made her question her decision. "Wait. You could still take Herbert and leave, Teguin. I was not thinking clearly. It might not affect him once you are away from this place. The damage could be ongoing, though; he has a fragile constitution—I know I am not making any sense, but I cannot confirm the cause unless I return to the warden's study."

"I will help you if it means there is a chance it will help Herbert." he replied. "He cannot travel the Wastelands like he is now and I will not leave without him."

"Then up the stairs. Hurry."

Panting, they reached a narrow landing halfway up the tower where the structure curved. Jade pushed open a large door, and they found the room ransacked with scattered and torn remains of bedding and broken furniture. An abandoned pile of possessions lay near the desk, with leather pieces of practice armor that were badly stained, a tumble of old boots, and a ripped doll with tufts of fleece spilling from its belly.

The only piece of furniture left intact was a large desk with its drawers wide open, its surface and sides scratched with lewd suggestions. Teguin flushed with anger. Jade stared at the desk for the second time that day. She gave herself a little shake, her lips trembling.

"There is some kind of punishing force at play here; a reaction against anyone who dares to use magic. Even I am not immune to its power. Such a weapon would likely be kept by the prison warden—" her voice broke, but she made herself finish, "in case of an uprising caused by magical means."

Teguin circled the room, stepping past the pile of boots and gear. "A Master Historian would say to focus on the past in order to answer a question in the present. We are in an ancient place created by our ancestors at the height of their skills."

It was a simple statement but she played along. "Right. Someone made an object to manipulate magic and control others." Bending, she picked up the ripped doll from the tumbled pile. "Such a creation is far too dangerous to be left to looters and monsters like Jarvin and his men."

Teguin looked between the room's contents and the stone walls that surrounded them. "The stonework in this place is strange; its color and quality are unique and different from the surrounding sandstone, and have you noticed, the walls and floors are free from any scratches or worn spots from regular use? No erosion."

A part of Jade felt hollow and numb, it was painful to be in this place knowing that Torven would not be coming back. Teguin turned the ring he wore on his finger and she winced. "Careful. That ring has its own enchantments and they are not well inscribed."

"Master Frost would not be happy to hear that."

Teguin's magic in the hands of Master Frost and her experiments. Another reason she would need to visit Praxis, and soon. Jade blinked as she watched a surge of magic pulse within Teguin, trying to break free as he said, "It is not a part of me, so I thought I could use it to—"

"No. Enchanted objects like the one we seek are made to fulfill their purpose, Teguin. It is not a person, and would not stop to judge what kind of magic is being used any more than it would seek reason."

"But there must be a way of controlling it! Is it not significant that simply having magic does not leave us bedridden by constant attack?"

In defiance, Teguin put out his hand and placed it against the wall. She gasped in horror, and braced herself for the worst, but nothing happened. Teguin swallowed but kept his hand in contact with the wall.

Teguin turned his head to look back at her. "Well, it must allow for some passive use of magic or I would not be standing here."

She gripped the desk with both hands and swore softly under her breath. "That was a damned hay-brained thing to do. Stone on stone, of course. A Seeker should know better." She shot him a furious look. "Do not count on that kind of luck often, Teguin."

Teguin jerked his head toward the scars on his hand. "There is no luck in stone, milady, only logic we do not yet understand." It sounded like something Torven would have said, and that made her smile until the memory of losing him returned.

With an eye on the walls around them, she sighed. "Well, at least we know one thing: the magic you have must be attuned to whatever this thing is, otherwise you would be in far worse shape than you are now; which gives me an idea. That ring of yours, how was it made?"

"Master Frost made the rings of glowstone and red powder from my magic. Once she learned more of my magic and what happened to my arm, she was eager to experiment with it to try and enchant objects. This was one of her better inventions; it reminds me not to overdo my magic because it glows, er, right before I do." His scars were clearly visible against the dark stone wall, and with his arm so tense they cut deeply into his hand.

Jade bit her lip. "I see now she was right to be worried; you seem to love taking risks."

"It is not about the risk. If it means learning more, means gaining important knowledge, then I will not hesitate."

"Well, we are closer than we were before to learning how they made these blasted objects in the first place and that is something. That ring of yours might be the key we need."

Jade waved her hands to indicate the room around them. "It was several months ago, but do you remember what I said at Praxis about like magic attracting like? Keep your hand on the wall and walk around. Let me know if anything changes."

"A slight tingling up and down my arm, but otherwise no changes so far."

"Wait, Teguin. Go back."

He backed up. Jade saw his magic race from his shoulder to sweep down into his hand and fingers as if trying to escape to a single point in the wall.

"Stop there and step away slowly," she said. Her attention was fixed on a point level with his shoulder. He tried to take his hand away, but it was caught fast against the stone, the finger with his ring strangely stuck in place. The ring had a dull red glow but she nodded encouragement while fighting the urge to panic.

Inspiration hit. "Pull your hand downward. Stay relaxed. No need to lose a finger."

With a ping, the ring slipped from Teguin's finger and lodged itself into the wall. A section of the stone wall imploded. The ring disappeared. Teguin took another step back.

Lady Jade walked right up to the hole and put her hand inside. With a look of horrified fascination, Teguin rushed forward. "What are you doing!"

She pulled out a cluster of clear crystal which fit neatly into her palm. There was a sound of tearing as she pulled a square of black cloth from a pocket of her dress, and put the crystal inside. Only when she had it fully covered and in her pocket did she look up at him.

The presence in the prison lessened. A change in the air. Teguin must have felt it too.

He was holding his breath, and released it. "That is what caused Herbert so much trouble? It looks like a child's bauble; a piece of frippery my uncle would have on a shelf for sale."

"Looks can be deceiving. It is a clear crystal. Seekers use them to scry for magical objects, but this is one of the purest I have ever seen." She held out her free hand to him for support, and as he guided her back to the stairs she moved more easily than before.

When he tripped over himself on the first step, she looked over at him. "I admire you wanting to help your friend, Teguin. I only hope you use the same determination to find my daughter."

They headed back to the ward. As they reached the hallway Herbert saved them the trouble. He met them at the bottom of stairs holding his staff and rubbing the back of his neck.

"What happened?" he asked. "One moment yer talkin' in the ward and the next I've taken her place on the cot." His eyes narrowed when he saw the familiar way that she held onto Teguin's arm. "Where were ye?"

Anger showed on Teguin's face for the first time that Jade had seen. She released his arm as he pointed at the staff. "Had to have a snack while you waited? We had to go and save your hide while you were unconscious. Did it even occur to you that Lady Jade asked us not to use any magic for a damned good reason? You could have been killed."

The corner of Lady Jade's mouth twitched, but she said nothing.

Herbert sputtered and tightened the grip on his staff until he found his voice. "It's an apple, not a bleedin' shank!" he yelled.

The sound of running footsteps heralded the return of Jarvin's men. Jade had a sudden thought. The sight of Torven's study in shambles was a warning. Seeker or no, she was vulnerable to the whims of Captain Jarvin. It brought too many risks to keep the clear crystal in her possession.

If it were safe with anyone, it would be Teguin. And giving it to him would cement their trust. She slipped it into his hand. "Take this. Keep it safe." She pulled away before Teguin could ask any questions and walked toward the soldiers.

She must have looked a mess, but Jarvin's soldiers hurriedly sheathed their swords at her approach.

"We heard shoutin'," said one of the younger men with an appraising look at Teguin and Herbert.

Lady Jade gave him a bright smile. "How noble of you to come to my protection. I have excellent news for Captain Jarvin; I am ready to complete my work. Would you bring me to him?" She had already taken the young lieutenant by the arm but he turned back.

"What about them?"

"They are free to go, and you may take me to the captain so that I may relay that message in person," she said with a wave of her hand.

"But—"

"Lieutenant, I wish to see Jarvin. Now. Good luck with your work, Mister Dorst. Mister Tanasen. Come and go as you wish, and Empress Bless you both." Without a second look in their direction she hurried away.

Teguin managed to put the crystal into his pocket without drawing attention to it. She had seen the anger written across Herbert's face before she left, but Teguin would know what to say to his friend. She had his word that he would keep her sponsorship a secret, and now the weight of that promise would bind them together, and keep her daughter safe.

19

AN INDECENT PROPOSAL

Feran threw open the door to Selina's study. The woman rose to her feet with her quill still in hand, a ruffled robe wrapped around her to ward off the morning chill in the room. She flushed, and her cheeks turned a bewitching shade of pink that matched her gown.

"Why, Feran," she said, "what brings you to Praxis and my rooms in such a hurry this morning?"

Feran went to her side and dropped to his knees. "You may think me impetuous as I was in our youth, Selina, but I cannot stay silent any longer."

Before she could reply, Selina's steward, Tirol, caught up with Feran. Gripping the door frame for support as he snorted into his drooping mustache, the man announced with a loud huff of offended dignity, "Merchant Dorst to see you, Headmistress."

Feran ignored the man. He knew the slightest break in his attention could be disastrous. The next few moments were of paramount importance to his future.

"I am a man of opportunity," he hurried to continue. "The time has finally come when I might bind myself to you in honor and prove my everlasting devotion. Choose me, Selina. Be my wife."

Ink dripped from Selina's forgotten quill and onto the hemline of her dressing gown. It spattered his breeches and the arm that rested against her chair. Without a word, Tirol closed the door with a heavy thud.

Selina was frozen in place. Her expression shifted and transformed from one emotion to another, transparent as clouds gathering in a storm. When she finally did speak, it was far from the impulsive and passionate reply that he hoped to spark.

"This is indecent, Feran. A woman chooses her man in marriage. She is not picked by him."

"Be honest, Selina," he said with quiet firmness. "Tradition has never interested you before."

Her nose crinkled as if a foul odor had reached her notice. "How could I accept the proposal of a man? It would shame my cousin, and, and—"

"Oh nonsense," he said, taking her hand in both of his. "You have always been special to me, and surely you can see the mutual benefit of uniting our families now that the Dorst name will be a noble one again?"

"Legan has accepted the pardon, then? That surprises me to hear."

That was a mistake. He should not have mentioned it. "Well," he hesitated, not wanting to tell her any direct lie. "Legan will come around."

"Come around?" Selina pulled her hand away. "Come around. I see. And in the meanwhile, you want a union so that my public support is behind you in case anyone questions the precious Dorst name."

Feran fought to keep his anger in check. "Must you be so sterile about my declaration? I put myself before you with no ambition in mind—"

"No ambition? You? Do not treat me like a blushing handmaiden," she said, her voice full of scorn. "How dare you assume that the moment you arrive I will do anything you wish; you must think me a fool."

Feran knew then that he had greatly misjudged her reaction. Was this only a passing mood? Had he made a grave mistake?

Mind reeling by the forcefulness of her rejection, he sputtered and attempted to recover. "My love, we are neither of us lovesick pups. Think of the power we would wield together. With my wealth and your influence combined we would be the equal of any noble family in the Imperium."

Selina seized a loose curl that fell over her shoulder. She twisted and pulled it until she winced. "We have always done well together, Feran. But what you ask is unnecessary. You see my lack of a husband as a weakness, but I assure you it is by my own choice. A very different kind of choice than you presume."

Embarrassment inflamed his cheeks until the heat spread like hot coals across his face. "I see now that I would be nothing but a burden to your status, *Headmistress*."

Remembering the quill in her hand, Selina threw it onto the desk. More curls came loose from the twisted bun that held them in place. "You assume that taking you to my bed makes you my first choice for a husband." She spat the last word at him like a curse.

Feran stood. He searched her face for any sign that she would change her mind. All of his plans were falling apart at a spectacular rate; first the Guild, then his own brother, and now the woman he loved. Their rebuttals and rejection fell against him like lashes from a whip.

"I thought you would see more value in our union," he said. "Clearly, I was mistaken."

Her expression softened. A tiny seed of hope planted itself. She patted him on the arm, but the conciliatory gesture stung almost as much as the refusal itself.

"Feran, politics and love rarely have any real connection." She turned to the window. "The Dorst name has not yet been cleaned of its tarnish. The Empress cannot truly embrace you or your family again until she has a renewed pledge of loyalty and good faith. In the meanwhile, you and Teguin both will have to accept that there are limits to the privileges bestowed upon you."

"The Empress is gracious and generous in all things," Feran managed to choke out the ceremonial compliment required of him. She was firm in her refusal after all. There was nothing more he could do to change her mind. "I will not continue to impose my presence on you, my lady."

He was shaken to the core by her rejection. How easily she turned on him, threw his words back in his face when he showed deep feelings of love and affection. Was he really so worthless in her eyes after everything they had been through together?

If he had any hope of fixing things he needed to leave before he made things worse. He would have to change his plans. Anger toward her would only lead to more distance between them and unkind words.

She was still at the window when he reached the door. "I will leave tomorrow at first light." He forced a smile as he looked back at her profile. "I must make several stops before I return to the capital. There is still much work to be done. Old friends to meet. Other choices to be made." If she would not help him, then he would have to find another way.

"Good fortune to you, Feran."

"Fortunes have their burdens." He chose to take her parting words as a challenge. If the value of their alliance was not enough, then he would have to find other ways to prove his worth.

Plenty of women would vie for his attention once he returned to court. In the end, Selina was doing him a favor by keeping his options open. Yes, that was the way.

Selina's affection and position would soon be dwarfed by other opportunities. He had made his own luck before. This was no different.

ANGER UNLEASHED

Herbert tugged at his boots. Rubbing at raw heels, he knocked out as much sand as he could safely manage without tumbling off the back of his lamat. The creature lumbered across the sand, turning without warning while Herbert clutched at his saddle to try and avoid adding new bruises to his backside.

These lamat from the prison were far larger than the young ones they left with the soldiers. Every strange noise they made set him on edge. Worst of all, this new lamat had also discovered the staff he carried was full of tasty green things to eat. When the nostrils of his mount flared and snorted, Herbert had precious little time to act before a long tongue flipped over to steal his next meal. A quick kick was the only way to prevent the lamat from snagging a bit of green sprout or sweet snow pea.

He didn't have much luck keeping his staff out of reach; the creature's tongue seemed to grow longer. With his boot half on, he heard another warning snort and gave the creature a smack with his heel but too late; the tongue pulled an apple blossom from inside the staff's bulbous tip. The lamat chewed and swallowed and hissed at Herbert.

Herbert hissed back. "That was mine fer later ye sack of sheep's piss."

The creature bellowed and for one horrible moment Herbert rose into the air, weightless. He flailed in a panic before he connected with the saddle again. A jolt of pain ran up and down his spine.

The lamat's fat neck turned toward him and an eyelid slid open until its yellow-rimmed pupil reflected his crumpled clothes and flushed face. If Herbert had any moisture left to spare, he would have spat right into that smug yellow eye. It blinked and narrowed. The deep growl from the creature vibrated up his spine.

Up ahead, Cergath turned smoothly in his saddle to look back at them. "Trouble?" he called out.

The request from Captain Jarvin to bring Cergath along with them was not a request at all, and they all knew it. Here he was, another unwelcome guide. What could they do but say yes? In Teguin's words, he knew enough about the negotiation table to recognize when to protest, and when to walk away.

Herbert heard another snort. He reached for his staff without thinking, but then Teguin's lamat was beside him, Teguin red in the face and pulling the reins and somehow managing to guide it along.

"How are ye leadin' yers?" Herbert asked, ignoring Cergath.

"This beast goes where it pleases. Be grateful yours is taking a steady pace. Mine must smell something up ahead." He lowered his voice. "Did you feed yours a moment ago?"

"Na'en by choice."

"Be firm with the creatures," called Cergath. "These lamat are used to soldiers, not... strangers. But they will cover twice the ground as those other lamat you brought."

Herbert would have loved for Rinzi to hear her lamat called slow. The woman was probably halfway home by now. This prison guard was quiet, but at least he was eager to help them find this missing girl.

His water skin was lighter than he liked. Where would they find more water in such a desolate place? Clearing his sore throat, he glared at Teguin's lamat.

His own mount gave a rumble and a flash of large teeth that made Herbert's heart skip a beat. Teguin's lamat took off again with a snort as sand flew in all directions. Teguin clutched his reins with a whoop of surprise and soon he caught up with Cergath.

Herbert suspected that Teguin liked the lamat more than he would admit. His friend even shared his meals with the creatures and, despite his denial, it seemed willing to obey him. Or at least, his didn't threaten to bite his legs off. Lucky sod.

Another snort from his own lamat warned Herbert just in time to block its pebbled tongue. He wished he had thicker boots with him, though he didn't dare check how many teeth the beast had behind its scaly jowl. Cergath had said something about multiple rows of teeth.

Night air settled around them. In the distance, Iral hovered over the dunes, bringing every ripple of sand into view. It was a depressing reminder that nothing green surrounded them. His staff was the only sign of growing vegetation in this desolate place.

Herbert missed the apple orchards of Tanasen estate. The thought of each heavily laden bough stung. Would the peach tree be recovered enough to bloom this growing cycle? If he closed his eyes, he could almost hear the sigh of leaves on the wind as they raced across the berry bushes and into the shelter of the forest at the edge of their land. Now, that was a good piece of land.

Cergath stopped atop a high dune with Teguin just behind him. By the time Herbert arrived, he was willing to avoid a snap of teeth by falling off his lamat instead of dismounting. Cergath looked over at him as he got up, brushing sand off himself, and said nothing.

Teguin stretched. "Three days and we still have not caught up with them. I see no trail to follow. I mean no disrespect, Cergath, but are you sure we are heading in the right direction?"

"It's a fair question, but we're making good progress. There is no way to track them by sight." The prison guard gestured around them. "These winds move sand so quickly that any trail made by man or beast is quickly wiped away."

"Then how do ye plan on us findin' them, some 'desert sense' of yers?" asked Herbert.

Cergath didn't seem to notice that Herbert meant to insult him with the question. Instead, he pointed to the mouth of his lamat. "See their tongues? They can taste the scent of another lamat on the air for ten, maybe twenty leagues. Usually they keep out of one another's way, but at the prison we raise clutches of them together, from when they hatch, to when they are ready to mate."

When Cergath patted the leg of his own lamat it bent obediently to allow him purchase. He was back on his saddle and pushing forward again before Herbert had time to ask any more questions. At this pace, they would cover the breadth of the desert without stopping for so much as a last meal.

Herbert grabbed Teguin's arm before his friend could do the same. "Doesn't like t'slow fer much, does he. This side trip of yers better be worth it."

"Missing Rinzi already?" asked Teguin. He clapped Herbert on the shoulder with a smile. "Cheer up. We will find the girl soon, and Cergath tells me we should be close to the only source of water only a few leagues ahead. Oh, and there is plant life too: Something called needle trees."

"Cergath might be callin' it alive, but I'll be needin' a sight t'be certain the man could pluck a pod from a linseed."

"You heard what the man said when we left the prison. Guards often hunt for their own supplies, both medicine and food. If it's alive out here, Cergath has likely seen it. We're fortunate to have him along."

"So Jarvin can spy on us?" snapped Herbert. "Take a look around, Teguin. There's na'en here t'see us bloodied and buried, same as that warden. We'd be better off alone."

Herbert turned away and strapped his staff back onto his lamat. He stared into the giant yellow eye of his companion and grimaced, his sore muscles straining as he settled back into his saddle again.

His thoughts drifted back to the prison and their sudden change of plans. It was one thing to help Teguin find word of Master Troug, but to run into Lady Jade at the prison was as suspicious as the sweetgrass porridge they served at the Traverse Inn. Had Teguin known that woman was at the prison all along?

Herbert was brought out of his thoughts by a loud snort, and an unmistakable flash of a pea shoot flew past his vision. The next snort had him poised, ready to strike with his boot. Then something strange happened; a groan escaped the creature and it picked up speed, throwing Herbert sideways in his saddle. Running smoothed the lamat's motion and before long Herbert grew used to the new pace. How long could it keep up this speed before tiring he didn't know, but its tail pointed straight behind it as it ran, focused and humming with excitement.

The water must be close. Herbert leaned forward in the saddle, eager to peer over the next dune and gain a first look at the closest thing the desert held to a tree. Would there be a forest, a lake, or simply a well?

What he saw was the strangest looking cluster of branches he could have imagined. From a distance it appeared to be a series of dead twigs sticking up from the ground with sharp, broken ends. This was no green thing.

By moonlight, Herbert could see no leaf nor budding blossom like that of Falden Province but Teguin was right; aside from sweetgrass it was the first sign of plant life still standing in the desert. Like everything in this place, the plant appeared to be a dense collection of dried out stalks.

The size of the branches was misleading. As he approached, they grew taller until twice, no, three times the size of a man. Herbert's lamat raced past Cergath and Teguin then shuddered to a halt, sniffing wildly. Herbert slid off, only taking the time to pull his staff free and bring it with him and away from that foul creature and its tongue.

There was a chill in the air of this place. Herbert could smell moisture around the branches. He would eat his own swollen tongue before admitting that Cergath was right, yet he was, there had to be water here.

Looking around, it wasn't on the ground but in the trees. No, it *was* the trees. These barren, lifeless husks held something precious. Herbert put out a hand, but hesitated.

The surfaces of the trees were covered by needles, each the length of his finger, sharp and hostile in clusters that covered nearly every bit of its thick skin. Now he understood why they were called needle trees; the needles could easily pierce flesh and deter the curious or thirsty.

Herbert went right for the longest of them. They weren't just protection, he reasoned, but fingers reaching out to touch and explore the world. Determined to greet the tree, he dropped his staff and reached for the closest cluster at the height of his chest. These needles were more flat than round, like a double-edged sword, and he found that he could run a finger along their underside without cutting himself if he was careful.

It was like greeting a stranger. The needles were an introduction to a brittle, bitter existence. Herbert couldn't blame it for a cold reception. It was a hard life—an impossible thing, really, to be alive at all in a place like this. And to contain water as well... what a treasure these trees guarded.

Before he could explore further, Cergath interrupted, holding out a thin tube. "Here, take one of mine. It's the only way to get past the needles and harvest water."

"Fair certain of that are ye," he snapped.

"Why don't we try another tree," said Teguin with a warning look at Herbert.

Herbert knew he should collect water and move on but, just then, he didn't give a flying leaf what anyone thought of him using his magic out here in the desert.

Who cared what this stiff old prison soldier saw? What a pleasure it would be to turn his head and make him wonder at something he took for granted. Herbert was tired of hiding his staff. He was tired of second glances, and tired of being one step behind everyone else and their plans.

He was here to explore the plants of the Wastelands and that was exactly what he would do. Explore. He rolled up his sleeves and knelt in the sand, not knowing or caring what would happen.

Fingers trembling, he slipped past the needles to touch the trunk of the nearest tree. He opened his mind to it as if it were one of his own trees from home, and that thought conjured the images closest to his heart. Memories of home, with berry bushes and their delicate thorns so different from the needle trees, apple orchards and their delicate blossoms, the fields of greenwheat, so thick they would hide the ground from sight on harvest days.

It was like waking a friend from a long, senseless slumber. Something in the needle tree *softened* toward him. That was the only way he could describe it. The needles were long as ever, but Herbert felt he was sinking into the tree through untold layers of age and dry ground.

This place was old. He could sense it; the plants were slow to grow and quick to keep what little moisture they found. These were no trees, but a different kind of plant that grew for such an age that it took many lifetimes of a person to reach a single, sculpted shape.

"Yer a beauty," Herbert whispered. There was so much he wanted to know. This was but one of several dozen giants, and with the scarcity of water it was hard to believe that they could all survive in such close quarters with one another.

"How d'ye do it?" he asked, not really expecting a response. He gasped when his thoughts joined with a new awareness. Green rimmed his vision.

Instead of Tanasen Estate, unfamiliar images formed in his mind and he moved past the needles, past the thick skin of the plant, deeper than the water held in caches, and deeper still until he found the roots that stretched half a league under the sand. Unexpectedly, he found a second layer of thin tough roots stretching outward in shallow tendrils not unlike the sweetgrass along the borderlands of Falden. These roots reminded Herbert of mushrooms, the way they grew and formed and connected with other plants nearby.

No wonder they grew closely together. These were joined, in a way they were all a part of one another, sharing resources, sensing life. The bonds which connected these roots intrigued him, and as Herbert tried to figure out whether or not they had the same origin a prick of pain stabbed him right between the eyes.

"Oy!" he cried. Blinking, he realized that the pain was not his own but the shared sensation of having Cergath plunge the tube into a nearby plant, draining it of its water.

"Careful of the needles," Cergath called out.

"Careful yerself," he said, rubbing his forehead, then called out. "Take only what ye need; it takes an age fer a plant t'gather a drink."

"They do not need it for anything."

"Of course," Herbert muttered under his breath, looking over the dried stalks. "When was the last time ye had the water t'bloom?"

Now that he knew to look for it, Herbert saw signs of the water taken from each and every plant in the grove, where the needles on the plant were gone. Carved and picked and plucked away to bore giant holes in the tree's defenses, allowing animals and people alike to gnaw and bite their way into the heartblood of the plant, draining it of its water until there was little left to survive on except a whisper of shared roots.

The pain in his head intensified as the water drained from the plant, and he realized that another pain was draining a distant piece of the grove. The same tool. Only one was theirs. Breaking away from the plant, Herbert fought his way through pockets of loose sand to where Teguin and Cergath were filling their flasks.

"We're not alone," he said. "There's others at the edge of the grove."

"It must be Lena," said Cergath. It was odd that he believed Herbert without question; the man must have suspected she would be here. His sun-tanned face broke into a smile, the first he had shown on their trip. He corked his flask and went to his lamat, whispering in the creature's ear. It thrashed its tail as it took off in the direction Herbert pointed before they had time to react.

"Wait now," said Teguin to the man's back, but it was too late. He was over the rise and gone.

Herbert was shocked that the man would be so impulsive. There were no obvious signs of anyone else. The rays of Iral were feeble, and Ferual was hidden behind clouds. No longer in contact with the plant, Herbert felt hollow and full of doubt. What if he was wrong?

"We have to hurry and catch up," said Teguin, fumbling with his water flask.

"Why bother? He'll be leavin' us behind the first chance he gets. I'm stayin'."

"It could be anyone out here getting water."

"Sure, there's loads of people out here just waitin' in line fer a drink."

"Herbert, he could be in trouble."

"Ye reckon he wants our help?"

"It's Lady Jade's daughter."

"His or hers, same difference with the way he rode off just then; that's clear as spring water."

Teguin rocked back and forth, clenching and unclenching his hands. "*Empress Bless it*, Herbert, with you staying and him going I have to leave one of you behind."

Herbert didn't see what all the fuss was about. He pointed to the needle plants, incredulous. "This is the safest ye'll find me!" The piercing look Teguin gave him made Herbert even more determined to stay right where he was.

Teguin jumped back onto his lamat. "Promise me you won't do anything foolish with your magic, at least until I get back? Feran used to tell me that a person is vulnerable in a place where they feel safest."

"Yer wastin' time. Go after him."

Watching Teguin leave, Herbert reached down for his staff only to remember it was on the ground back at the other needle plant. Alone. With his lamat near enough to smell it.

He whirled around and ran. It was easy to see the silhouette of his lamat and soon he could hear the sound he dreaded. Heart-wrenching crunching noises that signaled lunch.

"Drop it!" he cried, desperate. The creature backed away as he approached with a wary rumble. The staff, however, was still entangled in its massive jaws. Herbert didn't stop to think but placed his hand past the needles until the plant gave a small shudder at his touch. A moment later a hand full of the long spines shot out and into the creature's eye. With a hiss, an ominous cracking sound reached Herbert's ears. The sound had to be his staff breaking in two, he was certain of it.

Herbert howled in a rage that drowned out the lamat's hissing, and he dug his nails into the plant instinctively. Another round of needles shot out and embedded themselves in the creature's head. It slumped to the ground, motionless.

He scrambled to retrieve what remained of his staff. Pieces of the vine lay scattered in all directions. He was so focused on retrieving what he could that he didn't stop to check and see if the lamat was still alive.

Voices rang distantly in his ears. Herbert's fingers found the largest piece of his staff. The damage could have been far worse. It hadn't been snapped in half, but the growing plants on the inside of the staff were stripped barren, eaten away by the persistence of that long, dry tongue. The lamat still wasn't moving.

"Herbert?"

He looked up. Teguin's face was paler than the moonlit sand. He swayed where he stood.

With a guilty twinge Herbert got up, sand running off him like scattered seeds. Embarrassed by the fallen lamat beside him, his grip hardened on the broken staff. "Listen, I ken it looks t'be bad, but—"

"I want you to listen to me," said Teguin. He barely spared a glance for the beast. "There's something I need to tell you. We found Lena."

Alarmed, Herbert knelt to pull out his healer's bag from the fallen creature. "Is she hurt bad, then?"

"Not hurt, no, but Herbert—"

"So it's true, then." A man's voice made them both turn. Two new figures were silhouetted in the night, and that voice. Herbert knew that voice. Hated that voice.

A memory tickled the back of his mind. The smell of hot soured ale. The voice of his teacher, Master Jayce, brought him back to a stormy night at the Mulberry Inn. 'It'll be the Wastes for you I'm afraid.'

Lady Jade's daughter was not the only person to escape the prison. He knew that someone else had stolen a second lamat. But why did it have to be him?

A cascade of emotions rippled through Herbert. Anger deepened into revulsion. A small flash of green behind his eyes reminded him that this was real.

"Young Lord Tanasen," said Jameson. The man managed a polite smile, and even gave a bow that was in every way a mockery of the title.

The torment caused by Jameson at Praxis was an ever-present shadow cast over the memory of Olivia's death. Memories of Olivia, the first and only woman he ever loved, came back to him in a renewed flood. Words failed him.

Beside Jameson stood a young woman who even resembled Olivia; from the light hair to the outline of a delicate jaw. Fierce and alive, while Olivia was dead.

Teguin thrust a hand into his pocket, his eyes shifting in a wild dance to keep an eye on both of them at once. "I see your fortunes have much improved since we last met, Jameson."

Herbert's words felt hollow in his throat when he finally spoke. "Found yer way of leavin' prison, then."

"Oh, I have not been imprisoned. They had need of a healer. I made myself useful."

"And how many that ye healed found their illness suddenly worse?" Herbert spat. "Or was it enough t'have so many helpless souls at yer mercy, under yer will. How many died under yer hand?" Boiling beneath the surface, his anger gripped him by the throat until he thought he would choke on it.

The woman spoke for the first time. "Mason, what is he talking about? Who are these men?"

She moved closer to Jameson and it sickened Herbert to see her look at the monster with an expression of love and trust. So innocent. She had to be warned.

"Saw fit t'change yer name I see. Mason. Have ye told her about yer past, then, and shown her yer 'abilities t'spread rot and ruin?' It's a blessin' t'heal, but what does it say when yer the one makin' the sickness?"

Accusations spilled from him until he barely had air in his lungs but still, he kept going. "How d'ye make them trust ye at the prison; a sudden illness a few weeks into yer sentence?"

Herbert found Cergath's stoic expression and locked eyes with the man, determined to punch his way through and reach some kind of understanding as to how very dangerous Jameson was. "Spreadin', was it?" he asked innocently, spreading his arms to drop all but the largest piece of his staff back onto the sand. A flash of green in his vision kept him rocking from side to side with a hum of frantic energy.

The shortened staff flipped back and forth in his hands. He could not keep it still. "It's more yer taste t'start with the strong, break a guard or two," he continued, gasping for breath, "t'have their need urgent so they stop askin' questions and let ye prey upon the weak."

Those last words must have hit a mark, for Cergath stepped forward, his expression now unusually expressive. Concerned. His eyes were on the girl now. "Move away from him, Lena."

She moved closer instead, her eyes wide. "Mason, who is this man? Why would he say such awful things?"

"It will be alright, my love," said Jameson, his words sending a chill down Herbert's spine.

"*My love?* And here I thought yer love was given, like mine. Olivia's ashes scattered and barely cold, yet yer on t'the next pretty face."

It was like popping the cork on a soured bottle of ale. Jameson's face slipped from mild to monstrous. The moonlight all but vanished. Green and black danced across Herbert's sight.

Jameson did not speak, he roared. "I should have cut your throat when I had the chance!" He rushed forward and threw something dark and shapeless right at Herbert, the forms twisting and expanding in midair.

A kind of distorted seed pod he didn't recognize flew past his ear and landed at the base of the nearest needle plant. His heart sank as the pod grew in size, exploded, and spread a thick, gooey substance over it. The smell made his skin crawl. It brought back haunting memories of the ruination upon which Jameson thrived.

The rot spread quickly. Something hot and wet and sticky slapped over his mouth with rough hands. He was so preoccupied that he had taken his eyes away from Jameson, who quickly wrestled him to the ground.

He was just as strong and fast as Herbert remembered. "You shut your filthy mouth, Tanasen scum," he said again. "Don't you dare even speak her name."

Herbert struggled for air, his eyes watering. He still held the piece of his staff but he fought to stay conscious, trying to focus on his magic. A few twigs burst out of it to wrap around Jameson's arms. It was just enough of a shock to make the man loosen his grip in surprise, a choking laughter deep in his throat.

"Still kept this little vine of yours alive? Such a pretty little thing. So easily broken, like the rest of you. There's no masters to protect you now."

Herbert coughed and sucked in as much air as he could, scrambling away on hands and knees and leaving his staff behind. Half-blind from blinking green spots, he was vaguely aware of Lena struggling to be free of Cergath's iron grip, and Teguin arranging something on the sand.

Jameson's fist pounded into the side of his face and sent stars across his vision. The man pushed him up against the needle plant he was trying to reach and suddenly an entire cluster of its needles went right into his back. Herbert screamed.

The needles snapped off the plant and into his body, wriggling as if alive. There was no difference between his flesh and the skin of the plant. They were one. From tip to root he could sense the energy of life around him. He was strong. Complete.

The frantic struggle fell away as the plants shared his pain as he did theirs. He was Herbert, he fought to remember in alarm. Herbert Tanasen.

The rot that Jameson threw onto the plant left a sweet, wrong taste in his mouth as it got stuck between layers of absorbent tissue in the needle plant. Reaching inside himself, Herbert's magic touched the rot and stopped it in its tracks, hardening it like old sap.

Thick branches. Strong roots. These plants would endure. They both would endure.

Pain gripped Herbert. Someone was pounding his body into the ground, he caught the vibrations from the buried roots. It was an odd sensation, being so far removed from his body.

He needed to stop the pain, to fight back. Shock rippled through him as the plants reacted to his thoughts. They grew around him in response to his raw and basic desire to survive; that was one thing they understood.

Far from controlling it, Herbert faced having magic pulled out of him rather than giving it freely. A burst of emerald green flooded his surroundings. The needle plant's roots spread underground and locked together.

Shattered pieces of root from the needle plants erupted from the sand, grasping to rip and tear apart everything in their path. Needles whipped through the air. The ground heaved with such force that Herbert thought the dune might split apart.

An inseparable bond with the plants burrowed its way through his body as it took still more magic. Their needles grew back until he had nothing left to give them. The green vibrancy of light flashed into blinding brilliance, and the greenery of another place. A familiar place.

Fields of greenwheat rippled in the soft breeze, enclosing Herbert, who lay down to rest. Distant thunder released the first few drops of rain across the field. With a sigh, Herbert opened his mouth and let rainwater pour down his parched throat. Blessed release.

TEGUIN COULD NOT RISK PULLING Herbert and Jameson apart without knowing what was happening. In his experience, magic was a volatile creation and once two forces opposed one another it was deadly to interrupt. Dropping stones one-by-one from his pocket, he muttered as he tried to think of how he could prevent things from getting any worse.

Relic bones. What had driven Herbert to be so filled with rage; had he forgotten how dangerous Jameson could be? The man was strong, fast, and the madness that touched his eyes was like a rabid dog, enough to keep Teguin at a distance.

Jameson and Herbert both freely let emotions into their magic. At times like this they let those emotions control them, too, and that baffled him. Their struggle could quickly devolve into something far worse than a fistfight, and yet he had no idea what to do except to protect himself from the fall out.

Herbert let out a cry as Jameson threw him against the needle tree. The ground vibrated around all of them. Teguin thrust his hands into the sand to try and figure out what was going on, but he could see that Herbert was cornered and desperate and that boded ill.

It happened so quickly. Needle trees and sand exploded in front of Teguin's eyes—at least, that's what it looked like. The roots from the needle trees were shooting up from the ground and sand flew up around them.

Roots took hold of Teguin and attempted to pull him underground. He could hear shouts. The sound of blades cutting the roots nearby gave him hope that Cergath and Lena would be able to fend off the worst of the assault.

Herbert had lost all control. Appalled, Teguin reached out to the river stones, calling them back in a tumble until they formed a tight circle around him. He fought to keep his focus on the small circle, searching his mind until he found the sensation of hardened stone, solid and cooled. It was an effort to push his will through the stone in his hand and into the others, but he managed to pull himself free of the roots as the ground beneath him stilled. The roots squirmed but could no longer displace the sand to expand.

It wasn't much, but it was something. A stepping stone to keep above ground. In the distance he could see Lena cutting down roots with a sword that was too large for her small hands. Cergath struggled to free himself from more that were wrapped around his arms and torso. He was sinking slowly, and would soon be dragged underground or ripped apart.

Could Teguin use his own magic to rescue them? If he tried the same trick that freed him from the roots, he could risk losing control and encasing everyone in hardened sandstone permanently. No. It was better to use his own two hands.

"Hold onto him, I'm coming!" he called. As he bent to collect the stones, an ominous sound heralded a wave of spines that shot out of the trees in all directions. It was all Teguin could do not to bury himself in the sand and hope for the best. Somehow he crawled over to Cergath and Lena and the other needle trees, pulling himself free from shriveling plants and fallen needles.

Cergath wrestled to free himself from the grasp of the roots which no longer opposed him. Lena was in far worse shape. The roots had kept her standing to take the full brunt of the flying needles. Teguin caught her as the larger roots which held her shriveled back into the sand.

Her breath came in ragged gasps. There were so many needles piercing her body that even holding her brought their tips into contact with his chest. A numbing tingle ran along his skin.

When he reached to pull them out, Lena gave a slight shake of her head. "No." Blood welled in the hollow of her throat. There was nothing he could do for her.

Cergath knelt beside them, taking Lena roughly into his arms, indifferent to the needles and everything else around them. "Stubborn," he said with a gentle smile, "just like your father."

Lena tried to laugh, "Tell father, I fought for what I loved." Blood bubbled from her lips as she choked on the words, her eyes widening until they were dark. Vacant.

Cergath lowered her to the sand, moving her palms so they faced the sky and invited her soul to greet the Empress and her ancestors. Roots around them sank fully into the sand, the withered bits of rot and dried plant blowing away. A light breeze warned of dawn's warmth, coming on the lengthening horizon.

"Senseless," snapped Cergath, rising to his feet. "The warden was right, magic has no place in this world. It brings nothing but sorrow."

Teguin was shocked that Cergath knew the word magic at all. He would have liked to ask the man but this was not the time. He stepped carefully to where Herbert lay in the sand.

When he saw Jameson with Lena in the grove and recognized him, Teguin was hopeful that time in the Wastelands had mellowed the exiled man's taste for violence. Herbert had shattered that hope to pieces in seconds without ever giving Jameson a chance.

"Someone must pay," demanded Cergath. "Where are Mason and Herbert? I will tear the two of them apart limb-from-limb."

While Teguin was less than enthusiastic about defending Herbert, there was no point to letting anyone else lose control. The truth was he wanted to thrash Herbert himself.

"I am sorry for your loss, truly," he said. "But there is no satisfaction in beating a senseless man."

Teguin put a hand on Cergath's arm. The sight of his scars made the man recoil. "No, stay back. You are just as bad as they are, magic-wielder. I should have warned Captain Jarvin about you and Lady Jade when I had the chance. Then none of this would have happened."

"The only magic-wielder you should be worried about right now is Jameson. He and Jarvin could be blood-brothers with their love of violence and chaos."

"Fine. Search for Mason—Jameson, if that is what you call him. He has to answer for what happened, as does your friend. I will stay with Lena so that she is… protected." His voice grew tight and Teguin could see his hands were shaking.

Cergath managed to calm himself by gripping his sword hilt. He went and knelt over Lena's body. Teguin let him go. He wanted to be alone. With Lena dead, he had as much to answer for as Herbert and Jameson. More, even, for it was his promise to Lady Jade that was broken. What was he going to tell her?

No. He would think about that later when the time came. When he had no other choice. The sight of Cergath standing over Lena's body made him turn away.

That Jameson had not yet appeared was a comfort in itself. A man filled with such rage would not hesitate to continue his attacks if he were able. There were few places to hide here.

This was no ordinary place, where roads and forests and mountains cut through the landscape. There were dunes tall enough to block his view, yes, but they were in a kind of sunken bowl of these trees. Anyone running away up the sides of the dune would easily be seen even in low light. Which left an option that turned Teguin cold and hard as marble.

Jameson could be in the sand itself. Pulled underground. Buried.

Teguin kept his back to Cergath; it was better the man saw as little of magic as possible. The sprawled form of Herbert was just visible out of the corner of his eye. Teguin knew enough about his friend to know that Herbert might be asleep for days from such reckless use of his magic. But he would recover, more or less. As Master Frost would say, magic took its toll on everyone in different ways, but it was always a slap in the face.

Reaching into his pocket, Teguin dipped his fingers into the small black pouch of red powder and rubbed it into his hands until they stung with anticipation. He crouched until he made contact with the sand, opening himself completely in the search for any sign of Jameson. The scars running up his arm flared into life and Teguin lost himself in a moment of wonder, feeling the weight of the sand and each tiny fragment of stone pull his attention away from what he sought.

Shoulder throbbing, his thoughts spun in dizzying directions as he tried to sort through all the new information that rushed to greet him. It was the pain from his scars that brought him back to his senses. He needed to be more careful, and he needed to try again.

Quieting his breath like in his meditation, he could feel the vibrations from Cergath pacing in front of Lena. In the distance, their lamat clawed the sand. The excitement of the fight had startled several snake nests, causing them to empty. Teguin could sense no other movement.

He pushed further, sensing motion beyond the needle trees, and beneath where they stood. If he could feel the depth and breadth of the sand, then he reasoned he might sense the lack of sand as it covered objects—or people. It was a stretch, and the effort it took sent a tremor of pain up his arms. Sweat dripped from his brow as the first rays of morning sun gave him new incentive to hurry. With a surge of triumph, he picked out the most obvious shapes in the sand; roots from the needle trees whose shapes he knew from their sudden appearance; they had settled back into strange intertwining patterns, fighting the pressure from the sand to reach new depths.

Beyond the roots there was little but more sand and still more roots, far deeper than he would assume such things grew. It was a frustrating business. Teguin was soon ready to give up on this half-formed scheme.

He was not prepared to spend the day draining his magic when he had no idea what he was doing. He needed guidance. Where were Herbert's wild and surprising suggestions that so often resulted in success when he needed them.

With a sudden jolt of surprise, Teguin felt the distant sand tremor. There was a different quality to this new vibration. Not a creature which pushed or pressed down against the dunes, but it moved *through* the sand. What could do such a thing?

Whatever it was, Teguin was bruised, bloody, and exhausted. He would rather not find out.

He staggered to his feet. A connection with the sand lingered enough for him to walk with more confidence than he felt to meet Cergath's suspicious glare. "I thought you were going to look for Mason, not take a rest."

"I *was* looking for him," said Teguin, trying not to lose his temper. "But I felt something shaking the sand and it's moving closer. It must be quite large."

Cergath placed his palm on the sand and frowned. "Not one thing, several things. Listen." Cergath looked from Lena's body to the horizon. Sweat ran down his face, which turned pale. "Sand rays."

"Sand rays, are they dangerous?" asked Teguin.

"Nowhere to run. Not enough time to move her. *Blessed Empress*, we're doomed."

Teguin wiped a trickle of sweat that stung his eyes, only to realize it was blood from a cut on his head. "Cergath, surely we can defend ourselves. Sand rays sound like no great threat."

Cergath turned a blank face to Teguin. "What?"

"Sand rays," repeated Teguin. "We can fight them off. There is no choice."

"No choice... I will not beg for our lives." With a cry, Cergath drew his sword. But instead of turning to the dunes he tried to slice through his own armor.

Teguin yelled and closed the distance between them, horrified that Cergath would try to take his own life. He wrestled with the man, aware of every needle that found his skin, and how weakened he was from using his magic. Cergath had cycles of training and bulging muscles at his neck and arms; if Teguin had not used the unusual strength in his arm he would not have dared to take such a risk.

"Don't let grief consume you, Cergath!" Teguin said, "I need you to stand with me against what is coming."

The humming grew. Teguin's bones ached from the intensity of it as the glowstone in his arm flashed red. Whatever was closing in on them was moving enormous amounts of sand, slipping through the dunes like water. They were closing in fast.

Teguin was able to knock the sword out of Cergath's grasp with a lucky blow, which only made the man more frantic to reach it. He tried to dive after the weapon and Teguin had to throw himself into Cergath to keep him from falling onto the blade, by choice or by accident, he could not tell. They locked arms and Teguin's sleeve fell back until his entire arm was exposed, red and glowing from his recent use of magic.

Cergath froze in shock. The man's hesitation gave Teguin the time he needed to throw the sword a fair distance away. His fingers itched from the metal; what a distasteful weapon.

Cergath looked at the sword and then back to Teguin. "You have no right."

"And you are a coward, ser, if you think that death is an easier path than the one that lies before you."

The humming grew to such an intense pitch that when it stopped, Teguin reeled from the emptiness it left behind. Heart pounding, he blinked sweat from his eyes as their lamat roared a challenge.

Teguin thought that he was beyond surprise. He had seen all manner of creatures in the Wastelands. But the wave of sand that greeted his eyes was a marvel. They were not under the sand completely, nor were they atop it. Instead, a wide, gaping mouth opened to swallow the top layer of sand and send waves of it to either side once it passed harmlessly through slits in the mouth of the creature. Additional cuts in its sides reminded Teguin of fish gills and yet, these were no fish.

The lamat kicked sand high into the air at the sight of them, growling and snarling, their yellow eyes rolling in spasms. Claws fully extended, bits of froth falling from their enormous jaws.

He looked to Cergath, but the man did not rise to calm the lamat; he sat on the sand near Lena's body, head bent, intent on his own listless hands. Teguin fought the urge to run and keep running.

That urge fell away as a voice shouted from the approaching creatures, ringing in his ears as if spoken inside a large cavern. "*Siet, nezeni uns!*"

There were three of the creatures, and from atop the largest one's mouth jumped a woman, repeating the words again. "*Siet, nezeni uns!*"

The effect upon the lamat was startling. They shuddered, turned, and ran from the new creatures, heading up the dune and out of sight. Teguin watched their packs and gear tumble in all directions like stray coins, falling with heavy thuds into the sand.

"Wait," he shouted. "We cannot travel without them!" The loss of their mounts was a shock that he could not ignore.

Cergath shook himself as if waking from a dream, and would have broken into a run, but a dozen strangers surrounded them with nasty looking, curved blades in hand.

"It's no good to anyone if they're dead." One of the women had a crooked smile. "Sand rays and lamat tear each other apart if given the chance, outsider. Every sand walker knows that."

Compared to the claws and teeth of a lamat, these sand rays looked relatively harmless. But Teguin knew better than to judge the creatures only by what he could see. Their only means of escape was now out of reach and on the run, and he found himself eyeing Cergath's sword with a twinge of regret that it was well beyond reach. His use of magic had left him weak and vulnerable.

With a sudden start, the woman turned and went to another of the sand rays, disappearing inside the creatures mouth with a casual step that reminded Teguin of an Imperial rider; envoys of the Empress who spend so much time on a horse it was hard to tell where the rider ended and the horse began.

When she re-appeared, she supported the arm of an old woman who was bent in half and struggling to walk. They shuffled right past Teguin and Cergath to Lena's body.

"Is this the girl, Raima?" the old woman asked. Her voice was tight and dry, rasping like fingers upon dry parchment.

"She has a name," said Cergath. "Lena."

"*Relic bones*," Raima swore, "*mai-meia*, she has more needles than skin. Is there nothing we can do for her?"

The old woman knelt in the sand with difficulty, running her hands along Lena's fingers. "Gone. Lost, and where the water is strongest. It is an omen for dark days."

"What does she mean to you?" asked Teguin, worried that Lady Jade would have further trouble from these strangers.

"Who are you to question an elder?" said Raima, her eyes flashing in anger. "Outsiders have no place in the Wastes."

She gave Cergath a contemptuous look. "And neither do prison guards who patrol our home as if they owned the very sand itself."

"Peace, Raima," said the old woman. She looked over in Teguin's direction, her milky-white eyes unsettling. "Come here, man of the mountains."

Startled, Teguin found he moved to obey her. The woman held a hand up which had several fingers broken and mangled. She gestured to the spines that covered the ground and Lena's body. "These needles come from the air itself, yet none are missing from the plants around us. Explain."

Cergath spat on the ground at the woman's feet. "Tell her nothing; she's a desert witch."

With a cry, Raima drew a blade at her waist, its curve twisting to Cergath's throat.

"Raima!" Straightening, the old woman swayed as though the sudden effort might be too much for her wizened frame. "Remember your promise."

"But *mai-meia*—"

"*Siet.* The sun grows hot upon the sand. We will take them all with us. If they will not go willingly, bind them."

Teguin took a step backward. He didn't like the idea of going with them, but without their lamat they had little choice. If Herbert were conscious he might have tried to attack or escape, but Teguin was too tired to fight.

These were desert people living beyond the touch of the Empress. Who knew such a thing was possible. Why had Cergath not warned them of that possibility during their travels? The man's reluctance to speak of other travelers in the desert had sealed their fate.

Raima turned to Teguin. "What of you, outsider; will you come willingly?"

"My friend needs a healer." Teguin gestured to Herbert, who lay ignored upon the sand, skin waxen even in the desert sun.

"This isn't a negotiation," Raima growled, but the old woman held up a hand again for silence.

"There was another man with us who disappeared," he continued. "We must find him."

The woman nodded but Raima laughed. "Your second request is of little use. We found your lost man—or what was left of him, on a far dune as we approached. The sand rays caught the scent of his blood and brought us straight to it." A piece of a blood-soaked shirt appeared from the folds of her belt. "Which of you mangled him so, and how?" She looked impressed. "There was barely anything left, and yet he still—"

Cergath turned with a dry heave and gagged until he threw up.

Raima raised an eyebrow. "A weak constitution. Typical for a man. Live among the Blades awhile and that will melt away."

Teguin found his spirits lift at the mention of the Blades. If these desert people and the Blades were one and the same, then he would soon know the fate of Master Troug. If she was still alive, he could try and negotiate her release. He refused to speculate on what would happen if she were dead.

Wiping his mouth, Cergath held out his hands to be bound, but he refused to look at Raima or the old woman. "You will keep me with Lena, or kill me where I stand before I take another step."

Raima's lip curled back into a smile. "I will keep an eye on you, prison guard. And you will respect this elder, or I will cut out your tongue the next time you make such a mistake."

She turned to Teguin. "We will take your companion and tend to his wounds. But he spilled blood on our sand, and that will leave its own mark on his fate."

21

A CALL TO DEATH

Together, they walked into the heart of the desert. Elena stared off into the distance. "It is said that all Predestine monks hear the call to death like a song. I hear nothing. Perhaps it is lost on the wind."

"I hear only my thoughts," said the Lexicon, "which remind me of what I am about to lose. *Mai-meia*. Your memories, your knowledge of the old ways and the old language, you brought us many blessings."

"I brought you the teachings of a child, barely grown into a woman under the monks. Think of what we could learn if we came back together. Generations spent apart, reunited at last."

"I fear it is too late for such a reconciliation. Our differences are too great. We do not need their forgiveness, only some small part of their knowledge in service to our end."

Elena stopped to catch her breath. "Is humility too high a price to pay? What little parchment we have crumbles to dust in our hands. Even the stories we tell our children are empty words, the meanings forgotten. We fear the truth in our words might somehow bring the wrath of our Relics down upon us. Forgotten gods will not help those who lose their way."

"We have not forgotten," the Lexicon insisted. "The Relic teachings must be recovered, I agree. I need to speak with the monks, to have their wisdom, seek their guidance and yes, even reconcile our differences, if that is what it takes."

Elena reached out to find the hand on her arm and patted it. Her skin was soft, her touch light as a breeze. "Do not lose what is left of our past, or we will all live in half-truths and cold, bitter endings."

Her brow creased as she reached out her crippled hand to empty air. She looked around them. "Where are my children, so they might walk with me?"

Explaining the first time was hard enough. The Lexicon glanced behind them, but the ridge where her family had stood to watch them go was no longer in sight. "They asked that I go with you instead."

"Oh?" The wrinkles on the old woman's brow deepened as her eyebrows rose. "That is not our way."

"I must go with you to speak with the monks, Elena. They will see no outsiders, not even the Lexicon of the Blades, until they make the walk to death. I am not ready to make that sacrifice. Not yet."

"I see."

"Will you allow it?"

Elena's wrinkled face stretched into a smile. "I serve the Blades to the end, my dear. To the very end."

The Lexicon gave the woman an arm to lean on again, helping as best she could, hoping to learn more of what lay ahead of them. "Tell me of your dream. The monks appeared to you?"

Elena tried to laugh, her voice dry, hollow. "It will not help you find them. It is a calling, not a map. Dreams take long moments of reflection. They remind a lost spirit that there is a place for us beyond this life, if we are willing to forge a bond with the Relics one last time."

"I do not understand what you mean."

"The Relics have always been elusive, child. When it is your time, you will understand."

Elena had not called her child for a long time. Perhaps her mind was slipping faster now that she was facing her death. Shaking her head, the Lexicon guided them both up a ridge until they reached more solid ground.

The older woman looked around. "It is here that we will wait."

There were no markings or tracks to offer a hint of the monks and their whereabouts. If their guide did not arrive soon, the retreating sunlight would leave them in darkness. Alone, and on foot, they were vulnerable.

It was a terrible thing to wait for the unknown.

A walk to death was an old tradition, and not a popular one. Few Blades traveled in the deep desert in search of closure at the hands of the monks. Or perhaps it was that so few of her people reached a peaceful end to their lives. That was a sobering thought.

Elena turned away the offer of water. From her pocket, she pulled out a young scatter pod leaf, popping it into her mouth and chewing with relish. "Water only reminds me of my thirst. It brings no relief."

"Are you cold, *mai-meia*?" She had to do something, stay busy. It was time to build a fire. They would have to wait through the night and hope that someone would find them in the morning. It would be a mistake to leave Elena alone, even to meditate.

Searching her pack, a deep and inexplicable sense of alarm made her look up. Someone was watching them.

A robed figure stood further along the ridge, silent. Waiting. Though she could not see in the darkness, some instinct brought Elena to her side.

"Bid farewell to your family, and we will go," said the stranger.

"Wait," said the Lexicon. She held out a hand to prevent Elena from moving forward. "That is no way to earn our trust. Are you a Predestine?"

Crouching still, she pulled out a scatter pod and shook it, the sand lice within buzzing in annoyance at being woken. Light flooded into her hand as she stood and stepped toward the stranger. "You cannot take this woman with you unless you declare yourself."

There appeared to be only one of them. When she held up her light, the stranger flinched and retreated as if the brightness was painful in some way. She caught a brief glimpse of skin, pale as the moons, faded as if the stranger was not of this world.

Perhaps the legends were true, and the monks spent their entire lives in darkness, deep beneath the sands of the Waste. A hand brushed her shoulder and she started.

"Peace, Aileen." said Elena, her voice gentle. "There is nothing to fear."

"I am not afraid," she snapped, but that was a lie. There was something about the robed figure, a legend brought to life, that made her feel insubstantial herself, her aspirations buried in self-doubt.

Elena took the scatter pod from her hand and blew upon it, whispering until the light dimmed. "I come to you willing, monk, ready to face my end. But this woman will walk the sacred path with me. She is on a pilgrimage of prescience."

There was a long pause as the stranger weighed the woman's words. "Only a monk can claim such a sacred rite," said the figure.

"You cannot deny her sanctuary," Elena insisted.

"Only the elders can grant such a request."

"If she is on a pilgrimage, she has a right to speak with the elders, and if you bring her with us, she may make the request to them directly."

The monk made no reply, and stood as if riveted in place. The Lexicon worried that the request would be denied, that the very act of her being there would leave both of them alone again in the desert. She prepared herself for the possibility that her coming was a step too far, and a mistake.

Elena said, "You might as well take her with us, or I will not make it back with you if you have to return a second time." She tapped her temple with bent, shaking fingers.

"That would be a great loss for our people..."

The Lexicon could have sworn the old woman winked at her before wiping a lock of wispy white hair from her face.

At last, the robed figure moved. "So be it. I make no promise that they will see you, but you may come."

There it was, the opening she needed. Elena had given her the chance to do what no Blade had done since the fracture of the order. A meeting with the Predestine monks, a way to extract the knowledge she needed, and a chance to forge an alliance that would shake the very foundation of the Imperium.

22

ASYLUM

Luther's ears rang. So many voices around him. Hundreds, perhaps thousands of people were gathered in this place. After months of solitude it was overwhelming.

Here, the people of Dunmire flourished. Streams trickled into rock pools and vanished deep beneath. Low hills of tall grass rang with stomping circles of dance and greetings and laughter. Woven grass ropes and balls fell and flew over the heads of small children who begged and wailed to join in the game.

Luther's guide had to take him by the arm to keep him moving through the crush of bodies. The smell of charred vegetables and meat and bitter herbs made his mouth water in a familiar way. Walking across the open tundra was a startling contrast from the mountains and forests further to the south.

Bird and beast were larger yet tamer in Dunmire. There were dozens of creatures in sight, hovering and fluttering or settled down around their owners like seaweed covering a rocky beach. It was a strange thing to find creatures treated with such respect and affection. They might have been part of the family rather than the means to travel and eat.

Luther had never thought of animals in any other way but their use to him. He looked around in confusion. It was a striking difference, and one of many that separated the people of Dunmire from his own. He passed a horse and craned his neck to see the beast; it was easily half a man taller than those he was used to in the Imperium.

The Imperium. A knot tightened in his stomach. He glanced down at his hand where a bound piece of cloth wound around the Praelor's mark. He could still feel the mark biting into his skin. He could picture that cold, blue eye, fixed and unmoving. It unnerved him and he had to keep it out of sight. He could not look at it, not now.

With a grunt, his guide pointed to where the tall, dry grass gave way to lichen-covered stone. Gathered along the outcropping was a smaller crowd, more richly dressed and the only people he had seen who wore furs and animal hides like his own. In a way, they resembled miniature animals themselves, some prowling back and forth, others jumping from rock to rock in order to better see or speak. Several lounged on the ground in languid indifference, eyes half-closed and gleaming as they cast their gaze from one face to another with a calculating look Luther knew all too well.

As Luther traveled north, he noticed that each tribe or village had distinct words for actions and creatures that he did not understand, but they all shared the same common tongue as the Imperium. A few words here and there were pronounced strangely, but that, too, was no different than Imperial provinces back home.

The words for animals and the weather in Dunmire were more complex than he could follow when they were spoken quickly, but he only lost their meaning when he was exhausted or frightened. The conversations around him now were tense, with unfamiliar implication.

Every vein in Luther's neck tightened. His feet ached from his worn-out boots. He held his breath, and hoped that no one else could hear the pounding of his heart.

Luther bowed. His knees trembled until he straightened and forced them to lock in place when all he wanted to do was run away to the solitude beyond these grassy hills. He had to calm down and clear his head.

He was here. He would never get a better chance than this to be heard. A voice carried over the others and Luther started, meeting the eyes of one of the lounging figures, a man with a yellow glint in his eyes and a heavy fur wrapped around his shoulders.

"Be welcome to the Dunmiri, stranger and warrior-leader of the southern lands. You are well met at this Gathering. I am Gurn, leader of the Silver Wolf Clan, slayer of Gelnendram the child eater."

The man eyed Luther like a tasty morsel and grinned. Luther swallowed. Child eater?

Before he could think of what to say at being called a warrior and a leader, they were interrupted by a woman wrapped in a cloak of black with white and grizzled grey fur. "You give honor to a stranger before he speaks? Would you give him lands here as well, and let him take your women and children away?"

Another leader wrapped in thin, wiry hide laughed at the accusation. "Peace, Scythia. You speak of actions when this warrior comes with words. Would you send him away without hearing them?"

The woman named Scythia scowled. "You do not live as far south as I do, Lem. Their scouts harass our people whenever they get the chance. In the Borderlands, they make sport of our families and treat their animals like filth to be gutted without any *chusgari*."

There were murmurs of anger at her words, but the man raised a hand for quiet. "I am Lem, leader of the Boar Clan, slayer of Edramen and Bulrendum the pillagers of Brimtide. Tell us of your title and glory, wolf-slayer."

The pelt on his back weighed upon Luther like stone. His astonishment at the treatment he received by the strangers of Dunmire gave way to embarrassment. They thought from his pelt that he was a leader among his people.

Should he lie? No. He could already hear the Praelor's cruel laughter at the thought of him passing himself off as a warrior; he would not have the strength or the courage to slay a wolf, or any beast for that matter.

He did the only thing he could. Pulling the pelt from his shoulders, he took great care to place it at the leader's feet. "I come not as a warrior or a leader. I am a traveler. Luther Ferris is my name, and my family fishes the Iridian Sea."

"You are a slayer of... fish?"

"This is the warrior-leader the Imperium sends us?"

"And what of the wolf pelt! It has no honor to its name!"

Threats washed over him. All those cycles facing threats and the wrath of Praelor Thurst gave Luther a strength he did not know he had until he stood there with detachment, waiting for their silence.

When that realization hit him, the fear simply melted away. A question, a force more powerful than fear, took him in a firm grip. What punishment could these people devise to rival the finely-honed tortures of the Praelor? What pain could they inflict on him that could possibly surpass what waited for him in the Blue City?

Luther clenched his fist. Phantom pain flickered from the wandering eye. His skin crawled at the thought of what might happen next. He stood his ground.

"The Imperium is no friend to us," repeated Scythia.

"I agree with you."

Shocked, the woman stuttered in surprise. "You, you agree with me? Not only without honor, but touched in the head as well!"

Stretching, the wolf clan leader, Gurn, rose to his feet. "This stranger does not know our ways. If he is no leader then he has no right to speak at our council."

One of the older clan leaders struggled to rise, the hides along his back so old they looked more like rotten strips. "I would like to know what has brought him across the Borderlands, over the mountains and to our gathering, when on most other days he would find nothing but open skies and empty land. It speaks to me of a deeper plan. Something guides him, and means to watch over us as well. We should heed the timing as well as his warnings."

Lem also stepped forward. "There is no harm in hearing him speak."

Luther knew that he was not a man of silver words. He was so used to being spoken over that it made his tongue feel heavy and his mind slow to see the eyes that watched him. He had never dared to speak against the Praelor.

"I am the servant of a cruel man. A powerful man. A man who would poison the world itself if it brought him something he desired. I fear his greed and ambition more than any grief or pain or hunger that I have found in my life and so should you."

He managed to admit it. That was the hardest part to say aloud. Explaining why was somehow easier.

"This man has the ear of our Empress, who rules the lands of the Imperium as a goddess and tyrant, who destroys all who oppose her with an empty soul, black as a night without stars. She hungers for more land, more power, more to worship her divinity."

The words fell and tumbled from his mouth, spilling like pebbles down a mountain slope. "I come to you as little more than a slave, as an unwilling spy who sees more worth and beauty in this land and its people than I have known my whole life in the Imperium. I place myself in your hands and I ask for your protection. There are dark days ahead, and I would not wish your people to be blind to what threatens them."

With a gasp for breath, Luther swayed where he stood. It was like sucking out poison from a snakebite. His face was hot, his lips dry and cracked and yet it was wonderful. He never felt so alive.

Words flew around him, but he did not try to understand their meaning. A sense of deep peace settled in his chest. The weight of pain and fear was gone, melted away with the knowledge that the Dunmiri would know they were in danger. Now, they could fight the Praelor. They could prepare. They would know what was coming.

23

A DROP OF INK

Praelor Thurst recoiled from a horrible brightness. There was a wall of wide windows beside his bed. He sensed movement around him. With an unsteady hand he managed to grasp at blankets which weighed upon him like sand, and then at one of the many pillows which kept him sitting upright.

"Is he awake?" came a voice at his side.

When he inhaled to answer, pain shot up his throat.

"Who's there?" His voice shook as a reaching hand came into focus, the rest fading into the darker, blurred surroundings. "The light," he pleaded, "make it stop."

Shapes moved around him, but there was reassurance in the quiet. A small hand took his searching one. Blessed darkness.

"Praelor?" asked a voice.

He felt the softness of those hands, then tenderness as a second closed over the first. Their warmth, their touch, it brought such a strong emotion that he turned his face, trying to lean forward in order to bring clarity to those shapes in the darkness.

He had lost his ability to see well cycles ago. Vague shapes lost their meaning. When his vision dimmed too far, he grew paranoid that his surroundings were hallucinations instead of a trick of the light. He squeezed his eyes shut, but that only made him more desperate to know more of his surroundings. "Where am I?" he croaked.

"The palace. You had an attack."

"My flask, I must have my flask."

"There is nothing in it."

"Then I have to, I must—" he failed to finish his thought. A wheeze tightened the breath in his lungs and his heart quickened to catch up with his returning memory.

The Seekers. So much left to do. How would he find enough magic in time?

"Calm yourself, Praelor. Have you no other supply, no other store of ink or powder left?" The hands that held his tightened.

"There is no more to make. Nothing to save." The shame of his confession ate away at him.

"Why did you not say as much, do you know what will happen when you die?" said the voice with dismay, and Thurst realized with a start that he knew that voice.

Shame blossomed into tears which ran down his cheeks and filled his mouth with their salty brine. "Forgive me… Empress." He grasped for his memory again.

The flask was empty. Surely he had some plan in place, some enchantment saved for such a time as this. Plans within plans. If he could only focus long enough to remember.

He closed his eyes. The Imperial Watchtower and his quarters came to mind. The shelves, the drawers of his desk, the loose flagstones where he might have stored something as a younger man.

The stone floors brought a different memory back to him; one from his earliest days at the palace. A novice from Praxis, he came to court to work away his debt to a patron who cared little for reading and writing. They wished for a scribe to keep records.

There were no Masters, then. Only patrons and debts. It came to him in a rush; Thurst's own shelves contained a lifetime of precious ink. His legacy to the Imperium.

He kept his eyes closed, but tilted his head to the face inches from his own. "My records and books, the press in my quarters. Bring them to me."

The hands pulled away and Thurst heard voices in the hallway. When he woke from a doze, his senses pricked. Stacks of books surrounded him. His books.

How long had he been asleep? With dull thuds, the pages rustled and settled with a reassuring presence that calmed his pounding heart. The servants who brought them came and went. Soon the smell from the oiled leather covers permeated the room. He reserved leather for his most important work, and could never sacrifice those which he had bound and cleaned and cared for all his life.

There were others; volumes covered by softened cloth with waxen thread to hold the bindings together. Floral and berry scents brought their brightly dyed covers to his mind's eye like jewels. Journals, observations, studies where all were precious, but... he had to act.

At his left, he could hear pieces of the press click into place, reconstructed. Turning cogs, plates stacked, and soon a container would catch every drop of ink. This time he would have to press and squeeze and pull it from the pages instead of binding the words. How strange.

There it was again, that rattling wheeze in and out, in and out. Every breath louder than the last. It maddened him.

He was weak. Disgusting. Would he even have enough strength to recall his words and release the ink from its pages?

A cold anger settled into his stomach. All this time spent collecting magic, keeping it under tight control, and it was coming undone. This aging, wasting sickness held him at its mercy, constricting his breath, blurring his vision, and burrowing to take his magic away. He would not stand for it.

Stripping ink from books was a great loss. It wounded him to the core, but if he should die now, unprepared, the greater loss would be the knowledge he took away to the dark, restless place that awaited him. No price was too high to pay if it secured the future of his Imperium.

When a stack of scrolls fell into his lap, he cringed with a broken shriek of surprise. Another stack followed. Then another.

"Pardon, yer Praelorship," came a gruff voice, "where are yer stacks of loose bits t'be left?"

Thurst's gnarled fingers closed around them. "Here," he wheezed, scooping them up into his arms. "Leave them here."

The sending scrolls had slipped his mind. What news from Dunmire, and for how long had he slept?

He waited until the steps of the soldier drifted away and when the silence in the room was absolute, he unrolled the first scroll. His fingers drifted in search of ink. Trembling, he found the first spark of it and reached inside himself, drawing it from the page until the words filled his mind, absorbing the information it contained like a long drink of cool water.

He dropped the empty parchment and let it roll to the floor. Searching out the next, he pulled the words from the page with his eyes shut in concentration. While not all the ink was of his creation, it allowed him brief moments of relief from the gnawing panic that filled his chest.

The spy reports were simple and without substance, like stale breadcrumbs. Descriptions with clusters of families and tribes in Dunmire, and their larger gatherings for celebrations. Nothing was said of soldiers or the aggression that the Empress declared to be steps away from their border.

No mention of magic, either. What the Dunmiri possess they hide well, he thought as he pulled the coverlet and the next stack within reach. Magic was still there. It must be. They had to dig deeper, move farther, and push harder to get the information he—and the Empress —needed.

Thurst paused as his fingers ran over the last scroll. Luther. The man's messy, broad script fell across the page in bold, swift strokes, but barely filled a page. It spoke of mountains and ice melt slipping into streams, and ended with the kindness of its people. Was the man on a reconnaissance mission or a convalescence?

Unacceptable. He remembered the words he spoke to Luther before sending him on his first mission. There was no fire in the man's heart, no urgency. No conviction. What a waste for someone so young with so much life to live...

Thurst paused. He wiped a line of drool from his mouth and held stained fingers to his lips. A shudder ran through his body.

His eyes opened to the same shadows and formless surroundings, but he needed no mirror to witness the wide, eager smile that stretched across his own face. He swung an arm until it encountered the nearest stack of books.

He hesitated at the softness of the covers beneath his fingers. Mulberries, he decided after holding the top book from the stack to his face with a sniff. A deep purple cover, then.

The first few pages were agony. The thick paper would not fall away from its careful binding. But there it was, the ink waiting to be joined with him again. This time it would not be so easy.

He had no one to help him use the press. Crazed with thirst, he licked the pages as a dog would lap at a bowl of water, searching. A spark of magic returned to him and suddenly he wanted more. So much more. He stuffed the pages into his mouth and let the ink dissolve onto his tongue with a hungry snap of teeth.

The book fell apart in his hands. Pushing aside the scrolls in his lap, his fingers brushed once more against Luther's empty report. With a surge of righteous fury, he crumpled and threw it to join the other scraps.

Luther was a failure. This time, he would make use of that, and give the man the ambition he lacked. He needed to gain back his strength and once he did, the young Seeker would know it.

FAMILY TIES

Feran sipped an ale and spat it back into the cup. He was hungry enough to try the bread but that was a mistake, it was no better than the ale. Eyes burning from the foul odor of unwashed sheep, he tried to hold his breath as he waited, shivering, rubbing his hands together as he watched the door.

A meager fire burned in the hearth. His chair was closest to it yet he could not feel its warmth. There was nothing he hated more than being cold. He moved closer.

A woman passed his table with a hopeful sway of her hips and he reacted instantly, lips curling into a snarl that sent her shooting out of the room. The sooner he could leave this place, the better.

"Feran Dorst," came a shrill voice. He leapt up from his chair, looking wildly around. A woman peered through the grimy window. He waved both hands for her to stop yelling and join him, painfully aware that his name was not always welcome, even in Islip Province.

"Lady Morna, you haven't aged a day," he said, his face frozen in what he hoped to be an ingratiating smile when she came inside to his table. He tapped the tips of his fingers together and bowed his head, holding his hands out in a gesture of respect the woman's position had demanded before her exile.

"Oh Feran. Still holding onto your court charms after all this time? No one cares about that sort of thing here."

As they sat down, Feran had his first good look at her in many cycles. The woman's face was lined with care and guarded. Her eyes were just like her daughters, wild and brimming with life.

Time and bad circumstances had changed the woman, it was true. Dirt under her fingernails, the way her hair fell into her face. If Lady Morna had fallen on hard times then here he was, ready to lift her spirits. He remained hopeful she would see the value of his plans for both of them.

Why waste time. "Have you heard the newest Imperial edict?" he asked. "The Blessed Empress will forgive all the noble houses who spoke against her when they pledge a renewed vow of loyalty."

A hungry look flashed in the woman's eyes. "Is that so?" She picked at a tuft of fleece which stuck out of a ripped patch on her jacket.

Feran pictured the fierce, immaculately dressed woman who led House Reean; a spitfire of a woman whose voice was loud enough to make anyone obey. If she were twenty cycles younger… but no. Even then, he would detest that shrill voice. Seeing her like this was, in a way, its own reward.

Lady Morna gave him a long look. "Traveling all this way to bring news to an old woman? Feran, if I knew you better I might think you had another reason for coming."

"Will you accept the pardon and return to the Blue City?"

"Why should I?"

"Your family."

Her eyes narrowed. "They seem happy enough. Half-frozen to death, but stubborn and living on that mountainside of theirs."

"Have you been to see them? Visited?" asked Feran, shooting a dark look at any passerby who got too close to their conversation for his liking.

Her face darkened. "It's a long distance. Most folk stay in one place rather than galloping halfway across the Imperium."

"They are starving, Morna. Worst of all, they are too damn proud to do anything about it."

With a groan, the woman tapped the table with frantic fingers. "And you want me to save them? *Empress Bless*, did you come all this way to torture me? My only daughter married your brother. I send them what help I can though I'm no longer a wealthy woman. And now you came to me for coin—"

"No." Her put a hand on hers, covering the slim fingers that were cold as the windows and stone walls around them. "It is not an empty coin purse that brings me here. Quite the opposite. I want Legan and Iridal to join me, to share in my wealth and good fortune."

The speech was a good one, and the smooth flow of it was just as he practiced. "No doubt Iridal wrote you when I took Teguin as my apprentice. The man is like a son to me. I send them goods and supplies and I have lost count of the times I have asked them to come and live in the Blue City with me! And yet they do not come."

He shook his head, and was happy to see her lean toward him with that same hungry look. He tried not to smile. "I know that Iridal would see reason, but my brother… he is too proud. Must we all suffer because of it?"

Her voice was piercing even at a whisper. "There were times when I thought Iridal married the wrong son—"

"If you accept the pardon of the Empress, I would be honored for you to stay with me in the Blue City. You could be reunited with Iridal and live in comfort the rest of your days, if they would only agree to return."

Morna pulled her hands away from his as if stung, contempt freezing her voice. She threw her shoulders back and gave a full-throated, shrill laugh that set his teeth on edge. "Is that your game?"

She brushed back her hair. "Even if I do accept the pardon, I would rather chew on rat bones and slimewort the rest of my life than have you drag my family name even further into the mud. I wish House Reean had never chosen to ally themselves with the Dorsts and their stubborn need to be above the law and now here you are, simpering, oozing charm and passing off as something we both know you can never be. You have sunken too low, and crawled too far to be anything but a conniving, manipulative—"

"Enough!" Feran was too furious to see straight.

Lady Morna pulled off her torn coat to reveal gold embroidery and fine wool. With an expression of haughty triumph, she wiped a smudge of dirt from her cheek. "Are you so blind that you would use family as easily as a sack of flour to barter with, and to me? I have stable hands with more sense than you, merchant."

She rose from the table and straightened to her full height, eyes blazing. Shaken, Feran could say nothing in reply. Reeling from the small ways in which the woman had tricked him into thinking she was desperate, he found no words, only a haze of panic and confusion.

He rose, anxious to be gone as quickly as possible. In truth, he half expected the woman to strike him or at least spit in his face, and he would rather save what little dignity he had left by staying out of range.

He pulled at the high collar of his cloak, his face still burning. He promised himself that he would never let embarrassment overcome him, but Selina and now this woman had succeeded where many others had failed. He hated them for that.

Before he had a chance to recover, Lady Morna turned and left. The worst blow of all. Humiliation.

Cycles of being ignored by the nobles of the Imperium, and now even a fellow exiled house would have nothing to do with him. All his plans spiraled out of control and ended with nothing. Frustration consumed him.

A heaviness settled in his chest. Fury spread like ice under his skin. He had no memory of how quickly he returned to the Blue City or anything of the journey, but when his wagon reached the bluffs which overlooked the sea, his hands clutched a whip slick with blood.

WHERE LOYALTIES LIE

Teguin watched as a healer of the Blades changed the dressing on Herbert's wounds. Herbert had not woken, had not stirred, nor had he made a sound when they reset a dislocated shoulder. He twitched in his sleep—if sleep could describe the senselessness that took over the man's body.

Bandages held together by scraped snakeskin tightened and stretched as the healer tested them. There was a sloppiness to the work that made Teguin suspicious. Then he realized the man was not using magic to guide his skill.

At least, he gave no appearance of using it. Teguin knew the signs: a distracted, inward focus. Glazed eyes, with deep breaths that seemed to stretch for minutes at a time. There were ways to notice, even if he did not have the magic of a Seeker to see it form and change and manifest.

It was strange to have someone patch up Herbert other than Master Jayce at Praxis. Using magic with proactive intent and a sensitive awareness of their surroundings, Praxis was an unheard-of rarity, a safe haven for practicing magic, a necessity for their survival. As Teguin knew firsthand, using magic by mistake or in ignorance created disastrous results.

It was not understood why magic could affect wielders in such drastic and alarming ways. Some called it a draining experience, where the world around them faded away into a different awareness. Teguin felt that awareness himself, but tried not to sink to where he might lose control. Others called it a descent of losing one's mind. Magic use could lead to madness or death; he was not surprised by the accounts of curses in the rare histories he found at the Praxis archives.

Having a source of powerful magic was a challenge. With its presence came a need to know and explore its potential, and an acceptance that doing so would put his life at risk. Teguin did not choose to have magic, but he did find a deep and passionate need to use it, to understand why it existed at all. It was a risk he had to take.

From what he could tell, Herbert had a very different reaction than he did when using magic. They had spent hours together comparing their experiences. Teguin would argue that Herbert's magic used him with alarming regularity instead of the reverse. Herbert could bring his magic to life as naturally as walking or breathing. There was less planning and thought involved and more feeling, more filling the needs of the moment.

Why was it such a fluid and easy experience for Herbert? He could not conceive of magic coming that easily when he himself had to focus and concentrate all of his energy and attention to become aware of his magic, and only then try to influence something around him. He felt tired after such interactions, but looking at Herbert after his battle with Jameson was a reminder of the differences between them. It deeply troubled him, now more than ever, seeing the extent to which Herbert let his emotions feed into his magic.

Herbert had fallen unconscious many times while using magic. After he could do no more, he went into a sleep-like state that went beyond dreaming. This was one of those times.

Did he know of Jameson's death, and what had happened? To hear the Blades tell it, there was little left to recover. A surge of revulsion and horror sank in, and Teguin's stomach gave a lurch. How was his friend capable of something so violent?

Herbert's expression was one of blissful ignorance. Teguin sighed.

That look was such a poor reflection of his thoughts that suddenly he wished to leave, to be anywhere that did not remind him of what Herbert had done. The sight of his friend was too painful.

"Can I leave?" he asked the healer, turning to look around the room in some surprise. Other than Herbert, they were alone.

The man did not pause in his work. "Outside the door."

When the healer spoke, two men entered. Teguin followed them without looking back. His relief was so profound that he was more eager to leave than to ask where they were going. What could he do about it, except follow his escort to see where they led him?

Climbing through these caverns of sandstone reminded him of a story his uncle told him once about the Merchant's Guild. In the capital, the Guild kept most of their inventory in winding caverns which led would-be robbers to be lost. Without his magic he would certainly lose his way in this place.

There were many shared spaces. Like a rabbit warren, smaller rooms were hollowed out to expand and deepen the network. He ran his hands along the wall, enjoying the only magic of which he was capable of producing at will. It distracted him from thinking of what Herbert had done.

When he set off to explore the Wastelands and find news of Master Troug, he had not thought they would find the Blades so easily. That was careless. Uncle Feran had urged him to anticipate and plan multiple outcomes and possibilities just like a trade negotiation. Teguin appreciated the art of a good trade, but he saw this journey as he saw most things; a series of well-learned and practiced steps. Feran always told him that was why he had so much left to learn.

"Teguin Dorst, is it? I heard your companions arrived with injuries." A voice came from behind them. Teguin knew that voice. He whirled around.

It was the Lexicon. She made no move to attack, yet he braced himself, reaching into his vest for his powder. A pointed blade pressed into his back from behind. He had completely forgotten his escort was armed.

The Lexicon smiled. "I would not do that if I were you."

Teguin lowered his empty hands. Considering the strength of the woman, he knew from their last encounter that he could not overpower her, alone or with two other Blades breathing down his neck.

Without her gleaming bronze robes, her clothing was fashioned from a kind of unfamiliar fabric or skin. It was a simple cut similar to the shirts and breeches of farm workers, like the other Blades he had seen. If not for the metallic glove fastened over one hand, and the space given by those around them, in deference, he might have mistaken her for any stranger.

Teguin had not seen her after the attack on Praxis, where she had warned him what would happen if he tried to interfere with her plans again. What were her plans now?

"What do you want with us?" he asked.

"For now, I want you to come with me."

Teguin had little choice. He followed her to a hollow alcove that allowed them to sit down. Their escort left without a second glance, but he could still feel where the blade had pressed into his back.

The Lexicon offered him a drink from a flask. "I see that you responded to my invitation by crossing the Wastelands themselves. I am impressed."

Her greeting was friendly, her willingness to speak with him a mystery. He tried to keep his voice even. "The last time we met, you took Master Troug against her will and set fire to Praxis."

"Crude, but true in its essentials, yes. I would understand your anger, but believe me it was a message we had to send to the Empress. Would you like to see the bone reader?"

The answer to his unspoken question filled him with relief. She was alive. "Is she your prisoner?"

"She is our honored guest. If you join her in her work, you may also stay with us as long as you wish."

Teguin took a sip from the Lexicon's flask. He had to take a drink in order to keep his temper in check. Do not anger a host who offers you their hospitality, his uncle would have counseled him. Treat any uncertain situation like a negotiation. Set aside your feelings.

So, he did what any merchant would do to avoid commitment; he changed the subject. "I thank you for treating my friend. He was in a great deal of pain."

"From what I hear, his opponent will never feel pain again. To take life in such a manner is not without consequence. And your other companion, the Imperial soldier. He has threatened our people, and we do not take kindly to being threatened in our homes."

Teguin thought of the prison, and then of the prison warden lying dead at their feet at the hands of Captain Jarvin. "I do not know the man, but he has lost too much to have a clear head."

"I did not realize when we first met that you were a Dorst, but you have more reasons than most to despise the Empress. Your grandfather was executed, your family was stripped of their nobility, and your parents fled to live in exile. Have you ever thought about joining those of us who embrace a life beyond the limits of the Imperium?"

The question was so direct it took Teguin by surprise. No one had ever asked, ever hinted that he had a choice in the matter. Perhaps it was the unspoken conflict that existed between his uncle and his father which had led him to avoid the question.

He was a pren at Praxis, in the very heart of the Imperium. His uncle would give all his fortune to regain his nobility and have their family be a noble house again. The goodwill and favor of the Empress meant everything to his uncle and nothing but pain to his father. Where did that leave him?

It was lunacy to question the Empress and her right to rule.

A nagging doubt hovered over his silent complacency. His father never spoke of it, but Teguin's grandfather had played major role in a rebellion against the Empress. He was caught between opposites that until now, he had not dared to try and reconcile.

"I do wish to see her," he said. "Master Troug, I mean."

The Lexicon rose and motioned for Teguin to follow her. "I will not press you. If you wish to know more of why she is so important, both to us and to the future of the Imperium, we should talk more. But I understand that you are anxious to see your master again. Be warned, though. She has made a pact and sacrificed much to reach the goal we share."

Teguin did not like the sound of that. In the short while that he had known Master Troug, he had seen her tireless dedication to historical events of the past. What could she have found to keep her happily hidden away from Praxis? He had a hard time believing that she was happy living with this group of exiles, as the Lexicon called them.

Their path took them to a lower set of caverns larger than the ones he had seen toward the entrance. These chambers were old, and there was a strange smell to the place, a sourness of tanned hide and vinegar and still air that reminded him of the warehouses he and Feran used for storage. There were small globes of light resting in the walls and the Lexicon took one. With a shake, the pod threw light into the next room as they entered.

He took a step back.

Piles of bones as high as he was tall. Bones in jumbled heaps, pressing toward the entrance as though they longed to escape and see the sun once more. There was a new smell in this room, though if Teguin thought long enough to name it he might be sick.

The Lexicon stepped aside. Teguin moved back into the room toward an empty cot. "Master Troug?"

"Teguin?" A form moved toward him from the shadows. Hands reached out to him, but these were not the hands he remembered, delicate and soft and always stained with ink. These hands were dry and wrinkled and so pale they might have belonged to an old woman, not one in the prime of her life.

"Teguin. You came back."

Teguin stared down at the woman who was his master and tried to believe it was her. The voice was hers. But she was a wisp, a cup of sand herself, stone ground to pieces until lost.

"What did they do to you?"

Her gaunt face, pale as chalk. The surprise in her expression was genuine. "Do?" she asked. "Of all the questions to ask me, Teguin Dorst. I'm surprised at you. Have you seen this place? Do you understand the treasures we have uncovered?"

She turned to the Lexicon, who shook her head. "There was not time. He wanted to see you."

With a dry laugh, Master Troug tugged at her hair. "No time indeed. This place is timeless. Endless memories."

She continued to laugh, and Teguin reached out to keep her from falling. She weighed no more than a feather and her skin was hot to the touch. "You are unwell, Master Troug," he said.

"No, Teguin, no. I am fine. The search keeps me alive, burning bright as a pillar of light in the darkness." She pulled away from him, but the smile that reached her eyes was a familiar one.

Teguin realized his elbow threatened to topple a pile of bones next to the cot. His master worked with bones whenever she could at Praxis, but it unsettled him to see so many in one place.

With a deep breath, Master Troug opened her arms and spun in a slow circle. "Do you realize where we are?" The silence that followed her question was answer enough.

"Teguin, this is a cache of bones older than any at Praxis. Some are older than the founding of the Imperium!"

All Teguin could think of was his first day at Praxis, and of meeting Master Troug in the underground cavern of ancient stone, the shelves lined with precious books. Books, and one skull. He could see her face, glowing with health, and the wise gleam in her eyes as she asked him what he knew about the founding of the Imperium.

He sat down hard on the cot. How could he be so foolish. What would a room full of ancient remains mean to a bone reader, a Master Historian? As she said, it was a treasure trove. Here was an unending source of fascination beyond anything that Praxis could offer. His mouth went dry.

"You *do* understand," she said. "I knew you would. But there is more, Teguin. So much more."

"Teguin, you could help your master here," said the Lexicon, putting down the globe of light on the small table next to the cot. Troug blinked at the light, holding out a hand to block some of its brightness. Had she been underground this whole time?

Try as he might, Teguin could not think of how he fit into this discovery. "But I know nothing of your work here," he said.

"You know more than you think," said Master Troug. "The

archives at Praxis and in other collections revealed to us the path that led to the founding of the Imperium. The Relic Wars turned rich and fertile lands into ruins; these wastelands, a barren desert with no hope of recovery."

The Lexicon nodded. "What happened to the people who stayed behind and refused to join the Imperium? Did you ever wonder why the Empress banned travel in the desert? Why the prison exists in such a strange location?"

"Well, yes, but—"

"The prison was not always a prison, Teguin. It was a watchtower. For all we know, it was made by the Relics before their fall."

"How do you know this?" he asked, and Master Troug gestured to the pile of bones next to them.

The Lexicon poured a cup of water from the pitcher at Troug's table and pressed it into the woman's hand. "You push yourself too much, Lavinia. Drink. I will tell it."

There was no warmth between the two women that Teguin could see, but the bones brought them together. If not a bond of friendship then a shared obsession.

The Lexicon continued. "Creating the prison could have been a way for the Imperium to keep an eye on the desert and its inhabitants without drawing too much suspicion. But now, it appears our dear Empress is tired of spying on us. She has moved too many soldiers into the desert to be above suspicion."

"She had the prison warden killed," admitted Teguin.

"Warden Moonstone is dead? When?"

"Three days before our meeting the Blades," said Teguin, unsure of how much time had passed since their arrival. The strangeness of the prison made a certain kind of sense with the Lexicon's theory; its design was like no other building in the Imperium. But to have so many Imperial soldiers in the desert still made no sense to him.

Master Troug stared into the distance, her eyes unblinking. The Lexicon touched the woman's shoulder. "Bone Reader?"

"The prison, the watchtower…"

"She needs to rest," said Teguin.

"But Teguin, you are here and I—" the woman's voice faltered.

"Rest, Master Troug. I will be here when you wake." With a nod at the Lexicon, Teguin helped to wrap a small blanket around her before he left.

The quick changes in Troug's focus concerned him. She was not given to such changes in temperament, and her fragile appearance was yet another concern he wished to bring up with the Lexicon. She wore such a vacant expression as he left...

The work was important, yes, but why was she so determined to continue at a frantic pace? She was a mindful person; someone who thought through her actions to a degree of detail he admired. Her time in the desert had changed that and not for the better.

A breeze blew down the stairs. Still dark, their path opened and ended at the top of the cliffs with a night sky full of stars. Teguin sucked in greedy, grateful gulps of fresh air.

"I come here often to clear my head," said the Lexicon, sitting crossed-legged at the edge of the cliffs. "Such a barren place now, but picture what it must have been once. No cliffs. No rents deep in the ground but leagues of farmland far richer than Falden, and with cities so immense they reached to the sky."

Try as he might, Teguin could not picture the past. But he knew one woman could have seen such places in her visions. A bone reader could re-live the last moments of a person's life in vivid detail. How many lives had Master Troug seen in this place?

She sighed. "The deeper we dig in these bone piles, the closer we come to finding not only memories, but physical echoes and living proof of Relics and the wonderful things they did for our people."

Teguin crouched beside the Lexicon. Sand dunes stretched beneath the cliffs in fine ripples. Busy figures scattered across the sand beneath them, taking advantage of the few hours of cool weather before the heat of the day returned.

"Why are we in such a hurry to rediscover the distant past?" he asked. Master Lingermort would have made him lick the floor of the archives with his tongue for asking such a question.

The Lexicon's metal glove closed into a fist. "Relic bones." Her answer was as direct as her questions.

Teguin was unsure of what else a bone reader could do, but he saw what reading dozens, maybe even hundreds of human bones had done to Master Troug in a short period of time. "Does such a thing as Relic bones even exist?"

"What would it mean to you if we found proof beyond a doubt; if I could show you that Relics were real and not the imagined children's tale the Empress insists them to be? With Master Troug's work we could learn beyond any doubt or speculation that they existed. Teguin, we could learn how they died. What if we could dive into their thoughts and memories just like our own past?"

It was speculation and nothing more to think such a thing was possible. But if it were true… the knowledge would be priceless.

"Has Master Troug found someone who knew the Relics? Saw them?" he asked.

"Not yet. But we are close. If the Empress learns how close we are, we could be in danger of losing all the progress we have made. She would stop at nothing to steal what we have found or worse, she could destroy any hope of the discovery. An Empress cannot afford to make mistakes."

Teguin was torn. He thought of Praxis, and what they might learn if there were more than bones to be found here. Knowledge was meant to be shared, not hidden away.

"You are right, Teguin." The Lexicon said suddenly, rising. "The bone reader—Master Troug, is pushing herself too hard. While I am eager for her to uncover the knowledge each bone brings, there is no one here that she listens to like you. She asks for you often. Having you here would bring a tether to the present that she loses too easily."

A chilling breeze found its way through the folds of Teguin's cloak as they stood together.

"Think about staying," she said. "You do not have to decide right away, but you could be here to save her from the darker times ahead."

A chance of uncovering Relic bones. Witnessing the golden age of magic in the Imperium. Working with Master Troug, and learning once more about his own Destructive magic. It was a tempting offer.

He never thought he would be tempted to stay and yet here he was, already eager to know more about what she had learned while they were apart. And if he did stay, he could keep Troug safe from the Lexicon; despite her friendliness, he still did not trust that woman and her agenda. It was clear that Master Troug was in no condition to travel anywhere and if he stayed, there was no limit to what they could discover together.

UNBOUND

Feran straightened his best vest. Brushing strands of loosened hair to the side with shaking fingers, he swore as scented oil came off onto his hand in a sticky mess, fumbling with his handkerchief to wipe it off. Stiffened embroidery from his collar tickled the back of his neck, and it was only after he had left his warehouses that he realized his new boots were too small and pinched his feet. He tried to stay as still as possible while waiting to be received.

Muffled voices rose in the next room yet he could not make out the words. The door remained shut as the minutes ticked and turned into another silver chime on the clock. It was an insult he tried to take in stride, but the ignorance and insults from the Tanasens had barely been outweighed by the enormous profit he made as the only seller of their apples.

Without his guidance and experience, the Tanasens would have never been accepted so easily in the Blue City. Now that they were established at court, Feran remained in the background without acknowledgement or recognition and they avoided him like a biting insect, an irritation beneath their notice. He should have expected such treatment from Falden farmers but it stung all the same.

After months of planning, the eldest Tanasen, Nora, was to unite

House Tanasen with House Stenlin, cousins of the Empress with royal blood in their veins. Only two hundred cycles ago, Empress Iridalisan chose a man of House Stenlin to father many children. It brought the Stenlins to a position of power they maintained to this day. Desperate to find his own way back into court life, Feran had done everything in his power to help the Tanasens win favor with other noble houses.

House Stenlin was one of his proudest accomplishments. An invitation to the wedding was a condition of his help. It would be his first appearance at court since the exile of House Dorst; an opportunity well worth spending a fortune to achieve.

Savine Tanasen was an ambitious woman. She had not been happy with Darrell for signing a trade agreement with Feran while she was away in the Blue City. He had a much harder time keeping the Tanasens happy once Savine took control.

The woman refused to call on him, neglected to invite him to social gatherings, and when asked of Herbert's sponsor at Praxis, Feran had no doubt his name slipped her mind entirely. Worse still, he had no choice but to ignore the slights. Trading with noble houses was a kind of legitimacy that he needed now more than ever. He would do anything in order to ensure the Tanasens had no credible excuse to end their contract.

A woman's laugh confirmed Feran's suspicions. Darrell would never have kept him waiting. The laughter grew louder as the door connecting the rooms opened.

Lady Tanasen's round figure popped through the doorway and her pleasure was genuine as she rocked back on her heels in mock surprise. "Why, Merchant Dorst. *Blessed Empress*, have ye na'en else t'do but wait at our door?"

Feran stared at the chuckling man who stood at her side. The sight of elderly Merchant Milgebrant in the Blue City, and in the Tanasen's home, was such a shock that he forgot what he was going to say. He stood, riveted in place.

Inviting Feran's trade rival into their home was such a clear violation of trade customs that with a guilty bow, Merchant Milgebrant paid him more courtesy than the two had exchanged in a dozen cycles.

Feran had no doubt that he was meant to interrupt the meeting. It was a long way to travel unless... an agreement had been offered or already made.

Lady Tanasen took Milgebrant's arm. "Such a pleasure t'see ye." She rushed past Feran as she escorted him to the door, waving away the servant who held it open. Her shoulders threatened to burst out of an ostentatious array of blue and green silk that layered together enough fabric for three separate gowns.

Feran had never forgiven Merchant Milgebrant for cutting him out of all trading in Emerald Bay, the only southern port of the Imperium. He was so driven by the desire to snatch the Tanasen's crops from the pompous prick that every cycle after that he dedicated weeks of travel to Falden, spending any profits he made to steal Milgebrant's most lucrative sources of goods away from the other merchant with simpering and empty flattery. Milgebrant had not shown his face in the Blue City out of embarrassment after his son, Gileas, lost the Tanasen's contract. Oh, what a sweet victory that had been.

Feran knew he needed to scrape together a smile or a kind word, or better yet a piece of information that would make the Tanasen's need him again. But this last insult was more than he could handle. He did not ask why Milgebrant was there.

It was such a blunt and petty blow that he could not face the vulgarity of it. He was too furious for words. Silently, he walked to the door to take his leave.

Eyebrows raised, Lady Tanasen blocked his way, her voice syrupy with sweetness. "Yer leavin'? But Merchant Dorst, we have yet t'speak of why yer here. I am shocked ye haven't been t'see us with news of Herbert at Praxis."

Praxis. With no word from Selina since their falling out, Feran had not found time to find a new source of information. Traveling from one end of the Imperium to the other had taken its toll on his presence in the Blue City, and now that he had no new political support, the strain was starting to show in his trade alliances.

With a sniff, Lady Tanasen reached for a bowl of sugar lumps and popped several into her mouth, sucking on them as her plump chin wobbled. "We waited, but with na'en a word we had t'protect our family and good name. With the ceremony so near, it would be wise t'keep any hint of scandal out of the court."

Three more lumps of sugar. It was repulsive to stand there and listen to that awful sound. The woman's voice wasn't much better; her thick Falden accent was a strange parody of her surroundings and dress.

"I had t'hear it by word of Lady Marshton, ye see. Her son was in his last cycle at Praxis. He heard rumors of a special part of the school, a part that was shut down, the masters all but gone, and the prens sent away on mysterious errands."

"I was told not to speak of it." Feran had no doubt the woman squeezed her information from Lady Marshton like a snake squeezes the life and breath from its victims. At least she gave him the opening for a simple excuse.

With a sour look, Lady Tanasen put down the sugar bowl. "Am I t'have my information from rumors instead of the man who could, but refuses t'tell me word of my own son?"

"I would think your attention better spent on your daughter."

"That is na'en yer business."

"None of my—" this was too much for Feran. "You would be stuck in Falden with nothing but an empty title if it were not for me!"

He had never uttered an impolite word in the vile woman's presence. But Lady Tanasen did not bat an eye at the insult, and her reaction alarmed him more than if she had shouted for him to leave. She laughed.

"See, I spoke with a few members of the Merchant's Guild about our little arrangement. Turns out, our commitment t'trade with ye was pinned on Herbert bein' at Praxis until he was a Master. Now he's on his own, seems we've other options." Plucking another cube of sugar from her bowl, she started to hum.

First Selina, then Lady Morna, and now Lady Tanasen. Feran could have strangled them all. So, the woman finally found a way out of their contract.

He could guess which merchant at the Guild had offered her his help. Brexel had every reason to humiliate him, and just in time to keep any Dorst from attending the wedding with a public show of support. It was a consummate move. The woman was not adept at making alliances, but she knew all too well how to break them apart.

If he were a member of the Merchant's Guild, he would have had the right to protest with considerable support. With the Headmistress of Praxis at his side, he might try to claim the old rights of sponsorship would not allow a break in a trade agreement until the sponsor was repaid; but Selina would not help him. Not now.

He had no time to bring about his long-term plans. All the support and coin he had poured into the Tanasen family would bring him nothing without a noble title to fall back upon. It was time that he acknowledged who had the true power in this agreement. To his shock and disgust, it was not Feran Dorst.

Lady Tanasen's pursed lips stretched into a wide smile that made her look like a frog. "We'll have a justikar send word. Good day, Merchant Dorst."

Feran stumbled out the door. Narrowly avoiding the metal spokes from a slowing carriage, he hailed it and stepped inside. He could not forget Lady Tanasen and her tuneless humming and it haunted him down the windy, salt-stained streets while he clutched his head.

The shipments he held in his warehouses were not nearly enough to cover the trading for the rest of the cycle. His ready coin was already spent in favors for the Tanasens. Without the apple harvest from next season and with no guild to fall back upon for support, he would have no way to deliver on his promises. He was ruined.

HIDDEN IN STONE

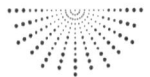

Teguin had to steady Master Troug as they reached the pile of bones she wanted. There was a tremor in her hand as she pointed. He crouched until his nose touched his knee. "This one?"

"The one beside it. Smaller, the one with a curve in it. Yes, that one."

The thought of picking it up made him uneasy. This was a person, once. If a bone reader could relive the last moments of a person's life by touching it... what else was left behind?

Using a square of cloth from his pocket helped a little, but it was what information the bone might contain that overcame his aversion. He pulled out the bone fragment without the rest tumbling and deposited it on the table.

Master Troug fell upon the bone with a sigh of delight. Her fingers danced over the stained shard. Holding it close to her chest, she stiffened with a shudder and grew still to the point where she didn't seem to be breathing.

A hand fell upon Teguin's shoulder when he would have hurried forward. He had not heard the Lexicon return. "She is in a trance," the woman said. "To wake her would be dangerous."

Troug's eyes were open but she did not blink. Teguin did not want to turn, afraid that the moment he looked away Master Troug would make some small movement in appeal for help and he would miss it. The Lexicon had no such concern.

She stepped past him and moved around the room to examine the piles of bones. "Are you going to stay with her all night?"

"Will it take that long?"

"Minutes, hours, even a few days if the connection is strong enough. I thought you would understand that being her pren. Death is never the same twice." There was a nasty inflection in her words.

"She likes her privacy. Or she did, once."

"Did you not stay with her when she was at Praxis? I am told it is the custom."

"Not while she used her magic, no." It sounded ridiculous to speak of privacy as he watched her invade another person's life during their last moments. It was true that Master Troug never asked him to leave while she worked, but she also never invited him to stay until now.

"Does someone else stay while she works?" he asked.

"We have a boy who keeps an eye on her. Will you—"

"Yes. I will stay."

The Lexicon raised an eyebrow. "As you wish."

SCREAMS FOLLOWED Nezt as he ran. The walls and ceiling shook from the footfalls of thousands in battle, and he sent a fervent prayer to the Relics that no one had followed him. Coughing, he wiped blood from his lips. Two, four, six knots kept the bundle safely closed. He had to make sure that nothing could escape.

Nezt skidded past the shuttle looms. Spare threads hung listless from where they were stripped of their woven masterpieces. He turned past the foundations of the gristmill, reaching rows of heavy barrels which pressed in around him like stacked giants, dripping ale foaming through cracks and onto swollen bags of wet grain which threatened to burst.

His long robes wrapped around his ankles and he stumbled, pulling to untangle the heavy fabric. Leader Tobin liked to keep the initiates slow and steady in their steps but now the heavy fabric swallowed Nezt and kept spinning him off the walls like a child's toy. His chest burned.

Was it pain or panic? He was too light-headed to remember. He had to get away, to go beneath. They told him beneath and then they died. His mentors, teachers; everything swept away above his head in a river of blood.

Tears fell and he did not regret them. So much life and all of them lost.

"Nezt?" His name, strange and familiar to hear.

Nezt blinked. There were faces peering at him from behind those barrels.

He pulled the bundle closer and his chest tightened. "I need to go deeper," he pleaded, looking past them. "A door—is there another door?" He had to find another door.

"Another door?" came the voice again, a strange and detached sound that floated beyond the angry yells of battle above them. Many of the voices he recognized but could not name, their dark faces melding with the shadows as they spoke.

"—There is no other way out."

"—We are trapped down here."

"—They left us here to rot."

"—No safe place left."

The cold reality of their words sank in. Impossible, thought Nezt. How could they send him here if not to go deeper?

An explosion from above brought the stacked barrels tumbling down around them, splitting and spilling their contents. Soured ale splashed over Nezt and with a scream, someone was crushed under a tumbling pile of grain. He had to get out.

Cries of terror were matched by new shouts in the room. Torches spat flame at the frightened faces of his friends. The battle had followed Nezt underground. The attackers were not battle-hardened soldiers but desperate men and women with fever-bright eyes, burning to cut down anything they could reach. Nezt had seen it over and over again, the stresses of bloodshed and horror making monsters of them all.

He backed away. The slippery floor brought a new kind of chaos as the ale sucked at his ankles, sliding him into the wall as he twisted to avoid the worst of the mess, ducking out of sight. Knees shaking, he tried not to make a sound.

It was all happening so fast that he almost missed it. The ale in the room with barrels spilling open and yet only his feet were wet. Pulling him against the wall, dragging him toward the only place where the liquid could drain. A hidden door. Another way out.

He did not stop to think. Without a word of caution or comfort he left his friends to be slaughtered, heard them crying out for help or for the Relics to save them—as if that would bring salvation before death. He slipped through the door and prayed that no one would see him go, that he would have a few minutes more to lose himself before he, too, was found.

On and on he ran, sliding down the passageways and hoping he would find a promised place to hide his precious bundle. There were twists and turns and places where cobwebs and dust mixed with the new river that rushed along with Nezt to some unknown destination, cycles of work and sacrifice to store a lifetime of goods for the dead and now he was moving past any chance of his own survival. The thought drove him wild with a frenzied need to complete the one and only thing he could achieve, to hide somewhere where no one would find him.

What comes after death? After seeing so much blood and violence Nezt did not want to know. The honor in death they preached was a recitation, a prayer he made every day to bring comfort to those close to their end, but there were too many battles. Too many bodies, and now there would be no one left to anoint them.

With the Predestine monks dead, how would the survivors bury so many dead and bring them peace?

His free hand ran along the wall and he let the darkness swallow him whole. The pain in his chest was both pain and panic, he realized. Each burrowed deep with sharpened claws, tightening their grip

There it was. A crack in the wall large enough. Out of sight. Safely tucked away.

Nezt did not stop. He pushed the bundle in and used both hands to crawl away from it and up another passage fighting against the spilled ale, fighting to breathe, reaching upward, rejecting the memory of this terrible place.

Clutching his side, he felt the sting of a forgotten arrowhead and pulled it out. With a yell of effort, he threw himself down another passageway, hearing footsteps sloshing down through the muck. His last thought was to bring them to him and away from his hidden treasure, to end it.

"Over here," he gargled. He no longer felt his legs and soon he stumbled and fell as hands crushed the breath from his body.

TROUG'S GASP was a desperate gargle that made Teguin's skin crawl. It was horrible to hear. It went on for ages. She spat a mouthful of… something onto the ground. It looked like blood.

Teguin shook the boy who slept at his feet. "Quickly, now. Fetch the healer."

Master Troug had made no sound or movement for so long that Teguin was meditating in a half-daze himself. A bit of food, an occasional moment to step out or stretch his cramped legs, but she had not moved or spoken. It was agonizing to witness.

Blinking with glazed eyes, she saw Teguin and her cracked lips parted. No words emerged. She clutched her side and tried to straighten. She touched her face and grasped at her throat and then pulled on her hair until Teguin took her hands gently in his own, concerned she would hurt herself from tugging so hard.

"Peace Master Troug," he said.

"I hid it," she said, her voice hollow. "I made it beneath and found the hidden door. Will you tell Leader Tobin for me?"

"Yes, of course," Teguin promised, and her hands relaxed. He had no idea what she meant but at least she was breathing better. She wiped her mouth and he could see a streak of blood on the back of her hand.

The healer rushed into the room. Muttering under his breath he looked at Teguin with a frown. "The boy told me he missed it. How did she die?"

"What?"

The man sighed. "I have no time for this. She wakes and touches where she was injured. What did you see?"

"Her side, her throat, her hair—so her head? And she spat out blood."

"Good. Now, you may leave."

"But—"

"Perhaps I was unclear. Leave. Now."

Teguin would have argued, but if he continued to protest he would keep the healer from tending to Troug. The man looked as though he might have something painful or poisonous in his healer's bag that he would use if he were crossed. It was odd to feel threatened by a healer. Teguin could see large needles sticking out of dried plant stalks as he backed away. Herbert would have given a piece of his staff to see inside this bag.

Teguin's heart skipped a beat. Herbert. How long had he been with Master Troug, and what had happened to his friend while he waited?

He ran for the stairs.

A PARTING OF WAYS

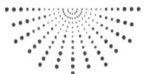

Herbert struck a small glowstone against the wall with his good arm, the other strapped to his chest with bandages. The makeshift sling threw him off balance. It was an awkward, clumsy attempt to patch him up and he resented that he could not fix it himself.

Smashing the rock against the wall gave him something on which to focus. At least it passed the time. Straightening, he winced as the bandage on his shoulder shifted and tugged. It must have been dislocated and reset from when... when he fought off Jameson.

Cursing, he tried to see the room in which he and Cergath were being held. The small stone was not cooperating. Herbert was so used to traveling with Teguin that he rarely kept a striking stone in his pocket.

It was a fool's errand with a stone this small. He expected to smash the glowstone to pieces rather than shed light in the room. At least it allowed him to vent his frustration at being kept in this dark pit of a buried cell.

His fingers itched to clutch his staff, but that, too, was gone. They better not bend a single branch of what was left, he thought darkly. If they did, he would know, and he would break a few arms of his own.

The feeble light reflected strangely off sandstone; the walls absorbed more than they reflected. Sand for hundreds of leagues and now they were stuck beneath it. Was it his imagination, or did the air taste foul down here? Herbert held his breath and struck the glowstone again.

"Leave it," snapped Cergath. "Who cares if there is darkness underground."

"Who cares? I care plenty when there's na'en a pocket of light fer a whole day. Longer, even. How long was I asleep?"

"Not long enough." The disdain in Cergath's voice rattled Herbert like a knife scraping tree bark. Herbert could barely see him silhouetted in the glowlight, kneeling on the floor.

"I heard them talking," said Cergath. "Some plant brings them light in the darkness and they will not leave one with us. They look at you like... like you and light are not to be in the same room together."

It was the plant and what he might do with it that worried the Blades, not the light itself. They both knew that. But Cergath refused to speak of what he had seen and Herbert could only remember what had happened in shimmering flashes of green: a dim recollection of roots springing from the ground.

Why would Cergath so easily accept this dark cell? If anyone understood what it was to be held captive it was a prison guard. Yet he did nothing.

Imprisoned with a useless prison guard. Just his luck.

"Where is Teguin?" he asked again now that Cergath was speaking to him. "Where are the others?"

"Others?"

"The girl, Jameson the bleedin' bastard, where are the rest of 'em?"

With a yell, Cergath rushed at Herbert and pushed him against the wall, knocking the breath out of his lungs. The man lifted Herbert with such ease that he cried out in shock and surprise. Pain from his shoulder made him gag. He saw a flash of green and felt a different pain, another strong set of arms holding his shoulders, fingers twisting around his neck.

Rough hands pulled them apart. There was a light blinding him. Blinking, Herbert saw a curved and nasty looking knife which kissed

Cergath on the throat until he backed away, hands raised and shaking.

"Enough of that," growled the woman. She clutched the blessed source of light; a large seed pod he had never seen before. The urge was too strong and Herbert lashed out with a desperate swipe to hold it.

"Do it again," she hissed, "and the next chamber I find for you will be sealed shut."

Cergath made a strangled noise. Herbert took it for manic laughter, but in the retreating light he could see tears streaming down the man's face. Cergath returned to the corner and would not turn around to face him.

"How is it that you do not remember?" the man choked out, his voice breaking. "How is it that such a violent, bloody end should visit itself on the innocent and yet the guilty sleeps like a newborn babe. Is there no justice left in this world?"

"What d'ye mean?"

"Mason and the girl are both dead by your hand, man." Cergath had tried, but could not say her name.

Mason. Jameson. Pain bloomed in his chest. Flashes of green tugged at his vision. Olivia was gone. Yes, yes of course she was. Dead and scattered.

And this other girl's name… what was it? He could not recall, and he found he did not want to know. He dreaded the knowledge as if its memory would bring back more than he could handle.

What had he done?

Cergath's anger hung between them in the darkness like the foul air, thick and stifling. There was the ring of truth in his words. They staggered Herbert yet, when he closed his eyes, all he saw was the glowing seed pod suspended, bathing him in light.

Herbert kept his eyes shut.

"Herbert?"

With a groan, he raised his head. His mouth was dry and his muscles stiff and sore from leaning against the stone wall while he slept. He stumbled as he stepped forward. He would know that voice anywhere. "Teguin. Finally."

"Here, they brought you food and water."

The guard from before stepped inside long enough to place a tray on the ground, then spun out of reach with a low growl, taking the light with her. She stayed near enough the door that Herbert and Cergath could see the tray.

They pounced on the food. Cergath spilled half the water down his front while Herbert tore into the dried meat, ignoring his protesting stomach. Mystery meat was no match for his hunger.

"Herbert, I tried to have them give your staff back so you could repair it but… that will have to wait."

"Wait? It'll take a lifetime if they ken what it is. The staff is gone, Teguin. That's the straight and narrow of it." It gutted Herbert to say the words, but who in their right mind would give such a powerful tool back to him? At least they had not destroyed it yet. He could feel its presence somewhere nearby like an extension of his arm, but it was only a matter of time before that, too, was ripped away.

Cergath dropped the water flask at Herbert's feet. "Enough about your precious walking stick. Teguin, how long do they mean to keep us here? And why are you free to walk among them?"

Something was wrong. Teguin was looking everywhere but at them. His friend was many things, but evasive was not one of them. Yet now he could hardly keep still, shifting in place and clenching his fist as if he expected a fight.

That was it. Teguin was tense as if he expected a blow. Suspicion prickled the back of Herbert's neck. "Where have ye been?"

"With the Lexicon."

"Leader of the Blades," murmured Cergath. "I should have known."

"She's alive, Herbert. Master Troug is here, and I've been with her, learning what she is doing with the Blades. She won't leave this place."

Herbert tried to manage a smile but it felt more like a grimace. "Master Troug is alive?"

Teguin glanced at Cergath. "The Blades are doing important work, discovering things that make our time at Praxis look like, well, like we were working in the dark. Master Troug has decided to remain here, and I have to stay with her. I don't trust these Blades, but I can't make Troug leave against her will."

Herbert could not believe what he was hearing. "She wants to stay? What about bringin' her back home with us where it's safe! I ken ye wanted t'find Troug and yer crazy dice toss paid off, Teguin. We should be headin' back t'Falden." Herbert lowered his voice until it was a whisper. "If we reach the Imperial soldiers at the prison, we can end the Blades once and fer all."

Cergath leaned forward too. "For once I agree with the man."

Teguin shook his head. "You would unleash Captain Jarvin on these people? The man is a monster."

"Olivia is dead because of the Blades!" How could his best friend abandon him to be a prisoner while he made his own plans? He fought to keep his voice low. "They deserve it. These people are killers."

"And what are you, Herbert?"

The question stunned him to silence. Is that what Teguin thought of him?

He had never thought of himself as a man of deep beliefs, yet the thought of Teguin defying the Empress and staying with these bandits filled him with disgust. "Might as well spit on Olivia's ashes, Teguin. This makes ye a traitor t'the Imperium. There's na'en a place in the provinces that'll be a home fer ye once yer marked. And with yer ties at Praxis, they'd mark ye fer certain."

"Praxis is in ruins. There is nothing left for me there."

"Then ponder on yer family, man! D'ye fancy Feran will forgive a nephew who runs t'the desert and joins a mercenary band which hates the Empress?"

For the first time Teguin looked unsure of himself. That hurt all the more; the man showed no remorse for abandoning Herbert or for dismissing their time together at Praxis and leaving him to fend for himself in the desert, while the guilt at leaving his uncle made him pause.

Teguin reached out to put a hand on his shoulder. "I urge you, at least listen to what the Blades have to say. It's true, I do not trust the

Blades or the Lexicon, but there is so much we could learn if we at least keep an open mind. I can't dismiss what they have to offer. The Blades know more about magic than anyone I've met in the Imperium."

Herbert recoiled and threw off the hand, though it hurt him to move so quickly. "I have all I need, Teguin. These people are only usin' ye. Have ye lost all sense? Trustin' that woman, that Lexicon or whatever she calls herself. She kidnapped Troug and bundled her off as if she were na'en but a sack of flour!"

"I admit their attack on Praxis was brutal. But what happened to Olivia was an accident."

"*Listen* t'yerself. Ye wanted t'find Troug and rescue her but now yer both stayin'? They have ye on their side in the blink of an eye."

"If you saw what they have here, what Troug has here, you would not question my choice to stay."

"And what is it, exactly, that they have here?"

"Stay, and you will find out."

"That's a load of sheep's piss, Teguin. Ye won't see me step in it or call it golden peach nectar. I'd rather call it what it is than drink the stuff, thanks all the same."

"You are not well enough to travel home, even if I were ready to leave tonight."

"If it's so easy fer ye t'leave me alone then I must be alright," he said, so angry he could barely see straight. The Blades had burned down Praxis and the man had the nerve to defend them, even join them!

Teguin continued to press him. "Your magic is out of control, Herbert. The Lexicon could help you before anyone else gets hurt."

Teguin saw they were out of water and pulled a flask from his side, holding it out to Herbert.

Herbert threw the flask back in the man's face. "Keep yer favors t'yerself. All this time ye wanted t'get back here and be with yer new friends, is that it? So eager t'explore the desert- gah! What a fool I was t'follow right along like a dim-witted beast t'the slaughter. Yer a right bastard."

Teguin swallowed his reply. Herbert could feel a hollowness in his chest as disbelief set in. This was happening. His best friend was betraying him.

"Go on, then. Leave us here t'rot. Traitor."

What good was a man who abandoned his friends whenever it suited? Herbert decided he was better off. Let the Blades have Teguin. If he turned his cloak so easily, he wasn't worth saving.

They needed to be taught a lesson. All of them.

A STEP TOO FAR

L uther marveled at how quickly they traveled south to the Borderlands. Traveling in the open without fear of capture lent as much speed to the journey as the horses they rode, though Luther missed his boat.

Was it really stealing if it had already broken from its mooring? Either way, the steadfast little craft had been a comfort. Luther would gladly have taken it again rather than ride a beast, even if the journey were twice as long, but the ice melt only pushed the river's current in one direction and this time Luther did not travel alone.

If given the choice he would have much rather stayed in the grasslands or journeyed father north to stay as far away from the Imperium as possible. The choice, however, was not his to make. South they went.

The clan chiefs had their doubts about his story. Luther could hardly blame them. Here he was, a stranger walking into a clan gathering to proclaim their doom was at hand, that they were about to be invaded, and that he was there without any plan except to warn them.

Why should they believe him? He was no warrior or hunter with tales of great courage and cunning. *Empress Bless*, he was there not to contact the Dunmiri but to spy on them.

The thought of the Empress jolted Luther out of his reverie with a guilty lurch. He was so used to proclaiming her name with every breath that the thought of her colored the weight of his betrayal, heavy and close to his chest, tapping like a hammer upon tiny nails. It was too late to take back his betrayal. All he could do was prove his words true or die trying. He doubted the Dunmiri were a forgiving people.

After his warning at the gathering, the clan chiefs had decided to send him back to the Borderlands with an escort to find some evidence of preparations for war. If successful, they would grant his request for sanctuary. That would mean freedom. A new home.

It was a tantalizing offer. But how would he find the proof he needed and escape back north before the Praelor found him? Looking down, Luther pulled aside the bandage on his hand. The eye was open and looking around as if searching and Luther could feel it burning into his skin with a renewed hold. He shuddered.

"Your injury, does it pain you?"

The voice from behind him startled Luther. He pulled the bandage back in place. "No, no. I am fine, Bregt."

The man guided his horse with ease to join Luther. "My people do not like to show pain, but a wounded hunter makes his people weak. It is better to be honest."

"But I am not—"

"Not a hunter; so you say. But it took courage to come to my people, your enemy, did it not?" Bregt's stare made Luther look away.

His reply was faint. "Yes."

"A messenger fights their own war. If words save the lives of my family then they are as valuable as any arrow. Our people are in your debt."

Luther smiled. He did not deserve those kind words. Firstborn son of the Boar Clan chief, Lem, Bregt came with a dozen men to investigate the truth of Luther's claim.

Strong, handsome, confident. Bregt was everything Luther wished he could be. More agonizing still, it was effortless for the man. It bothered him to distraction, thought it was a comfort to have someone on his side for once. Bregt believed that he was in earnest, but he would have to convince the rest of the clan chiefs in order to gain his freedom.

Why was he hiding the proof he needed? If the Praelor saw him, so be it. The risk was worth the reward. Luther fought to swallow, and with trembling hands, he unwrapped the bandage.

The eye was no different than before. Wandering. Out of focus. He held his hand out to Bregt, and waited for an exclamation of surprise, a cry of horror, a reaction to prove that magic was real.

"I do not understand," said the Dunmiri.

"What do you see?"

"A mark of spilled ink."

Luther's heart skipped a beat. "Is there no shape?"

"It is like a cloud in the sky."

Luther let the wrappings fall to the ground. A new wave of despair rose like bile in his throat. The eye continued to move, it's gaze uncertain, as lost as Luther felt.

Then Bregt stopped his horse. "Quiet." In one fluid motion he dismounted and slid a short spear from its sheath.

Luther held his breath. Half their traveling party was gone. A whistle came from somewhere to the right and though Bregt relaxed, a frown fell across his face as a woman walked into view.

"Scythia," said Bregt. He shoved the blunt end of his spear into the ground. "Why have you come?"

A cold fear gripped Luther. Chief of the Badger Clan, the woman vehemently opposed his request for asylum and rejected his warnings. A short axe swung lazily in her hands as she looked them over.

"I have no need to explain myself to you, Bregt. These are my lands by right." She had to tilt her head to look up at the man who towered over her.

Even with her attention elsewhere Luther backed away, unsure of her intent.

"These are the Borderlands," replied Bregt in an even voice. "You have a right to them like anyone, but this task was given to me."

"Is this your first trip beyond the mountains as a man?" scoffed Scythia. "You do not have enough warriors with you. I would understand if you have forgotten the thrill of the hunt since you prefer to ride in the grasslands, where the view is clear in all directions."

"I can keep an eye on one man."

"Fine. Please yourself. You stopped listening to me a long time ago. But I will be keeping an eye on this *boderi* make no mistake. He smells of death."

With a scowl, the woman disappeared back into the woods.

Luther noticed that the men were staring at him, refusing to meet his eye. "What is a boderi?" he asked.

"It is a—what do you say in your tongue... bad spirit? When a creature dies, it goes to find a new home. Most find peace, but if a spirit grows lost or angry they can become *boderi*—ah! Cursed, yes. A cursed spirit."

"That sounds... bad."

Bregt shook his head. "Do not take it to heart. My mother does not like many people. Not even her own children."

"Your mother?" Luther tried to swallow but there was a lump in his throat that got in the way. "Is she not a different clan?"

"It is not uncommon. Children can happen after gatherings... you understand. The children choose which clan to join if their parents do not wish to remain together. I chose to be with the Boar Clan. Is it not the same for your people?"

"My people do not have clans. How do I explain... we have noble families related to the Empress, or ones she favors. Our women choose whether or not they will keep their family name, and the fathers or their children would never choose where they go."

Bregt coughed into his hand, but Luther suspected he was trying not to laugh. When he recovered, he looked around to make sure that no one else could hear them. "The women of your clans, your people, they must be strong to command such control over their men."

"I would not know," said Luther. "But the Empress has two daughters of her own, and while I do not know them I would say they command both respect and fear from the people."

"My mother would like to hear that. And do you think these daughters will bring war upon us to honor their mother, this Empress?"

Luther stumbled over a tree root. Embarrassed, he scrambled back to his feet again and wiped the mud from his hands as best he could. He was enjoying their conversation so much that he had forgotten the reason they were there.

War. Such an ugly word.

He cleared his throat. "It is the Empress alone who makes the decision. Her daughters, well, they carry out her wishes as law I suppose. All who are under her domain obey."

"You do not."

"I... that is true." The skin on his hand stretched until it burned with the mark from the Praelor. "Coming to you was the first time I thought I had a choice."

Bregt nodded as though he understood. Luther wished he did, too. The closer they came to entering Imperial land the more he felt a weight return to his shoulders. He jumped at every broken twig under his worn boots, the lonely bird calls taunting him with whispers and trills and cries that sounded similar to why, oh why, oh why.

Up ahead the valley would open into a series of logging camps that Luther had passed on his way into Dunmire. If they were still there; the few villages this close to the Borderlands were more like broken shanties that moved where there was work, clearing and scouring what they could to get by one more cycle. The Praelor liked to boast that there was no need for the Shattered Mountains, that the Borderland patrols were enough of a barrier to prevent any serious threat by the Dunmiri.

But what about the reverse, and what protected Dunmire? Luther knew all too well that as their knowledge of magic grew it extended the physical reach of Imperial power and influence. The Praelor was fair proof of that.

He smelled the fire and smoke right before he saw it drifting above the trees up ahead. Then came the screams. Bregt said something Luther did not understand and mounted his horse.

Three of the men stayed behind with Luther, shaking their heads when he moved to the horse intending to follow Bregt. The sound of a piercing scream made him less enthusiastic about moving closer but he still wanted to know what was happening.

It was an odd coincidence to come across a skirmish right when they arrived. Was it too much to hope that a random Imperial patrol would be proof enough for the Dunmiri? Luther paced and plucked at the harness of his horse, too restless to simply stand there.

He must have missed a signal to come ahead. Moving as one, the three men mounted their horses and gestured for him to follow. They rode until they reached a large clearing of cut trees, their trunks smoldering and the damp, muddy ground steaming from the unexpected heat.

Scythia had not left to return home, she had gone straight to the nearest Imperial encampment and raided it. Luther could see Bregt and Scythia facing one another once again but this time, Bregt was bellowing something that Luther could not understand; his accent too quick and heavy with anger. Around them lay scattered bodies.

A few survivors knelt in the mud, bound and bloodied. Luther's heart sank. He would probably join them soon enough.

Bregt saw him coming. With a shake of his head, he slowed his speech so that Luther could better understand his heavy accent. "These are no soldiers. Why do you slaughter them like animals?"

"At the last snowfall our village lost four children to their knives. And for what? The sheep they watched, then slaughtered without skill or mercy to the poor creatures." Scythia wiped blood from the cudgel and pointed it at the survivors.

"We traded with them when they first arrived. Welcomed them to our camps and into our homes." She spat on the ground. "The moment the weather turned rough they became animals. So we treat them as animals."

"But I do not understand," said Bregt. "You opposed Luther at the gathering when he said the Imperium wished for war."

"Oh use your ears, Bregt. Anyone who betrays their own people will soon turn on others like a rabid animal." She glared at Luther. "Be gone, *boderi*!"

"Are you finished?" Bregt said. "Because we are not here for revenge. This is not a group of soldiers. That is why we are here."

"Fine." She spat on the ground in front of the captured. "Where are the soldiers?" She pulled a small dagger and rammed it into the shoulder of a kneeling man. He screamed while the others wailed and begged for their lives.

Heat from the burning forest seared Luther's throat and stretched his skin. The smell of burning flesh hung in the air. He would have spat on the ground if there were any moisture left in his mouth.

He needed to leave this place. Cool, clean air would do the trick. Clear his head.

Another cry and the man fell to the ground. Luther wanted to run away but when he sprang into action it was to throw himself at Scythia's blade, screaming something that must have been words but were drowned out by the ringing in his ears. Shocked, she let him take the blade.

"Soldiers," he heard himself babble. "Look around you woman, this is not a place of war but of hardship and struggle and suffering. And here we are, adding to it."

He meant to throw the weapon away. He would have loved to break it in half or throw it into the nearest river if he could. Instead, it fell out of his shaking hands.

Scythia recovered quickly and sneered at him. "Where is this war of yours? I cannot see it."

Luther had not mentioned anything about magic. At the gathering he half expected they would simply reject his warnings and kill him. Afterward, he could not think of how to describe or show evidence of magic to the Dunmiri in a way that would make them understand what he meant

Magic was the catalyst, the change that would upset the balance of power. It was a real possibility that even from a distance the Empress might be able to conquer Dunmire. That was why he was here.

Luther had no active magic of his own. No fancy spells or shifting rocks, no levitating water or bones to knit back together. To see but not influence was a constant burden. So how was he to prove it existed and what would he tell Bregt and Scythia, that an unseen force that he could not show them would be the downfall of their people?

No. He needed something solid. And for that, he needed time.

Should he use the sending scrolls he carried? That would have sent a message to the Praelor, which was the last thing he wanted even if it would show what, a message written from the air? His scrying crystal would simply look to be a crystal; a valuable treasure perhaps to them but the magic it magnified would not reveal itself to idle curiosity.

How very confusing. It was difficult for him to imagine what others saw in the presence of magic. He could watch as the essence of magic unfolded and took shape, transforming in front of him. To others magic simply was, or was not; the interaction and result might as well be unrelated.

Luther yelped and fell to his knees as Scythia pressed the tip of her blade into his shoulder, so close he could feel her breath on his face. Then a different cry passed his lips as a burning pain seared his finger. The Praelor's mark.

The magical eye came alive, grasping for the binding hold it had on Luther. Writhing and enthralled, Luther cried out and clawed at the bandage on his hand, falling to the ground. He was too afraid to look.

Was this the point at which the Praelor could feel him again? There was a sense of wrongness in the mark, a searching hunger that sank into Luther's skin as never before. He was only dimly aware of Bregt and Scythia standing over him arguing and he did not care.

It was better not to see the magic erupt from the eye. Better to block out the image of its curling tendrils as they surrounded him, unbidden and wild, filling his lungs with frozen calm. Best to believe he could still have the luxury of choice.

His mind settled into a haze he well remembered. There it was, a feeling of numb and detached indifference. He closed his eyes.

HEADS WILL ROLL

A s Lady Jade rode into the Blue City, fury clung to her skin like the salt that coated the misty streets of stone. A sea of soldiers at her back and a hundred prisoners shackled between them. Not one of them dared to look her in the eye. By the light of the moons she made out the gilded sign of the Golden Limpet ahead and slowed her horse.

"Ride on, Commander. Report to the general and keep them separate from the others until you hear from me."

"Your will, Seeker," said the man.

"The Will of the Empress guide us all."

Faces pressed against the windows overlooking the street. Those at the Inn turned to watch her. She refused to acknowledge them.

The innkeeper smiled when she entered. "Lady Jade, you honor us with—"

"My room and a hot bath."

The smile faded into a nod. She ignored those who waited for her to share news of the soldier's arrival. Even the innkeeper, usually full of conversation and paid well to share it, kept out of her way except to bring her a drink and to her room when it was ready.

All the sand and sweat and dust from the road melted away with the steam from her bath but when she emerged, her anger remained.

Cycles of sacrifice, and with two cruel blows she had no family left to protect. The pain brought clarity to her grief.

A wisp of magic escaped her bag. Jade kept the sending scroll tucked away. She knew every word it contained by heart. Drinking her wine allowed her to ignore the scroll, but the thought of lying awake in bed for hours brought her back to her silk bag in search of its punishment.

The temptation to destroy the message returned as she unrolled it, unable to look away. *Prison hawk intercepted. Your daughter, Lena, is dead. Herbert Tanasen used magic to kill her. We arrived too late but will bring her to the monks. We will walk with her as our sister. The purest form of life is found in death.*

She grimaced. No mention of their failure to keep Lena from harm. No apology. How like the Lexicon.

The words would never bring her comfort but she could not bring herself to erase them. She pulled out a squished quill. The vial of ink at the bottom of her bag was one of pure silver, the crystal stopper twisting out of its protective sleeve to reveal blue liquid that swirled around in search of escape. Only a small amount was left.

Jade had plenty of time to think on the journey. She dipped her quill in the ink and wrote quickly to keep the words settled on the page. *Arrived in the Blue City. Need to speak with you. At the Golden Limpet.*

Threads of blue magic threatened to drift into the air until she blew upon them and the magic settled on the page. She waited for the message to reach its master, rubbing her back where the prongs of the chair pressed into her sore muscles. What she really needed was a few hours of sleep.

She dragged herself over to her bed, but the act of lying down was like a splash of cool water. The window beside the bed gave her an excellent view of the street, and she left it cracked open.

WHEN THE KNOCK came at her door, she straightened and winced as her arms tingled and complained; falling asleep against the windowsill was not her best moment.

"Lady Jade?"

"One moment." She opened the door and stepped back in surprise. The Imperial Palace guard took the movement for an invitation and stepped inside. She swore the guards looked younger every time she returned. Oh, to be young again.

"I'm here t'escort ye when yer—that is, yer ladyship..." he tried to explain, looking everywhere but at her.

Jade realized she neglected to put on a dress before opening the door. It was the first time in weeks that she felt the urge to laugh. It was amazing how so little mattered to her when she let go of the need to impress others.

"Yes of course," she said. "Let me change and I will be with you."

"Y-yes, yer ladyship," he stammered and backed out the door.

The carriage and the direction in which they headed left Jade little doubt that it was to the palace and not the Imperial watchtower that she went. How odd. It was true that she and the Praelor rarely communicated, but she found it strange that he would neglect to mention a move to the palace.

Stranger still, he made no reply on the scroll. The Imperial soldiers would have arrived by now. Was her arrival at the palace a mark of some misstep or offense?

No. It was time to stop reading between the lines. She would wait to see what brought about the change.

Glowstones illuminated the deserted corridors. Escorted by half a dozen guards, Jade had an odd premonition as she went deeper inside the palace that something else was wrong.

There was an emptiness to the place that Jade found alarming. The Praelor was a person who contained more magic than anyone else she knew and yet she could not feel his presence. The Empress favored those with magic and kept them close. To be surrounded by so many yet feel so little was alarming.

"Are you sure we are going to the Praelor?" she asked one of the guards.

"Just down the hall, milady," the woman assured Jade. When they arrived, her escort saluted and left her there alone before she could ask them any more questions.

She walked into the room and gasped. Magic stood out better to her in the darkness. Veins of it clung to the walls in a woven mess of color as if shriveled under a hot sun.

There was a sickness to it. Somehow corrupted, tainted by many different people with magic of their own. How was such a thing possible?

At the height of his power, the Praelor radiated magic like a constant swirling fog, but thick and viscous, more a sweet syrup than a thin haze. It pulled and stretched around her when she visited the Praelor as a young girl, too naive to realize that only she could see it. Now it was dried up inside of him, like an artist who left out their paint for too long.

"You came," a voice from the bed wheezed.

Speechless, she went to his side.

"How do I look?" he asked, his voice like dead leaves, so forced it pained her to listen to it.

"You're all dried up," she said.

His cough was so slow she could hear him fight to breathe between fits. "Never could lie to me," he said.

"I never had to, Praelor."

When she moved to the other side of the bed, she slipped on piles of ripped pages and broken books which slid out of her way. She saw a touch of magic from the pages when she leaned in to touch their broken spines, but it was less distinct, like shards of mirror glass holding a familiar reflection. The pages were empty.

"This body cannot sustain me any longer," Thurst hissed. "But there may be another way. A way to move on again."

She struggled to grasp his meaning, and shivered. If anyone could cheat death, it would be a man with the Praelor's talent. Sitting at the edge of his bed, she could see the inside of him better than the outline of his shadowed figure, like two parts of the same whole moving slightly out of step with one another.

"I need you to help me prepare, Jade. You always were my favorite."

Used to the coating of magic that clung to her from others, she was puzzled to see nothing reach out; this corrupted magic appeared to avoid her touch. This gave her a strange comfort. Would she be impervious to this magic, just as she was hopeless to directly influence it?

"I will want something in return," she found herself saying. It was worth the risk.

"Ah," he wheezed in a broken attempt to laugh. "Demanding favors from a dying man? I expected nothing less."

"I have a few conditions. But yes, Praelor, I serve the Empress in all things."

"That is interesting to hear." His throat constricted. Patches of magical residue in his throat widened and cracked and shifted when he swallowed.

"What is it you want from me, Praelor?"

In the darkness, his cracked lips stretched into a smile.

FALL IN LINE

Herbert rubbed his shoulder. "Did ye have t'swing wide?"

"You were in my way. Next time move faster." Cergath shouldered a stolen pack and glanced over his shoulder as they moved across the sand at a crawl that set Herbert's teeth on edge. It was agonizing.

To avoid notice, they walked perilously close to the cliffs, turning at the last possible moment so the Blades passing through on their own business would not see their faces and know them for strangers. A number of people had gathered to harvest and trade and hunt what they could find during the early hours of the night, but the alarm had not yet been raised about Herbert and Cergath and their escape.

Compared to their imprisonment, the open desert seemed almost friendly. Herbert was so on edge that at any moment he expected an alarm would sound and they would be set upon and recaptured. If Teguin was willing to let the Blades have their way with him, the man would hardly care if he were killed when trying to escape. Herbert chewed on his lip until he tasted blood.

There were so many raw emotions flooding his body that he could not stop shaking. Forget Teguin. All he should care about now was going back to Falden and forgetting this piss-poor desert ever existed.

He had underestimated Cergath. When a moment of inattention gave them the window they needed, he took it to free them both. Herbert owed him. He hated the man for that.

They were moving out of sight and out of reach from the Blades, and Cergath would not stop when Herbert suggested they rest. The man headed with confidence toward some new goal that Herbert could only try and guess. As if he knew Herbert's thoughts, the prison guard whirled around and grabbed him by the shirt with a menacing tug.

"The only reason you are with me and still alive is that I took an oath." His voice broke with emotion. "That is all I have left, but give me one good reason and I will leave your carcass for the birds. Clear?"

Hot anger flooded Herbert's cheeks. "So where are we goin', then?"

Cergath released him. "Not far. I mean to come right back and deliver the full fury of the Imperium on these bastards."

Herbert laughed, his dry lips cracking further. "And how, exactly, are we supposed t'be doin' that? Na'en a scrap of food, one weapon between the two of us, and me barely able t'stand upright."

"What makes you think I want any help from you?"

"The lack of any other option, fer starters." He didn't want to help Cergath, not exactly. It was more that he wanted to repay the debt he owed the man so he could get as far away from him as possible. If he hurt the Blades in the process, even better.

"Listen," he said to Cergath's back. "Ye hate me. I ken that. But if yer aim is t'pound these Blades t'dust then I aim t'help ye see it through."

Cergath snorted and glanced behind him. "And what about your friend? Are you that eager to see him dead?"

"Indifferent is all. Stubborn ass, he's made his choice." Herbert shook his head to try and clear his mind and focus. "Far as I'm concerned, he can rot with all the rest."

"I see. One more thing," said Cergath. "You travel with me, then it will be up to Captain Jarvin to pass sentence on you. You agree to admit the whole of what you've done. Two people dead at your hands and no holding back. It's that or die alone in the desert so make your choice now."

That startled Herbert into silence. Cergath stared at him with cold, unblinking eyes until he gave a slow nod. What else could he do?

Herbert struggled to keep up with Cergath's frantic pace. Breathless and angry, he stumbled often, reaching out in expectation that his staff would be there to steady him. Leaving his staff behind was a cruel blow.

He had no desire to make another from scratch when there were too many parts to replicate the original faithfully. The roots and seedlings and plants layered upon one another gradually, growing and intertwining to become one in its own unique way. Even if he could make another, it would never be the same. Half those plants came from the greenhouse that he and Olivia had crafted together and they were irreplaceable, the greenhouse now a smoldering ruin thanks to the Blades.

While the moonlight did little to hide their progress, Herbert looked over his shoulder less often. His breathing grew easier. No yell or challenge came.

Cergath kept his eyes to the sky instead of looking behind them. It was a contagious motion and Herbert found he was looking up as well. "What is it?"

Cergath ignored him. Stranger still, the man stomped as hard he could as they walked, sending shivers of sand cascading down the dune.

Herbert steadied himself as sand drifted and slid around them. "Ye've lost yer head," he snapped. "Won't sand rays feel all that commotion?"

"It doesn't matter." Cergath continued to jump. He looked ridiculous.

An answering shiver of sand made Herbert yelp as wriggling baby snakes burst out of the dune. With a grunt of satisfaction, Cergath grabbed a handful of the creatures.

Herbert gagged at the thought of eating a snake raw. He wasn't that desperate. Not yet. About to say as much, he stopped when Cergath threw one of the snakes high into the air and whistled a sharp trill.

The snake fell and burrowed back into the sand. Unperturbed, Cergath threw another into the air and whistled again. There were many things he wanted to say to Cergath while watching this performance. Most questioned his sanity. He never had a chance to say them.

A bird shot over the sand dune like an arrow and scooped up the third snake with a trill that mimicked Cergath. Stunned, Herbert watched another snake launch into the air. The bird took it to the ground, landing at their feet with a soft trill. It looked up at them when it finished eating.

Cergath crouched to stroke the bird. "This is how patrols stay in touch with the prison. This is how we track escaped prisoners and this, Herbert, is how we send word to Jarvin that the Blades and their stronghold have been found."

Reaching under its belly, Cergath pulled away a small pouch tied to its leg. "When Captain Jarvin finds this place he will grind it to dust under his bloody boots."

Herbert smiled. With a man like Jarvin on their side, Teguir would lose and the Blades would fall.

FORGOTTEN TIES

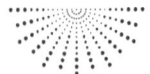

The Lexicon stood in an audience chamber. She was deep inside the lost and long forgotten city of the Predestine monks, and it was a place of decay and neglect. Meditation and wisdom were clearly more valued than fresh air. But she would give anything to learn the secrets of this dismal place, to know with certainty that an alliance would bring her the resources she needed to stop the Empress in her tracks and prove that the woman was no goddess of prosperity.

For all she knew, the Relics were no gods. But she would rather worship the memories of old bones than a royal family that wanted to murder or enslave anyone who disagreed with them. A light pod burst to life in the room.

Shadows closest to her vanished. Walls of carved reliefs took her breath away. At first she thought they were layers of swirling pattern without meaning, but the longer she examined them the more its patterns transformed. People with wide open arms framed landscapes of farms and swirling trees, with fields full for harvest, and clouds that must have shone were they free of dust.

She recognized these patterns. They were of a similar style to the cavern at Praxis in which the Emperor's Horn had been hidden away. The thought of the Horn was an urgent reminder of why she was there.

Putting aside her pride was not easy, but she remembered Elena's words. The woman was gone now, given over to death, her last wish honored. The Lexicon had been granted her audience with the Predestines.

She appealed to the bent figures seated on a bench against the far wall. "Elders, the events that separated our people need not keep us apart. We need your guidance and your wisdom."

Their pale faces were hidden in shadow still, their outlines swaying or leaning, the smell of decay overpowering. It made their lack of reaction all the worse when they refused her request without reflection or emotion.

"You do not act with that wisdom in mind," said one of the monks. A wrinkled finger pointed to her metal hand. "You wield knowledge and magic like a gathering storm, dropping ice and lightning to bruise and scorch the lands. Even your title, *Lexicon*, brings an insult to the purpose of our order. Leave us, and do not return."

When they asked her to leave, she became even more determined to stay. She had to choose her words carefully. Resist your anger, she thought, taking a slow breath.

"I come to you in humble supplication, not with judgement of your ways. We are in need of deeper understanding."

Another elder spoke. "Peace and understanding come hand in hand. Without both, there is no worth."

"And what if peace is impossible without the violence you despise? You do not see it yet, Elders, but our lands and people are under attack."

"Explain."

So the Lexicon told them of the current Empress and her involvement in Praxis. Praxis, with its archives of lost and stolen magic and the cultivation of those who could wield its power. She told them of Seekers, eager to see if they knew what one was, and explained their role in finding Artifacts. The discovery of General Empreen's Horn—and how close they came to losing it—made the elders murmur to one another, and when the Lexicon explained the Imperial presence of Captain Jarvin and his men at the prison there was a marked silence.

The Lexicon touched her hand to her forehead and heart in a gesture of respect. "I know you think of my people as lost to the old ways, but we do not wish to turn our backs on tradition. We simply wish to be strong enough to fight back."

One of the elders spoke with stilted and pained slowness. "In isolation there is ignorance—"

"—which makes you vulnerable," she interrupted. "By refusing to take action you leave the most valuable treasures you guard hidden from sight, but unsafe."

"And how would bloodshed keep us safe?"

"I do not know that it will," she admitted. "What I do know is the Imperium will not spare your lives, respect your traditions or leave anyone to follow them. Are you so unwilling to fight that you lose everything?"

The elders stirred at her words. One voice carried over the rest as they spoke their thoughts aloud. "If the Relics will it to be so, perhaps it is our time."

"But how can we know?"

"It could be a test of our will."

"We must meditate on the signs."

The Lexicon listened. She brushed the metal of her gloved hand behind her back. At least they felt enough concern about their own skins to reconsider her request.

"The affairs of others are none of our concern," said one of them.

"We are your people," she insisted. It was an insult to present such a picture of weakness, but she was desperate. "Does the absence of a few hundred cycles mean that you will turn your backs on your own children?"

"Children will act as children do…"

She bit back a response. Her silence held some value, for when they did reply, there were more in favor of listening than ignoring her request. "We will consider the matter, and have a room made for you, daughter of the monks."

"I accept your hospitality with thanks."

It was better than being sent home empty handed. She only hoped they would not keep her waiting long.

THE RED BUTCHER

Cergath watched Jarvin's soldiers arrive for the second time.
Their numbers were formidable. Enough to invade a small province, and ridiculous for as small and desolate a place as this. He knew
with a sickening thrill that in a few hours' time the sand would be
covered in blood. These were dark days.

The prison warden, his friend and sworn commander, was dead.
Now the warden's daughter, too, was gone. The prison was empty and
here he was, allied with the man who killed the warden in cold blood; a
man who would lead them in a new crusade to bring death and
suffering.

He took small comfort in remembering that they were Imperial
soldiers, one and all. The warden gave his life to prevent a costly battle
between their guards and Jarvin's soldiers. All the while, a common
enemy was building in strength. Uniting to eradicate this threat was a
cause he would gladly sacrifice his life to achieve.

There would be worse days to follow so long as men like Jarvin
stepped in to lead, but Cergath vowed that if it brought them victory,
then the price of that victory was all he had left to honor.

"Reporting in, ser."

"Sanders?" Cergath turned to see his second-in-command salute with a wide grin. Behind her, many of the prison guard saluted and stood at attention.

"Captain Jarvin sends us with his regards."

"Where is the captain?"

"With the rest of our troops, preparing to attack."

"Without speaking to me first?" he said, stunned. His report to Jarvin had been brief and without detail. An enemy encampment underground was not a place to rush into blindly.

Sanders must have seen the alarm on his face. "The captain intends to smoke them out by lighting fires at the entrances. He ordered us not to go inside."

"Fires? With what?"

"Well, with some of our tents, supplies and…" she looked around uneasily. "The Empress has issued an edict. She sends word through the Imperium that we are now blessed with some kind of gift. They call it magic. It comes to the worthy through Her will, and brings us victory today and in all the days to come. Today, the captain tells us we will be blessed with fire in the desert." Though the woman's words were hesitant, she spoke with a hushed reverence.

Magic. The warden had used that word with disdain and mistrust, as something to be cast aside. Herbert had shown him the darker side of magic, and to hate and fear those who used it. Now the Empress herself proclaimed it a good and righteous thing.

He looked at his guards. Good and decent Imperials to the last, ready to do their duty. They did not understand this magic blessing and yet they embraced it as a promise of their victory. He knew it to be a curse, yet it was blasphemy to reject the proclamation of a holy gift.

Battling his aversion and disgust in silence, he touched a hand to his heart. "The Blessed Empress touches us with Her Divinity to aid us in our time of need. We are Her chosen."

"Her Blessings are known," replied the guard in unison, mirroring him.

Cergath looked around, and noticed that Herbert was gone. The man must have snuck away while he watched the soldiers arrive. But a killer would not escape punishment so easily, he would make sure of that.

"Sanders, have you seen the man who traveled with me from the prison?"

"Who, healer Tanasen?" said Sanders.

The irony of that title made him furious. "Yes. Him. I want him by my side for the battle." He would have to keep an eye on Herbert until he could force a confession in front of captain Jarvin.

Sanders looked confused. "Are you injured, ser? From what I heard, he was allowed to take command of the other healers."

"He spoke with Captain Jarvin, then. What did he say to the man?"

"Ser, I was there only a moment to take orders," said Sanders, shading her eyes as she looked around to wave over a silent stranger. "We should get into position. Captain Jarvin sent a scout with us who found a foothold in the cliffs thanks to new information."

He barely heard her words. If Herbert confessed without him there the captain could easily forgive him without knowing the full extent of the man's dangerous nature and his, his filthy magic. That could not happen. He would not allow it.

"Follow the scout," he said. "Go to the cliffs and have him return to Captain Jarvin for me. I will meet you there."

"Ser?"

"That's an order, Sanders."

She straightened. "Honor in battle."

"Honor and victory."

He would bring Lena's killer to justice. He would not, could not allow freedom without consequences. It was unacceptable.

The thought of finding Herbert and Captain Jarvin kept the preparations for battle far from his mind. He sensed rather than saw the soldiers around him. All he would say was the captain's name, following the pointing hand or shrug to the next Imperial. It was the hottest part of the day, and there was no shade. Sweat gleamed on their reddened faces. Cergath had spent half his life in the Wastelands, and felt neither the heat nor the sting from blowing sand.

He was a man carved by the desert, honed by the hunt. When he saw the command tent he made no effort to think through what he would say to Captain Jarvin for sending his company into the cliffs on their own. It was just as well. The effort would have been wasted. No one was inside the tent.

Cursing, he shoved the canvas flap aside and found the nearest soldier. Badly sunburned, the man yelped as Cergath caught him by the arm. "Where is Captain Jarvin?"

"Give ye a bleedin' silver t'find him," the man whined, looking around them. "Been waitin' fer ages."

"Try the healer's tent," he said, the idea occurring to him as he said it.

Another large tent was in sight of where they stood. Its blue-dyed folds flew wildly as a few soldiers struggled to hammer the tent pegs back into place. He followed the soldier until something caught his attention.

He froze. A figure ducked out from behind the tent. The man did not look over his shoulder and took off, running toward the cliffs, blue cloak billowing.

"Not so fast," he muttered. He broke into a run. Fists clenched, he forced his breath to slow and match his even strides.

Herbert had a head start, and his pace was hard to match. Cergath knew that there was little chance he would catch the man before he disappeared underground. That didn't slow him down. Anger kept him moving, his body pushed to the limits of its endurance.

The Imperial tents and soldiers were a safe distance from the cliffs. At least Jarvin had the sense to make sure the Blades were unable to drop rocks or worse upon their heads. It took little time for Herbert to reach the first series of sandstone piles, and Cergath ducked behind an outcrop just in time to avoid being seen.

He had to take a drink and wipe the sweat from his brow. When he looked again, his spirits sank. An empty expanse of rock. Herbert was gone.

"Curse it," he pounded a fist against the nearest rock. The very thought of giving up now was repugnant. He climbed to where he lost sight of Herbert and examined the rockface. It didn't take long to find a crevice just large enough to allow a person entry. He could still make out the faint sound of scraping boots, and unlike the soft shoes that the Blades took to wearing, these left a mark where the stained leather had rubbed away. Cergath climbed back into the Blade stronghold.

~

IT WAS A FAINT SENSATION. Herbert knew it was there, yet it hovered at the edge of his awareness like a biting insect. His staff.

It was there, he knew it was there. Tantalizing and teasing and just out of reach. Was this a trap? A test? The ache of missing a part of himself brought his imagination to life in a paranoid fantasy that he could still rescue and repair it.

There was only one way to find out. He had to go back. And for that, he had to get away from Captain Jarvin as quickly as possible without suspicion.

When the captain saw him enter the command tent, he sneered. "Yer pardon, lordship, but ye'll have t'leave and return t'Falden or wherever else ye call yer home. I ain't responsible fer nobility, see. The Blessed Empress will be havin' my head if I let ye come t'harm."

Herbert let the words sink in, forgetting his annoyance at the strange, almost comedic use of a noble title. It was strange how eager he was to leave for home until someone told him he could not stay. He would have been all too happy to leave, but on his own terms, and not without his staff. A league of soldiers would not keep him away.

"Leavin' when I ought t'serve is a violation of my duty, Captain. The healer's oath I took goes beyond some noble title and protection." It was a bald-faced lie, but Herbert hoped it was enough to win his freedom.

The untrained son of a noble house had no place in battle, that was true. But a healer was a rare commodity. While soldiers could dress a minor wound, a healer could prevent dozens of deaths or cure a spreading sickness that could cull a thousand men in days. Healers were worth their weight in silver.

Avarice glinted in Jarvin's eyes. "As ye wish," he said. "We've few healers, that's fair certain."

They were interrupted by the arrival of two soldiers dragging a young boy between them. The boy's head lolled to the side. He looked unconscious until he sprang into life with a cry, pulling a small curved blade from where it hid in a shirt sleeve. Jarvin caught the boy by the throat, but not before the dagger cut into his arm with a wild swing.

Jarvin laughed. His fingers tightened as the boy choked. Eyes rolling into the back of his head, the dagger fell and Herbert plucked it from the sand, putting it safely out of reach.

Herbert made to inspect the cut.

The captain shook his head. "Ain't bad enough t'bother."

With a smile of delight, Jarvin threw down the captive and knelt to plant a knee firmly on his chest, waving the other soldiers out of the tent. He uncorked a waterskin and poured its contents over the boy's face. A scent that reminded Herbert of ripened peaches poured onto the sand. With a wheezing howl the boy came back to life as he tried to wipe it from his eyes.

Jarvin leaned until his weight induced coughing, then a desperate silence. "That's better. Listen t'me, lad, fer I've little time at the moment."

His own dagger was smaller than the Imperial blade that Herbert saw most soldiers wear. He was surprised to see the captain's blade stained with blood and filth when he drew it. The boy's eyes widened.

"D'ye ken who I am?" Jarvin asked, his voice low and pleasant. Not waiting for an answer, he slowly tore a piece of the boy's shirt until it exposed his belly. "I left a man t'die in a pool of his own blood. They called me the red butcher fer it. I liked the name, ye ken, so I kept it."

He lowered the blade of the dagger. A trickle of blood ran down the boy's side. Herbert wanted to look away but a sick fascination kept him frozen as a silent observer.

Mouth trembling, the little spy said nothing. Tears escaped his reddening eyes. The trickle of blood quickened as the captain leaned forward, then back again so the boy could breathe.

"Best tell me where I might find a quiet way into that pile of stone over there."

Words erupted from the boy. Every breath a struggle. Each time he stopped, Jarvin sliced a small cut in the boy's side and he cursed or cried out to add detail to the directions. With a sudden sob, the Blade stopped speaking.

The blood on the sand looked different to Herbert now that it was the blood of an enemy. Pain and suffering were useful tools. The death of a single person could save thousands. Strange, he thought, the inner workings of a man like Captain Jarvin no longer seemed the mystery they once were.

What were the deaths of two people? Nothing. Dry leaves on the wind.

A hand clapped him on the shoulder. "Yer na'en a noble born, are ye Herbert Tanasen."

Herbert stiffened, but there was something new between them. Respect. "Na'en a birth or choice of mine."

"I caught as much. Yer a steady hand t'be sure. What d'ye reckon, is the lad t'be healed?"

Herbert looked at the body of the boy, or what was left of it. It was nothing to him. "Would be a waste."

Jarvin laughed, his face luminous. "That it would, man. That it would. Death, pain, we endure the mess of it all in service t'the Empress."

"Blessed Be." It was an awakening, this feeling of solidarity. This was what it meant to be a part of something more than himself, just as the needle plants relied on one another in the desert.

Jarvin dismissed Herbert with a wave and a wide smile.

Now the Imperials knew another way into the warren of tunnels, Herbert was not about to wait for it to be filled with the smoke and flames the captain described.

If he went before dark, he could return before anyone had the chance to miss him. His staff was the only piece of home that he had left in this barren place. Green and alive with a vibrancy all its own, it was the first real magic he had done for his own benefit and his alone.

It was a drink of cool water in the scorching heat. It was the one thing that could bring him comfort from all the pain that was slowly eating him alive. He had to have it back.

Cleaning up Jarvin's mess, Herbert scrubbed the blood from his hands and wiped them on the sand. The captain saw him as a tool now, one already put to use. Herbert headed toward the blue tent—the color of a healer's ward, and ducked through the back.

He ran toward the cliffs, his cloak turned inside out to show the healer's blue in case there were any questions. No one stopped him, though he hesitated and turned at the entrance to the cliffs thinking he might be followed. No one in sight.

With a sigh of relief, he snuck through the opening in the rocks that the Blade scout described right before his death. The touch of sandstone made Herbert think of Teguin; would simply being in contact with the sandstone be enough to draw notice? With anyone else Herbert would think such things impossible, but Teguin had a quiet concentration that made it surprising when he suddenly did the unexpected.

Damn him. If Teguin had only come with him they would be halfway home and in good spirits, heroes to the Imperium for uncovering the hidden den of these bandits, these cowards. Now he had to lose his best friend as well.

Soon as he had his staff, the soldiers could burn the whole place and everyone in it. His steps slowed. Without the presence of Jarvin that fragile sense of solidarity weakened.

To help others in need, that was a healer's oath. Here he was, condemning a whole cluster of folk to their deaths. Were the Blades truly less human than Imperials?

What about criminals and prisoners? He could not condemn Jameson for thinking less of those he treated at the prison unless he shared the man's beliefs. A healer's oath, did that apply to bandits and thieves? Murderers? He swallowed hard.

The darkness in the passages made no difference. Now that he was underground, the pull toward his staff was gently tugging him, stronger with every step he took. Hurry, it seemed to say. So close.

Close enough to be surprised when a blow struck him on the back of the head.

Herbert tumbled to the ground. In a vain hope that whoever wanted to bash his skull in might think him already dead, he made no effort to fight back. When a second blow failed to follow, Herbert opened his eyes.

Cergath was purple in the face. The man clutched his chest and in a moment of sheer stupidity Herbert reached for his healer's pouch, thinking only that the man would fall over dead without some tonic to help his heart. Then he realized who must have hit him.

"What're ye playin' at!" Something wet and sticky was on his hand when he touched the back of his head. If only the room would stop spinning.

"Running off the first chance you get," gasped Cergath. "Should have known you would come back to help them, to warn them, to…" the man had to stop and catch his breath.

Herbert laughed. The idea was so insane that he found no words to protest the accusation. His laughter consumed him until he, too, ran out of breath. It was a struggle to regain his balance, but he managed to stand again by leaning against the wall.

They stared at one another with wild eyes. Herbert kept his back to the wall in case Cergath decided to hit him again. Even winded the man had unnatural strength, and Herbert was no match for a fight while injured and without his staff.

A faint buzzing sensation from his staff turned into a loud whining, matching his need of it with a presence that honed his dizziness into desperation. Herbert kept one eye on Cergath and a hand on the wall to move slowly backwards. He needed that staff, now more than ever.

"What do you think you are doing?" said Cergath, staggering after him.

"I want my staff back before we burn this bleedin' place t'bits."

"Your staff… you came back for that wooden stick?" The look on Cergath's face was an insult in itself. Of course he would not understand.

"I'm touched yer stuck like a burr t'the notion I like these traitors, I truly am. Did ye decide I wanted t'warn them? See me cryin' out fer help when ye nearly bashed in my brains? Now we're almost there so I beg of ye, either finish what ye started or let me go on my way."

Cergath kicked the wall and let out a string of curse words that Herbert would have admired from anyone else. As it stood, he was fair certain that Cergath would stubbornly follow him. He didn't care. Despite a throbbing headache, he kept moving forward.

Cergath stayed close on his heels. It would be a waste of breath to point out that despite their scuffle and loud argument and a good length of time underground, no one was there to challenge their presence. They were alone.

That meant that the Blades were elsewhere, their attention focused on something more important than Imperials wandering in their tunnels. That was worrisome. Not knowing where the Blades were, Herbert felt eyes around every corner. When he got out of this place, he swore he would stay above ground for a good long while.

The staff was in a small room that felt more a storage closet than a chamber. Herbert was so attuned to the feeling of plant life in the room that he instinctively reached for the small round lamp that someone had left behind at the entrance. It came alive in his hand with such force that it exploded, sending the tiny glowing creatures flying in all directions.

Cergath made a noise of disgust and backed away. "Sand lice. Disgusting."

A burst of light was all Herbert needed. With a sigh of pure bliss, his fingers closed over the staff, now more the size of a club from that damned lizard's last meal. The remaining plants were wilted, and the missing plants would be a pain to replace. At least the heart of it was intact. It was his once again.

The sound was so faint he barely heard it. Cergath made the strangest noise, half gasp, half sigh. Attracted to the fresh greenery of the staff, the sand lice burst once again into full illumination when Herbert called for the leaves to bud and start to regrow for a bit of comfort. The lice burrowed into the staff.

Dim light shone on the woman who pulled her dagger from the

body of Cergath. Herbert knew he ought to recognize her face, though to remember why only recalled the same haze which encircled that whole cursed mess in the desert.

The woman made to step over Cergath into the room, but the prison guard was not quite dead and reached up to catch her leg. "Murderer," he choked.

"I will be, soon enough." She let Cergath slide to the floor and cleaned her blade.

A sick feeling grabbed Herbert. Cergath was looking right at him as the fire in his eyes dimmed. Whatever Raima thought, the prison guard meant him. *He* was the murderer.

The woman might have a weapon, but the advantage of surprise was gone. Finally, he had the chance to face a Blade and seek vengeance for Olivia's death. Vines and thorns erupted from his staff.

And what are you, Herbert?

Murderer.

The words of Teguin and Cergath forced their way into his thoughts as the thorns tore into Raima's arms, growing as quickly as she cut them away.

A faint smell of smoke. He needed to escape before the Imperials put their plan into action. Herbert pushed the Blade aside, and ran for his life.

BONES TO ASHES

Teguin paced the room, rubbing a crick in his neck as he stepped around the bones. He was almost used to them. With a dry crackle, he stepped on one that was badly stained and it turned to splinters under his heel. He shuddered. Almost.

"Could you feel what was inside the bundle?" he asked, trying to imagine the wounded, staggering form of Nezt as described by Master Troug.

"Not really, no. And he dared not open it to look inside. But that betrays its importance!"

Teguin wanted to believe it. He wanted more than anything to believe that it was possible to find another piece of the Relic Wars; a Greater Artifact of equal importance to the Horn of General Empreen. But he had to remain skeptical. With Troug this excited, he did not want her hopes so high that a disappointment or failure broke her spirit.

"Describe it to me again," he said.

With a sigh, she closed her eyes and leaned back against the wall. "If that will help. But Teguin, these were places that have no bearing on what you and I see today. Another time, even in the same place, might as well be another world."

"Was there anything not made of cloth or wood?" he asked.

"Scraps may be left but there's little chance we would recognize them easily, not without moving every bit of sand around us."

"What could have survived for such a long period of time? Small miracle the bones are here. Scraps of clothing that escaped flood and flames, but no. Looms are made from wood and that would long be gone. The barrels, too."

"It was pure chance they managed to find anything at all," he agreed.

"Random, thoughtless digging for a little more storage, a little more space underground, and these bones were what they uncovered. Teguin, we both know that to look for a specific, hidden magical object is work for a Seeker. We have no way of getting one here to help us."

Teguin thought of Lady Jade, but that glimmer of hope died as he remembered the woman's daughter. He had promised to find and protect Lena. How much greater would his debt be now that she was dead?

He shook his head. "We have no way of knowing that would work. Even if it was precious to the Predestine monks, that does not guarantee it would have any magic at all."

Shoving his hands into his pockets, his scalp prickled as soft black fabric rustled in his fingers. He pulled out the bag. "With everything that happened, I forgot. There was a crystal hidden inside the prison. An Imperial Seeker gave it into my care before we left."

"Let me see it." She pushed aside the remains of their meal until there was enough room on the small table.

"It had a strange hold over those who used magic within the prison," he warned as she pulled out her own black pouch. "Herbert had some kind of fit, and I think Lady Jade did too, she was barely walking when Herbert and I found her in the healer's ward. I had no problem with it, but at times it is hard for me to tell when I use magic or if I act purely out of instinct."

Teguin found it hard to say Herbert's name after word had reached him of Herbert and Cergath's escape. By now, Herbert would be nearly back at the prison. Would he travel back to Falden alone, or would he go to trial for the murders and remain at the prison?

From what Teguin saw of Cergath, the man would already have executed Herbert for what he had done to Lena if he intended to take revenge. But anger did strange things to a person. Herbert was plenty proof of that.

Pouring the contents of her pouch into an open palm, Troug rattled the pile of small black rune bones in her hand. "One of the most difficult parts of magic is the determination of when we choose to act and be a catalyst for change, and when an independent force using magic around us has an effect independent of our wishes. The lines between magic and our senses are blurred to the point where we do not see most of what happens until the act is done. Yet I wonder, Samara."

"Who?"

"Teguin, I mean. I wonder…" The small bones soared into the air and fell into her hand with a soft clatter. "There is so much we still have to learn about magic compared to our ancestors. Think of the Greater Artifacts we have yet to discover, and those that we have in our possession. From what we experience, we know the Horn concentrates any magic around it to devastating effect. To design such a weapon would take such a rare combination of skill and enchantment. Uncommon to us, but a thousand cycles ago? I am not so certain."

Teguin had found Troug remarkably lucid in the past few hours, but he did not know this Samara. It was a slip that reminded him of how fragile her condition was, and how close she could be to forgetting who and where she was. It was impossible to take back the sacrifices that his master had made for the sake of progress.

"Is the Emperor's Horn here?" he asked, eyeing the crumbled bones as if he expected a skeletal hand to be clutching it.

"Ashes above, no! I have not seen it, nor have I asked. As far as I am concerned, the further we are from that piece of Destructive magic, the better off we will be."

Teguin agreed. The last time it crossed his path, the Horn had taken his and every other scrap of magic and thrown it back at them with enough force to collapse the underground caverns of Praxis and kill a friend. Searching for another Greater Artifact was no guarantee of safety, true, but he did feel safer with a bone reader at his side.

Troug unwrapped the crystal. Caressing her rune bones, she flicked them between her fingers. These rune bones were nothing like the splintered shards of bone around them, for their polished pieces were exactly the same size and shape; they pulled in his gaze as he watched them, dark as obsidian against the paleness of her wrinkled hand.

"You never told me why your bones are black," he said.

"You never asked." Troug patted at her shirt and the table before she reached into her hair to pull down a pair of bent spectacles. As was her habit, she answered Teguin's question with one of her own. "Did you learn enough of the Relic Wars in my absence to know why we burn our dead?"

"Master Frost was never as interested in history…" Teguin started to make excuses, then stopped to think about what he knew. "We all learn about the ceremony of ashes when someone close to us dies; about our desire to cleanse the body and rise like the Imperial phoenix from the ashes." He started to place a hand over his heart as a sign of Imperial loyalty before he realized that here of all places, that was a foolish thing to do.

Life was hard in the mining town where he grew up. Turth was a small village that had a few dozen families, but held a ceremony of ashes at least once a cycle. More often, if the winter season was a bad one.

The ceremony they held at Praxis when Olivia died had the same elements, yet it was more elaborate with scented candles and herbs and fresh flowers along the altar. But that was probably Herbert's doing, Teguin remembered with a pang. His friend was—had been—devoted to the woman.

Rune bones rattled across the table. Troug and Teguin leaned in to look, Teguin not knowing what to expect. Troug was too absorbed to continue their conversation.

With a gasp, she picked up two of the rune bones and threw them again.

They fell back to the table. Vibrating, each of the rune bones snapped together, joint to joint, twisting to fit in an oscillating pattern around the crystal. One by one, the runes stood out against the blackness as their etched marks glowed.

The crystal burst into a display of light and luminous color, expanding in size and levitating above them.

Warmth fell over Teguin like a cloak. A humming filled his ears. Sweet as music, the vibrations echoed in the small chamber with enough force to resonate in his chest.

In an attempt to plant his feet, he looked down to see the ground move out of focus, his feet shifting beyond his balance to slide until he would have, should have, fallen down. But there was no longer ground beneath his feet. They were both floating toward the crystal.

It was inescapable. Shielding his eyes, he saw Troug reach for the glowing source with joyful abandon. Though he could not say why, the idea of her holding the crystal filled him with dread.

He grabbed her arm just as she touched it. Light encircled them. Blinded, he tried to call out for her and see if she was injured but no sound escaped.

Teguin's senses awoke with a vengeance. The air that pushed against him was damp and heavy as if on the edge of a rainstorm, and the sudden change in temperature, the smell of pine needles in the air, the taste of charcoal and freshly caught fish, were all drawn-in by a single breath.

When the blinding light faded, Teguin was on his hands and knees. Discomfort turned into amazement as he shook off the pine needles. Beside him, a stream ran with clear water, its rapids competing with the birdsong in the trees.

Teguin knew before he turned that a path behind him cut through those trees. If he left the stream, he would come to a cabin in the woods barely large enough for a bed and a kitchen table. His mother and father would be there waiting for him, waiting for the fish he had caught. This place was as familiar to him as the day he left. Yet he could not accept it. It was impossible for him to be here.

Such fragile creatures, said a voice, its presence a shimmer in the air that forced its way into his lungs with a pressure so intense Teguin thought it might crush him from the inside.

Such brittle bones, came the voice again, *but so long since I felt the pleasure of new memories.*

The scenery shifted around Teguin in a swirling haze until he found himself in another memory, standing on a precipice of rock beside the Imperial Palace in the capital, looking out at the sea and marveling at the endless color and the violence of its waves. It had been a thrill, glimpsing the edge of the world for the first time. The bitter salt in the air was just as hard to breathe as the mountain air, and Teguin stood far closer to the edge of the slope than he remembered. Try as he might, he could not step back.

A rush of wind hit his shoulders. He closed his eyes and expected to lose himself over the cliffs, but a new force wrapped around him from behind. Rather than topple forward, he prevailed.

Opening his eyes again, he stood in yet another memory, a dinner where he had served Earl Pedergent. Looking down, he held a plate of roast fowl bones and a bowl of cherry pits. Surrounded on all sides, the shock of these faces, vivid, yet younger by at least ten cycles than he knew them to be now, was contradictory to the last detail.

Sweat and perfumed oil dripped down his skin. Heat rose from the feasting table, every sensation more intense than he could bear.

I see the turn of the cycles brings new prosperity at last, said the voice, ripe with amusement. There was a quiet menace that carved into Teguin with its honed edge.

Enough, he wanted to say. It is too much. I cannot bear it. But the air in his lungs tightened its hold as the room spun to settle into another of his memories.

A taste of mulberry wine. Laughter and the company of a good friend spread into the firelit night, one of many spent at the Mulberry Inn. But the laughter's echo was hollow and unending. The fire burned low until he could not bear to be in the room with its burgeoning shadows. Teguin drank, but he could not lower the cup and the wine kept replenishing itself, filling more than any cup could be fashioned to hold until he was drowning in the excess of it.

It is a meager feast, these memories, but there will be more to come.

Teguin fought to stay standing. As the subverted moments faded, he sucked in a grateful gulp of air. It was wondrous to breathe again.

The pressure on his chest was still there. New awareness sunk in, and a realization brought his stiff and heavy limbs moving to the hands that pressed into his back, grasping with a weak and urgent appeal. He turned and caught Troug as she sank to the ground.

Submit.

"I will not," Troug insisted. With a whimper, she shook her head.

You forget whom you serve.

Eyes wide with terror, she pulled Teguin down until she could whisper frantically into his ear. "When I am gone, you must hide my body where no one can find it. Except my longest finger. You must take that with you, a part of my memories must live on." He pulled away and looked at her.

She tightened her grip on his hands. "Promise me you will do it, Teguin. My rune bones have to be kept safe."

"I will." Her request rang in his ears but refused to sink in fully. Her eyes had a glassy, faraway look. She was gone.

The pressure came back tenfold. Teguin clutched his head. He managed to yell but the world came crashing back into focus around them with a sharpness.

What might have been a hailstorm of broken bones floated softly to the ground as each and every bone fragment in the room crumbled into fine powder.

You dare to defy me. I will have my revenge, I swear it!

The rune bones tumbled to the floor in a heap by Troug's side, their illumined markings faded. They looked different somehow, their polished surfaces reduced to dusky charcoal.

Bone Reader, came the voice again, softer as though muffled.

The cloth. With shaking arms, Teguin dragged himself past the lifeless body of Troug to the table upon which the crystal rested. In total disregard for the chaos around it, the crystal and table were exactly the same.

Secret Keeper.

Teguin took great care to wrap the black cloth back around the crystal without touching it. The pressure in his head lessened. It was a blessed release.

He put the rune bones in the second pouch and placed it in a vest pocket. The worst part was yet to come. He had to act quickly or he knew, promise or no, he would not be able to do it. Pulling a pouch of stones from his pocket, he took out a piece of flint with a sharp edge. He straightened Troug's arm and with one quick cut, he severed her first finger.

His throat was dry as dust. The thought of what he had done, even at Troug's urging, made him sick. But he took care to wrap and put it next to her rune bones with heavy heart.

Speak to me.

Teguin shook his head in a futile attempt to silence the whispers. Every word released a little more of its hold, and he found with great relief that he could ignore the pull of that horrible voice.

He collapsed next to Troug's body. What remained was only a shell. He looked into her open, unblinking eyes one last time.

There were no words to describe his loss. Her dedication far surpassed her physical strength, and the desire to cultivate knowledge and magic made her stronger than anyone he had ever known. Without her passion and sense of purpose, he would have to continue his studies, and their work, alone.

The scars that ran along his arm radiated heat. This dimension of pain was new to him. It had been a long time since he last drained Destructive powder from his shoulder. The ring on his finger was glowing and pulsing, warning him.

He would find a healer to help him with Troug first.

No. A healer was the last thing she wanted. A ceremony to cleanse her was out of the question. He had to protect her memory and her body was, her bones were…

He sat up with a groan. White bone powder coated the floor, the bed, and it stuck like paste to his arms and legs and covered the rest of him too, he had no doubt. Probably best not to think much about that.

Troug appeared to repel the powder. There was a small halo of bone dust outlining her body, which brought up still more questions that she never had the time to answer. Teguin dragged his cloak from where it lay and shook off the dust to give her some kind of wrapping.

She deserved more than that. He braced himself when he touched her, half expecting the white paste of bone powder to do something to her, for better or worse. Nothing happened.

Brushing a hand over her eyes to close them, he bowed his head. "Bones to Ashes and Blessings upon you, Lavinia Troug."

She was heavier than he expected. Stumbling out of the room, the pain in his arm and shoulder would have to wait. He focused on a new appreciation for simply being alive. All that mattered was giving Troug a burial beyond the reach of those who would dare to touch her bones.

He did not trust that the Lexicon would understand. Teguin knew that he was in no place to understand it himself right now, but, if it was important to his master, then he would respect her wishes. He followed any passage which led deeper underground.

At some point he kicked off his boots to feel the sandstone as he went. Alone, the small comfort of sand and stone brought him serenity as he struggled to make the best of where he was and what he could find. The pounding in his head worsened.

Slipping into darker places, he was too large, the way too narrow to move with ease. There was no way to gain easy passage, so he used one of the first tricks that Troug had taught him. With no one to witness the act, he used his magic to connect with the sandstone and grind openings in the settled layers of the wall. Fissures moved in gentle curtains of fine sand as they fell open to let him pass through a collapsed tunnel.

At the end of it, Teguin squeezed through a widening crack. With his senses still heightened, the bitter and tanic odor of decaying leather was strong here. Leather?

He placed Troug's body on the floor with tender care. On the ground beside her, he found a few bare scraps of parchment, and a piece of rotten leather cord which broke apart under his searching fingers. Teguin clenched his scarred fist.

While he could not command his arm to turn into glowstone the way it did when he lost control of his magic, his scars gave off a faint red light in total darkness. The effort it took reminded Teguin of how tired he was, but he did not care. His ring burst into life in protest, and it was just enough by which to see.

There, tucked into a series of smaller cracks, was a hidden piece of the past. In his excitement Teguin almost reached in to scoop it up, but felt the ghost of a whack to the back of his head by Master Interlaken at the thought. First lesson of encountering an Artifact of unknown origin, especially if you cannot see it: do not touch it with your bare hands.

Feran would have appreciated his solution. Though the thought of his uncle coming underground into a Blade stronghold was about as likely as a carriage ride in a snowstorm. His uncle was fond of wearing specially made vests in order to carry things he did not wish others to know he had.

It was fashionable for merchants, and it was also a clever way for anyone to hide valuables they did not want to be easily stolen. Teguin had one made in a similar style to his uncle, with even more pockets. It was perfect for hiding evidence of his magic.

The pockets were made from the same black fabric that Master Frost designed to keep magical objects contained. With a few careful tugs they were easily removable. One of them held a folded piece so large that he once used it as a makeshift blanket in a pinch.

With a smile, he pulled it out and dropped it on top of the discovery. She may not be alive to see it, he thought, but Troug would be happy all the same. And if no one found this small bundle in a thousand cycles then, as a tribute to Nezt, his master would rest here in its stead. She would have liked that. There was a rightness to it.

He rewrapped the bundle as best he could. Then he took care to tuck his cloak around her body.

"I do not know in the end if you believed in the Relics or the Empress or in any higher power as cause for worship," he admitted in a low voice. "But I wish you peace in your new place of rest, and will honor your memory all the days of my life."

With that, he tucked the newly discovered bundle into his vest. When he reached the widened part of the collapsed passage, he brought out his pouch of red powder. Pure Destructive magic. The heart of his power.

This is no different than a door, he reasoned. If I can grind it into sand, I can harden it, heat, shape it into a different form if I can explain my need. How hard could it be?

He used most of what he had left to dust the wall. The heat from his arm and shoulder helped to keep his focus on what he wanted from the stone; to remember the origins of molten rock deep in the ground, to feel that presence and transform it. Heat poured off his body.

The color of red glowstone crept up his arm, twisting through his scars. His ring turned a brilliant scarlet.

"I know," he muttered to himself, "but let me do this one last thing."

Lightheaded and dizzy, he watched with deep satisfaction as the opening glowed, darkened to a deep grey, and expanded until it was a single, thick slab. "Rest well," he whispered to the stone.

A faint whisper replied.

Speak to me, and I will find you.

COLLECTIONS

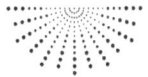

P raelor Thurst watched as Lady Jade pulled out the vial from its
silver case. The urge to grab the ink and drink it all, to smash the
glass and lick every speck of it, compelled him. He leaned forward,
then fell back against the cushions as coughing spasms shook his body.
There was such pressure on his chest his throat closed, making it
impossible to swallow as he fought panic.

"Are you sure about this?" she asked.

"Only a drop. This is all that is left. You are not to give me any
more, no matter how much I beg for it." How disgusting, that he was
grateful to be weak. Such weakness was the only thing keeping him
from losing control.

He could not fail. If he failed, all those books and manuscripts, all
those binding spells would be for nothing. In order for this to work, he
had to amass as much magic as he could to strengthen his hold on this
world.

His mind was clear, but the tightness of his breath kept him from
sleep and slowed his chances of recovery. Time was running out. This
pathetic excuse for a body would no longer hold him back.

"Bring in the next," he said.

Beside him, Lady Jade fingered a silver necklace with a large crystal pendant. A line of rope bound each string of prisoners, whose bruised and bloodied faces stared at them with fear in their eyes. Jade paced, and a line formed on her delicate brow as she examined each one of them. Some she dismissed right away, while others kept her occupied for long moments as she tilted her head, stepped back, and considered something that only she could see.

"Extraction," she said.

They all looked the same to Thurst; empty shells.

"Extraction," she said again.

The next one was a woman, bound, but in a prison guard's uniform.

"What is this?" he asked.

"Caught in an attempt to help the prisoners escape," said Jade, her voice dismissive of the question as she considered the woman. "Interesting. There is something to explore here. Move her closer, open her mouth."

The woman struggled, her mouth forced open for when Lady Jade let a single drop of ink fall from the vial onto her tongue. Thurst watched for any reaction, expectant, daring to hope.

Lady Jade tapped the top of the crystal vile against her lips as she waited.

The prison guard coughed, choking. Her face turning an ugly shade of blue. She collapsed.

Jade picked up and moved a larger crystal vial in front of the woman, kneeling. She pushed on the woman's stomach to release her dying breath. Then she quickly put the stopper on and nodded.

Thurst saw nothing but an empty vial. "Well?"

Jade sighed. "Not as promising as I hoped, but I saved what I could."

The soldiers dragged away the body.

"This is taking too long," he said, "we need to quicken our pace."

"To do that we need more ink, which we do not have. Do we?"

He tried to swallow. "If I did, it would be gone by now."

"Bring in more prisoners," said Jade, turning her attention back to the bound men and women.

"This is the last of them, milady," said one of the soldiers, keeping their eyes on the floor.

Jade considered those who remained. "Extraction, extraction, extraction, and wait." She squinted. "Is there anything to you at all? I thought I sorted through these already. Ah well, if there is nothing to take, then send this one to the Borderlands, I am certain a labor camp would take him."

When Lady Jade mentioned any other sources of ink, Thurst licked his lips, recalling the manuscripts and books whose ripped pages lay in a pile, the ink sucked away. He forgot how sensitive she was to unbound magic, and how sloppy his own weakness had made his actions of late. He dismissed the soldiers.

There were difficult choices still to be made. He was not prepared to confide in Jade about everything. The woman was crafted from the same metal as he, and he knew full well the power of a fresh, younger mind.

His experiments over the cycles had brought him so close to resurrecting the forgotten laws of magic. Those who refused to help him he bound to his will. With patience and persuasion, he was able to extract magic, and concentrate it to supplement his power for moments he needed it the most.

Now that his body was failing him, his magic was almost gone. He needed to take the next step. Not even death would stop his plans.

PROOF OF NOTHING

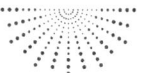

Luther gulped down the water in his flask. "It was nothing," he said, wiping his mouth with a ragged sleeve. He only wished he could remember why Bregt was so concerned.

"Nothing," replied Bregt, overemphasizing the word. "What is this… no-thing."

"What, the word?"

"Yes. There is some-thing; always, there is a thing. One thing, many things, but no-thing?"

The question was such a basic one that Luther was at a loss how to explain. He clutched at the reins. All he had to do was keep the horse moving forward without falling off.

"Put a hand in your pocket," he said when he was able to think about the question. "What is in your pocket?"

Bregt pulled out a piece of wood, the bare carved outline of a horse taking shape. "For my daughter," he explained with a sheepish smile.

He could not resist smiling at the sweet gesture. "What else?"

There was a wrapped piece of dried meat, a small carving knife, and both joined the wooden toy. Bregt looked over them. "These things."

"Good. Now what is in your pocket?" Luther pressed a finger into his head to try and relieve the pressure that kept stealing away his focus, making him forgetful of where he was.

Bregt put his hand back inside the pocket. "My hand."

"And?"

"My hand."

"Well, take out your hand. Now, what is in your pocket?" Bregt started to put his hand in again but Luther shook his head. "No no, I mean no hand, and no-thing," he emphasized the first part of the word." It was like reasoning with a child. A child the size of a small house.

Bregt thought for a moment. "No-thing. This is a strange word."

"But why?" he said, baffled.

"How can you know what is there? If my hand is in my pocket, then my hand is there. But with no hand, how do I know what is in my pocket to answer you?"

"I…" Luther paused. This was a more difficult question to answer than he realized. His heart was pounding so hard he could feel it in his throat. Faint dizzy spells faded in and out as sunlight cut through the lingering smoke. So thirsty.

"Where are we going now to find this proof of yours?" asked Bregt.

Luther hesitated. Was he supposed to be leading them? He no longer remembered.

There was no proof. Was there? His thoughts were a cascade of what to tell and what to hide and, most importantly, how to explain so that the Dunmiri might understand.

He was a Seeker, not an Imperial spy. He knew nothing about encampments and where the Imperial patrols would ride. The attacks may not even come from the patrols. Should he tell Bregt there was no proof?

The trust he had with the man was tenuous at best. He would not risk breaking it unless he had no other choice. Choice was a strange word. He rarely had the luxury of choosing anything.

The threat was magic. His frustration brought him back to the fundamental problem of telling the absolute truth. Perhaps a demonstration of magic would be enough.

Even the mark of the Praelor was an ink stain, a faded mark. It would not help him prove that magic existed. Hiding it had been a useless gesture, after all.

He needed to find something; that was plain. He pulled out his scrying crystal, a cluster of clear stone which pointed upward as he held it in the palm of his hand.

Scrying for magic required intense concentration. It was like viewing a world of vivid detail, colors and textures almost painful to witness. In people, it always seemed slightly out of focus. Luther did not have the gift of reading a person like some Seekers, but he could find objects crafted with magic, even if they were hidden.

A gentle tugging sensation pulled at him to change his direction. It might turn out to be a longer journey than the tolerance of the Dunmiri, he thought with a sinking feeling in his stomach, but he had little choice.

He clutched the crystal, and nudged the horse to the right, half expecting his mount to turn back, or refuse to move. "This way," he said.

To his great relief, the horse obeyed. Bregt moved to follow. "Scythia will stay to clean up the mess she made," he said. "She will ride to join us. My mother does as she wishes."

"Imagine my surprise," Luther muttered under his breath.

Leaving Scythia behind, but not for long. He was certain she would return. All he could think of was what that woman might do to him if he failed to give her satisfactory proof.

The Praelor was so far away that his punishments began to look like the better option. The smell of smoke and charred bodies followed them as a reminder of Scythia's return, and as they rode away from what remained of the Imperial village he worried that it would not be the last to fall under Scythia's wrath.

THE COST OF VICTORY

Herbert raised his shortened staff in the air, joining the swords of the soldiers in a cheer. Victory was theirs. No captives, no sign of survivors.

He passed the other healers who served in the Imperial legion, all were smiling and laughing while bandaging a few burns for the Imperials who got too close to the flames. Those were the only wounded.

In the moments leading up to the fight, word spread of how Herbert found and reported the location of the Blades. He tried to correct the first soldiers that approached him, but the sudden death of Cergath meant nothing to them. It was a strange feeling to be admired and cheered by a group of strangers.

The respect and acknowledgement as a brother in arms brought him back to the command tent with a feeling of elation. Was this a vision of the future; a magic-filled world, where no Imperial soldiers lost their lives and the Empress let those with gifts move freely and use it in her name? He would pledge himself for a lifetime of battles if they were all like this.

"That's fine work, Tanasen," said Jarvin, looking up from a map, nodding with approval. "Yer a hero, bringin' these vermin what they deserve. The full weight of the Imperium down on their heads is a clear sign we've Her Blessin' this day. Far as I'm concerned, it's all thanks t'yer loyalty. I expect half the Imperium will hear of it on our return."

Herbert's grin slipped. This was all Cergath's doing, not his. He remembered his promise to Cergath like a dream, like so many other painful memories he wanted to forget.

"What's the matter, man?" said Jarvin, handing him a flask. "We ain't a soldier gone exceptin' that prison guard friend of yers."

"Friend? Captain, we barely bent the grass between us." The flask contained a sweet wine that was a giddy delight to drink after missing a few meals.

Jarvin laughed. "Bent the grass, is it? Yer a Falden man right enough. Reckoned that the first time we spoke. I used t'plough the fields at Eldenwerst, out near Ferncliff. Which patch are ye?"

"Far t'the south," said Herbert. "Almost clear t'the Eigel wash, but ye'll see Waith and the Ash Mount as well if the weather's right."

Herbert passed back the flask. The sweetness of it stuck in his throat as Cergath overshadowed their celebration. He knew that if he was going to tell Jarvin about Jameson and Olivia—no, Lena, and how they died he would do it now, in this moment, or he would never speak of it again.

What good was a promise to a dead man, he reasoned. Nothing would come of it. Why would a man like Jarvin even care how two strangers came to die in the desert? People died every day by wandering in the Wastelands; it was a dangerous place.

Teguin and Cergath must both be dead now for all he saw underground. He could leave all the pain and sadness behind him.

"Pity about yer other travel companion. Ye said he was gone. Captured, was he?"

Herbert nodded. He had not told anyone of Teguin's betrayal. What did it matter, when the man had paid for the change in loyalty with his life? There was nothing Herbert could do about it now.

Jarvin passed the flask. "Least I can do is send ye back with an escort until we've orders of our own t'march home. What'll yer plans be, then. Back to greener pasture?"

"First there's a trip t'the Blue City I've been avoidin'," Herbert admitted. "Then home again fast as I can."

"Avoidin', eh? Ever been t'the capital?"

Herbert shook his head. Between the heat of the day and Jarvin's flask of wine he was sweating through his shirt. His stomach growled, and his fingers wandered up and down his staff as he weighed whether or not Jarvin would be afraid of seeing new magic if he had something to eat from it. The man had seen magic in battle that day. But what else, and what kind?

Hungry was hungry, he decided. The top of his staff bulged and bloomed as the tent went slightly out of focus. New branches erupted from the top of the staff and bore fully formed apples while their skin shone as if polished. *Empress Bless*, how he missed the feeling of trees around him. A faint scent of blossoms hung in the air.

Jarvin went pale. "Ashes above. That's a sight."

Herbert tossed the man an apple and tried not to think of all the times Teguin had stood with him just like this. "Tastes better than it looks."

Jarvin rolled the apple in his hands. "A real, damned piece of fruit in the desert. Yer a handy man t'have around, Tanasen. This magic of ours, it'll bring our enemies down on their knees. Ripe fer the slaughter."

Herbert plucked another apple from the heart of his staff and bit into it. Lips tingling from the tartness of the juice, he smiled. An end to hidden magic. He could get used to this.

MARKED

Alone sand ray rose and fell upon the dunes. The distant cliffs were nothing more than a somber haze, softened by smoke. If not for the circumstances of their escape, the ride would have been a thrill for Teguin.

The survivors from the Imperial attack fit on this one creature. Hundreds of Blades had been left behind, entombed beneath the smoking cliffs. It was a horrible and efficient way to die and be buried. Master Troug would have unexpected company after all.

Their movements turned ripples of shifting sand from one dune into another. Their passage was not something to track, Teguin thought. He hoped.

Raima's bloodied wrists kept catching his eye. The wounds were distinct and unmistakable. Herbert was the only person he knew who could use thorny vines as a weapon.

"It is no trouble," Teguin said to Raima. "I've some bandages left and—"

"Save it for someone who needs it." Her words were clipped and her hands gripped the top of the ray's mouth as she leaned forward to check the beast for some sign unfamiliar to Teguin.

"There is no shame in being surprised by someone with magic," he said, stating what he thought was an obvious point.

She released the animal to snatch her dagger from its sheath. It glowed in her hand and blinded him, he had to look away. He heard a hissing sound and when the brightness faded, he saw burn marks around her wrists.

"You think I need your advice about magic?" she said, eyes flashing. "I grew up with the Lexicon. She was like an older sister. I walked beside her as she made her own legion of followers, all magic wielders."

"Where are they now?"

"Dead, mostly. Or in hiding." She put away her dagger and with a lurch, the ray rose up from where it sank in the sand. "Go and play with your pebbles elsewhere, Dorst."

Teguin flinched. He looked down at his hand where he flipped three or four small stones between his fingers. Damn river stones. Always wanting to roll somewhere.

He went to put them away until he saw a little girl watching him, eyeing the stones as they drifted along the scars on his hand. A cut across her face had matted hair and dried blood twisted together. Blinking, she kept shutting her eyes and wiping her hand across her face, swaying from the motion of the ray.

One of the river stones stayed out as he opened what was left of his healer's pack. He searched until he found a small bit of sticking plaster beneath the clearmoss that had saved his life from the smoke underground. Flicking the river stone through the air, it spun and hovered in front of the girl just as it would in a river's current. She gasped.

"Go ahead," he said. "You can touch it."

She reached out a finger and it danced away from her. She made a small sound of wonder and pulled back.

"Reach out your hand," he said.

Her fingers opened until the stone had enough room to settle in her palm. He was pleased to see it fit well. By then he was close enough to take a look at her face. She needed to see a healer, that was plain. They all did.

"You can keep it if you hold still," he said gently.

Enamored with her new prize, the girl closed her eyes and ran her fingers over it again and again while he worked to wipe the blood from her face. The patch was too small to do much, but it kept the wound from opening further.

"There," he said. "Better?"

She pulled at his sleeve until his arm wrapped around her.

"She wants you to pick her up," said Raima from behind him.

"Oh," he said, flushing. "I'm not very good with children." The little girl climbed onto his leg and then settled herself into the crook of his arm with a sigh. He looked around. No one spared a glance for the girl. If she had any family alive, they were elsewhere.

The girl was light as a piece of silk his arms, her little heart beating against his chest as he tried to keep the worst of the sun off her face. How many children had died today? The attack had been savage. Intentional. Innocent lives brought to the bloody mercies of Jarvin.

Herbert must have known what would happen. What would he do next, and when would he realize that all of this was his fault? They both knew what kind of man Captain Jarvin was, yet Herbert lost no time in summoning that bloody butcher.

Teguin was at war with his own feelings. Would he be happy to learn that Herbert was alive, even if he was responsible for bringing the Imperial troops down on their heads? It would be easier to let his anger erase their friendship, but he wanted to know why Herbert and Cergath caused so many to die.

He knew he could reconcile why his closest friend had murdered two people. A loss of control. Magic could bring out the worst in people. All he could do now was focus on getting the survivors to a safe place.

After the encounter with the crystal, Teguin continued to notice his surroundings to a distracting degree. The child's hair told their story in blood and smoke, the matted ends tickling his chin every time she moved. Heat floating off the sand, a relentless fire washing over them without mercy.

He shifted the girl from one arm to the other and moved his legs to find a more comfortable position in which to sleep. The rolling motion from the ray was a comfort, yet his empty stomach was a poor companion. He pulled more of his shirt to shield his new friend.

A tugging from beside him made him jerk away. Raima was kneeling and pulling on his shirt. She wore a look of concentration that alarmed him. "What is it?"

"Your shoulder," she said in awe. "You bear a marking of the old language." She traced a strange line along where his swollen shoulder bore its red stain, then pulled away.

A tremor ran through Teguin. The whispers were few and far between but the crystal in his pocket was pressing into his leg, leaving him breathless with fear.

The sand ray shifted down to dive and with a curse, Raima slid back to the crest of its mouth once again. He dared not look at her, but as he rolled away he could feel her eyes burning into his shoulder as they moved deeper into the heart of the desert.

BY THEIR SILENCE

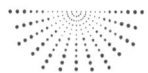

The Lexicon threw open the door and her glove scraped against the heavy stone with a shriek of protest. "What do you mean by letting our people wander in the desert? We are under attack and there are wounded. They may be dying!"

One of the elder monks lifted a hand and she fell silent, fuming. How dare they treat them this way in the wake of a massacre. They had left the survivors alone to suffer.

"You must understand our position," came the weary reply. "We are cautious by necessity. Imagine the dangers of allowing an unknown group of refugees into a place kept safe only by its secrecy."

"You suspect they are spies?" she sputtered. "But these are all people of honor, those who have vowed and pledged and sacrificed to serve the Relics."

"They are fleeing an attack, yes, but saving a few survivors could bring the entire Imperial army down on our heads."

"You know the movements of the Imperial army?" The Lexicon was instantly alert and suspicious. If they knew the Imperials had a thousand soldiers moving through the desert, they had neglected to share the information. She would have warned her people, prevented the slaughter.

"We have a way of following their progress, yes."

"Yet you did not tell me." She only had news of the attack when it was over and only by overhearing a patrol report.

By the time she realized how many soldiers had gathered and where they were, it was too late. By their silence, the monks had prevented her from warning her people. Such arrogance. What gave them the right?

"It makes no difference," said another elder. "What would it do to have warning or reinforcements from yet another place in the desert? It would reveal our position or worse, our existence in exile and hiding, safe from discovery for a thousand cycles. All in a misguided attempt to save a hundred doomed souls."

"Five."

"What?"

"There were *five* hundred souls in those caverns. And more on patrol, besides. How many have you in hiding? How many women and children do you have to replace your own precious council when you pass on?" Even hooded, she could tell from their voices that every monk which sat before her was an elder in more than name.

The elder cleared his throat. "Yes, well, you must understand that we have a pledge to protect our own."

"I do not understand, Elder, but I promise you one thing: I will remember it. Those dead and in danger are your people every bit as much as those protected within these walls. Why do you deny our kinship and history as if it never existed? You have no idea," she fought to say the words, "no idea what you have lost by your decision."

"And you have no idea the value of what we have here to protect."

"Tell me, was the life of a bone reader worth your silence?"

"Wait," said a new voice. The figure rose. "You might have a Bone Reader with you? Do they have rune bones?"

"Quiet, Edel."

"Why have a Bone Reader at all?"

"Because there was a crypt," said the Lexicon, watching the weight of her words sink into their shadowed faces. "Our city, which your indifference burned to the ground, was a place of rest and meditation well before the Relic Wars. I say was because now it is either destroyed or all those bones are in the hands of Imperial soldiers who care nothing for them. Shall we guess whether they threw them in a pile or desecrated them first?"

Bones were the sacred duty of a Predestine monk. The keeping of them was a lifelong duty and what ancient bones remained held a reverence that far outweighed living flesh in their eyes.

The blind fools. Silence followed the Lexicon while she paced and tried to control her temper. For all she knew, Lavinia and Teguin and Raima were all dead and here she was, arguing with monks so out of touch they may as well be stone pillars.

The standing elder, Edel, turned to the others. "Let them in."

"But sister—"

"Let. Them. In." The words were spoken with such finality that the others shifted where they sat.

The Lexicon choked back a scream of frustration while the monks murmured and whispered like the rustling wings of insects she longed to crush underfoot.

"It is agreed," came the answer. "But escort them to the outer sanctuary. None shall descend without permission."

"I will go to meet them," she insisted.

"Bring the Bone Reader down to us."

"If they live." The Lexicon left before she could say the many other choice words that rested at the tip of her tongue. She could only hope it was not too late to save them.

TEGUIN LISTENED for the shallow breathing of the little girl. Her face was red as glowstone, and she was feverish. Without water, she wouldn't last much longer. None of them would.

Teguin leaned toward Raima and rasped, "They must have seen us by now. We need to turn our attention to water and a safe place to rest or we will not last another day."

"No." Raima tried to push away from him. She was still kneeling after two days of guiding the ray. Unwilling to move aside and let another take her place, her muscles failed her. The impact of her fall sent a shudder through the ray.

She stroked the creature's hide with a bloodied hand. She murmured an apology. It was the first time that Teguin had seen tenderness from the woman. When she looked up at Teguin her eyes were bloodshot, her skin as cracked and raw as his felt.

"You do not understand," she said. "There is no water here. Not unless the monks share it with us. It is to them we go for help."

"And if these monks do not—"

"Then we die, here, at the bidding of the Relics."

"The Lexicon will fight for us," said an older woman with bloodshot eyes. "She will send help."

"We are forsaken," wailed another. "The Relics want a sacrifice. They want us all to die."

"Look there!"

Up ahead, a pile of clothing revealed a corpse half-buried in the sand.

Raima swore. As they grew closer to pass it Teguin understood why; the man had died the previous day and all they could do was leave him upon the sand without the decency of a proper pyre upon which to burn the body. They were riding in circles.

None of them knew where the Predestine monks were. Beyond a vague knowledge of the Shard, or the heart of the desert, there was no trace of them. The desert would keep their secrets unless the monks wished to be found.

Teguin blinked. It was an eerie sensation, hovering over the sand dunes with the heat rising to distort the world around them. Like floating in the air, or riding at the edge of the sun half blind and crazed with thirst. In the distance, the blurred edges of a sand ray reflected back at them.

He blinked again. It was another sand ray. Not an illusion, real. Their own sand ray tremored.

Raima snapped back to attention.

Teguin tried to move his legs, but they were numb from being locked in the same position for so long and he feared dropping the girl. His bare feet were swollen. When he tried to wiggle his toes the only feeling that returned made him wish they were numb again.

"It is the life after death," murmured someone behind him. "Come to greet us for our journey."

There was a wail, a chorus of moans. The child in his arms whimpered and covered her ears.

"Relics be praised," said Raima.

Teguin saw it, too. Sunlight glinted off the metal glove of the Lexicon like a silver beacon.

"We must not stop," he warned Raima. "You told me the sand ray may not move again if it rests."

"I know what I said," she snapped. "I will keep it moving, and sacrifice a drink of water to the sands in its honor if it should fall."

How could the woman justify such a waste? So great was his thirst that he could barely breathe. But the ray that waited for their arrival shuddered and rose to move away from them, swooping to dip just low enough to taste the top layer of sand.

Both rays would be unable to dive beneath unless the riders relaxed their grip on each enormous, hollow mouth. The vibrations between the two creatures settled like a hum in his chest. It made his ears tingle, his skin itch. He distracted himself by watching the girl who was rubbing at her eyes, blinking, her mouth slightly agape as she saw the other ray floating across the sand.

She took out the river rock and clutched it, rubbing the smooth surface against her cheek. Her dry lips moved, but so little sound came out that Teguin had to lean in to hear the words.

Faster they go in a crooked row,
when they will dive again no one will know.
One and two friends with a third now in tow.
Faster they go in a long crooked row.

THE FIRST RAY dove into the sand and vanished from sight. They were moving to follow. Teguin shielded the girl as best he could in a vain hope they would stay on its back before they, too, disappeared without a trace. He expected the sand to swallow and smother them. Instead, they discovered that a large hollow space existed just a few feet underground, if they knew just where to dive.

Their ray shuddered and collapsed, sending its riders sliding off. Hands pulled at him, cool and soft with damp cloths draped over his face, his chest, his arms. He hardly felt them take the girl from him. When he murmured it was not in concern, but with relief.

Behind his closed eyes, dark sun spots flashed and filled his vision. He tried to adjust to the low light of the underground. Cool air washed over him. When he removed the cloth from his face, he pulled himself up to an impossible sight.

An entire underground city. Built from midnight blue stone, the outline drew the eye and demanded appreciation. Clean lines cut strange, angular marks into the wide columns soaring into pointed arches.

Outlines for a hundred windows filled spaces between the columns, but each looked to be sealed shut from within. Teguin knew the many shapes of stone, and he studied the construction of buildings in great detail whenever he traveled to a new place in the Imperium. While this city was strange in its style, the rules of weight and structure were no different.

These columns could not be the only foundation of such a vast expanse of walls. The foundation was not visible, and he suspected that far more of the city's splendor lay hidden beneath their feet. The city was so darkened by its burial that it would disappear against the night sky.

It was a masterpiece of construction. The stone unlike any sandstone in the Wastelands, though it vaguely resembled the same strange stone which built the Imperial Palace. How did it get here?

Teguin half-walked, half-crawled to the steps and set his hands on them, seeking a connection with the strange stone. A jolt of energy shot up his arm like a burst of lightning and knocked him onto his back. When the ringing in his ears faded, he heard a voice in his head.

Call to the bones.

Teguin clutched his belly. Ashes above, that jolt was like a kick in the ribs. He needed to sleep for a few solid days, but the strange energy from the stone had revived him like a keg of tarish brew. He wanted to run, not walk, and explore the rest of this mysterious place.

"Teguin!" A figure leaned over him, the touch of her metal glove like ice against his burned skin.

"Lexicon," he groaned, trying to sit up.

"Where is she?"

He knew who she meant. "Gone."

"Bastards," growled the Lexicon, "I will—"

"No, it was before the Imperials attacked. There was nothing I could do."

"I counted on you to protect her." Emotions transformed the woman's face. Anger, grief, frustration. It was gut-wrenching to see.

"I did, until she no longer let me."

"What do you mean?" She helped him to stand, but there was a sharpness in her voice when she pulled him close to whisper, "Do you have her rune bones?"

Of all the questions he expected, this one took him completely by surprise. "Her rune bones?"

"Not so loud! Do you have them?"

"She entrusted them to me."

His answer brought a change to the Lexicon. She pulled away. Her expression transformed. He knew that look. His uncle would walk into a trade negotiation looking like that, like he was squaring off for a fight.

"Can you walk?" she asked.

"Lead the way." He could only imagine how terrible he looked, baked and scoured by the desert, preyed upon by a strange voice. The Lexicon was far from finished with him and until then, he suspected he would not rest.

She handed him a flask of water. "Drink it slowly, and come with me."

He hobbled after her, taking each step with a new appreciation for the boots he left behind. The stone beneath his feet was wonderfully cool, yet it held a harshness. Unwelcome, that was it. Like a door slammed in his face.

It was his own fault, barging in and making a connection right away, too curious to take a moment and study the place. That was careless. Reckless. Not his usual, cautious self.

He tried not to think about connecting with the strange city again, and decided it would be best to wait until he rested. It was enticing, though. They were surrounded by stone which had sand hovering to protect and hide them, encircling the city almost like a cocoon. Not buried, but enclosed.

It was an empty, restless place. He could sense this stone held more secrets than he had cycles left to live. Yet it was a comfort to know that such a place of true beauty existed in the world, and would long after he was gone. If only Master Troug could have lived to see it.

What a latent display of power. There were no signs of life. What had happened in this deserted city, built to be home for thousands?

The door they came to was guarded. Teguin looked to the Lexicon. She only waved her glove in a dismissive gesture.

"Step aside."

"Only the Bone Reader shall pass," came the reply.

"We bring word of the bone reader," said the Lexicon.

The door opened. "I will escort them to the chamber."

It was a woman's voice, but Teguin could see nothing of her form or face beneath the strange clothing she wore. Was it a mask, or merely a hood which cast a shadow over her face? He kept a respectful distance but there was a strangeness to the woman, to these monks, that put him on edge.

Through the door, a smell of decay surpassed even the archives of Master Lingermort at Praxis. This was a place of death and shadows, of silence and mute stone. The room they entered took his breath away.

The murals at Praxis were one thing, but the reliefs here stood out to him even in the low light. He was so distracted that he failed to notice they were not alone in the room, and would have walked right past the other hooded figures if one of them had not spoken.

"You honor our hall. We are the Elders, leaders of the Predestine monks. This may mean little to you, Bone Reader, for you look young in your journey, but we hope in time you will—"

"Oh, but I am not..." Teguin shot a nervous glance at the Lexicon, who crossed her arms and stood there without any indication of assistance. Negotiations was putting it lightly. He was a pawn in this game, and had no intention of being drawn into a bitter rivalry between the Blades and these monks, whoever they were.

"I am no bone reader," he said, touching a hand to his heart. "That was my master. I regret, that is, she is no longer with us."

"But this is terrible!"

"We are lost once again."

"Do you have her body? Without rune bones, they cannot—"

"That is enough," said a voice beside Teguin. Their escort glided past him. "We cannot bring back the past. Do you not sense it, brothers and sisters?"

She turned to face him. "You have rune bones. And what is the abomination you harbor? It taints the very air we breathe."

Teguin could feel the weight of his crystal, stretching the fabric, struggling for release. They felt the presence of the rune bones and the crystal, even through the black fabric that shielded them? Master Frost would be very interested to know that.

He knelt and pulled the black bundles from his pockets. The finger, he kept hidden, for they did not ask for it. They might have her rune bones, but until he knew what they planned he would not reveal he had a part of the bone reader.

"Do you know what it is?" he asked as he put down the crystal.

"I only wish we did not. The sight of it is as unwelcome as the heaviness it brings to this hallowed place. But perhaps it is better to have it here, within grasp, rather than let it into the hands of one who might wield it." The look Edel gave him at the last words made him want to slink away in shame.

"What are your intentions with our people?" said the Lexicon, breaking her silence. "If you claim no interest in the Blades and our mutual survival, we will take our leave, with everything we brought. You show little interest in our goals or our wellbeing so we will go. You will never see us again."

Teguin had some idea that these rune bones were important, but he wished he knew what game the Lexicon was playing.

Another of the elders stirred as she reached for the black wrappings. "Your intentions elude us, Lexicon, but we cannot deny there is some small truth to your earlier words. Our paths are intertwined. No matter how much we find your violence distasteful, we cannot have you leave with those."

"Is that a threat?" murmured the Lexicon. Her metal glove tightened into a fist.

Teguin knew that the crystal was new to the Lexicon. She had no idea that it was the cause of Master Troug's death, but she saw the way the monks reacted to it and perhaps she, too, sensed its power. Their reaction was one of caution and alarm. Clearly they knew more about it at a glance than he did by having it travel in his pocket.

Should he have left the crystal behind? It had a hold on him despite everything that it did to both him and Master Troug. The crystal was an unknown danger to the Lexicon, but what little he had learned had turned him into an ally of these monks.

"There is no reason for us to leave," he said. "By now the Imperial soldiers will think that we are all dead. Why change that when we can combine our knowledge and preserve what we found? Though the bone reader is no longer with us, I know she would want us to stay and explore this special place, a living part of our history. It will honor her memory."

He saw what the Lexicon could do with Greater Artifacts. If this crystal was one of those, then he wanted to know more about it. These monks seemed to sense its power in a way that impressed him. If they knew more of the past, then think of what he could discover about magic if he stayed with the Lexicon and the monks together.

"It is rare to see an outsider honor the memories of the dead," remarked one of the elders.

"Not as rare as you might think," said the Lexicon.

"The crystal must be protected at all costs," said another.

"If you stay," said Edel, "we will make your people welcome. But they will follow the path of the Predestine monks, not the Blades."

"An alliance requires allowances on both sides," said the Lexicon. "We wish to know of the outside world, and we will learn your ways, but leave when we are ready."

"You leave us time and again, and now you return. Is that not lesson enough?"

The Lexicon snapped her teeth into a smile that made Teguin's skin crawl. "Your word, Elders."

"We require more time. But we will discuss the details of this alliance you offer."

Teguin's eyes fell back to the crystal. "I would like to study your archives while I am here, and continue the work of Master—the, er, the bone reader, by researching what she shared with me before her death. Would that be possible?"

There was a long pause. "If you study our ways, and have the utmost respect and care, we will honor the trust that your master placed in you. In exchange, you will allow the use of these rune bones. Until our alliance is final, you will be brought to rooms while your people will be well looked after where they are."

The Lexicon gave a short bow. It was odd to Teguin, watching someone other than his uncle negotiate like this. There were striking differences. The Lexicon used threats and power plays, whereas Feran preferred to charm and bribe in order to get what he wanted.

When their escort led them to rooms, the Lexicon refused to leave until she had a word with him. As soon as the door shut behind them, she whirled around. "Teguin, I hope you realize that this is a dangerous place. Do not trust these monks."

"Lexicon, I can safely say that the only thing that interests me right now is sleep, the chance to live another day, and honoring the memory of Master Troug. When you care to share your plans with me, I will gladly listen. Otherwise, I am going to bed."

The only reply the Lexicon made was to turn and storm out of the room. Under other circumstances, he might have laughed at the irony. A few weeks ago he would have readily fought the Lexicon rather than listen to her advice. With Herbert and Master Troug gone, he would have only his instincts upon which to rely. That meant he was in a whole lot of trouble.

He rubbed his shoulder and winced as heat coursed through his fingers. What was he going to do about this rune mark? He remembered the way Raima reacted when she saw it, but without a mirror glass he could not see the change. It was never a simple matter to ask a healer for a second opinion when magic was involved. Without Herbert, he would have to fend for himself.

Bone Reader.

Teguin jumped. That voice again. He assumed, even hoped, that with the crystal out of his hands the voice would also vanish. His heart sank as the whisper came again.

Secret Keeper.

"At least we agree on one thing," he muttered.

Taking off his vest, he pulled out the long black bundle from a deep side pocket. There was a rustle of parchment. Teguin opened the fabric and watched the flutter of frost-grass paper, each page so fine that he could see his hand on the other side as he leaned forward, absorbed in this new discovery.

He had never seen such a delicate example of writing outside of Master Lingermort's archives. An unfamiliar language ran across the page. Another mystery he would have to solve on his own. He tucked it carefully back into his vest.

To find such a treasure in the wake of Master Troug's death left him with no time to see what Nezt tried so desperately to hide before his death. Now, he would have the time. And with it, pay tribute to the last sacrifice of his Master by reading every last word.

THE DEATH OF PATIENCE

F eran tugged at where brambles caught his roughspun clothing. He eyed the cave entrance, then pulled up the hood of his cloak and waited.

A low fog lapped at his bowed shoulders and fell to cover the mountainside in mist. His skin itched like Denari fire ants. Damp and cold, two things he hated. Yet here he was, crouching in the muck and frozen ground and bending the knee to the wilderness. He hated this place.

Even the cloth he pulled from his pocket to wipe his face was damp. The thought of a hot bath and the finespun linens of his bed only made his surroundings worse. He was getting too old to travel the roads of the Imperium.

Longing for the comforts of home, he prepared a list in his head of all the luxuries he would enjoy upon his return. All his life he had worked to regain the privileges of his childhood and the noble class into which he was born, but while wealth had returned with tireless work, the privilege was gone. Stolen. Just out of reach and kept locked away by others who sought to punish him.

Once, he had thought that wealth alone would soothe his wounded pride. Now he knew better. Wealth was not enough. It never would be.

He craved the respect that other noble houses owed him. He had worked too hard to be excluded from court and treated like some kind of filthy cur.

Dawn streaked through the gnarled trees. Quickly—too quickly for his liking, light brought the brush around him into sharp relief. Feran tensed at the sound of snapping twigs.

He struggled to pull the dagger at his side. With a chirp, a bird took wing at the sight of him crouched in the underbrush of its home. Feran silently added roast fowl to the list, just under a hot bath and a soft bed.

How much longer could a man stay underground? Was he mistaken about the cave entrance? No. He was certain there was only one.

Words were like charms to Feran. He used them well but when that failed? Well, why waste them on deaf ears?

He froze. A scraping echoed up from the cave. He held his breath as he watched the entrance.

Dropping a pickaxe and bucket, blinking against the dawn as if shocked to see sunlight once more, a creature of darkness and shadow emerged, made strange by the sweat and dirt and mud that coated his body with filth. A thrill of horror passed through Feran. The cold metal of his dagger slid smoothly from its place of hiding. The time for words and threats and promises was over.

Feran crept forward. Silent and undetected, closer now until he could see the fresh scrapes and bruises along the man's arms. Lines of sweat ran down the neck in muddy rivulets.

It was remarkable how easily the dagger sank into his brother's back.

Surprise. One last breath. Freedom.

A TASTE FOR REVENGE

A hollowness held Jade in a vice. Her rage twisted and seethed like heat from burning coals. She could not accept losing her daughter without a fight; not after everything she had sacrificed.

"We have many friends in common," she said to the man in front of her.

"Enemies as well I reckon."

The man was not at all what Jade pictured. He was quiet and soft spoken. While the scars on his hands and face reflected well what she knew of his work, his mannerisms revealed a gentle soul. Jade could read people, and this man seemed to live in constant defiance of his own nature. Remarkable.

"I heard it was you who put Praxis to the flame," she said, knowing full well because of her part in it.

The man's eyes hardened with suspicion. "That was work fer a friend, not bitterness as ye may well believe."

"But that is what I need, *Burn* Bastian. Bitterness. Flames, and plenty of them." She watched his face as it transformed in shock. She named him on purpose, sure he would recognize who she was by it. Few among the Blades knew his true name, and those who did used it sparingly.

He bowed low. "How might I serve ye, great lady."

"You know Falden Province well?"

"Well enough."

"Then you will have heard of the Tanasens and their recent turn to fortune." The words caught in her throat. It was odd to be the master of someone else's fate for a change; it took a different kind of strength to be detached and remote while doing her own bidding.

Her grief was a transformation. It burned until it left her deadened. It was too much for her to bear. So she cast it out for a better master, an insidious plan of action that kept her moving and focused, to hone her rage into a weapon she could wield.

Bastian scratched at a long thin scar, which ran down the side of his face from his temple to the corner of his mouth. "Plenty of folk seek vengeance, milady, but few seek me special t'deliver on it."

"My daughter is dead. I wish to see the man who did it suffer."

"So it's a blood revenge, then." His face impassive, Bastian twined his fingers together and touched them to his mouth as a gesture of prayer. "How would you like it done, a daughter or sister, a wife or mother?"

"Nothing so quick."

Jade knew better than most how losing family inflicted a deep and sharp pain. She wanted that, but not yet. First she wanted the Tanasens to feel fear licking at their heels, to wonder why and for what reason, frantic with the need to know why their lives were falling apart and all the while never suspecting that it had little to do with their petty politics.

Death was too quick for her liking. She wanted to be there, to see it happen and pretend that their fear would be a penance for her loss, knowing all the while that nothing would fill the void of her malice. But if it prolonged their suffering as she suffered, all the better.

"His family has an estate in Falden with a new house to demonstrate their nobility."

"Right. Burn the house then t'start?"

"No. The house you will keep standing. Not a piece of wood nor block of stone is to be harmed. The heart of that place is the orchards and fields. Burn them."

The shadow of a smile touched her lips. "Burn every green and growing thing."

BLOOD, BLUE AS INK

P raelor Thurst needed help to lift his full flask. It was finally ready. Surrounded by the best healers in the palace, he knew there was nothing they could do except fetch and carry and hold up this wasted body during its last moments.

It was a hard choice to make, sending the Seeker on her way. Without Lady Jade, if something should go wrong, he would be as helpless as a newborn babe. He would die, and with no options left.

All the magic in the world would not keep this body from falling apart. The flask touched dry, cracked lips. It was ink, of a sort.

The blue radiance of pure magic drawn from him was muddied now, according to her magical sight. Dozens of colors. Magic, but extracted and drawn from those too weak to use it.

He swallowed. The mixture burned, and it sank like glue down the throat in a thick slurry. Desperation created a certain lack of refinement, after all. That's what he taught his whole life.

Thurst had always thought of himself as a meticulous craftsman. Experimenting, calculating, changing, and enriching his work until he achieved a pleasing result. Now there was a certain irony to swallowing a clumsy medicine made by his own hand. It tasted awful. Not long, now.

It was time.

With a shaking hand, he used a heavy golden quill to scratch out a name, the person which his every calculation revealed as a pathway to freedom and a new start. Ink poured from him across the page. The name sank deeper into the scroll until it pulled and dragged his awareness along with it.

Darkness. Voices calling out in shock and fear. So many voices.

Memories bled through the parchment. Faces flashed and fled quick as rain until he heard only one. With its final gasp, breath left the shriveled body.

A golden quill dropped and rolled onto the bed. A heavy flask tumbled to the ground. Not one drop of ink spilled from either.

There was nothing left to save.

LUTHER POINTED to a stack of stones piled by the road. The tugging sensation he felt when magic called to him had brought them to a crossroad. It must be close, he thought, for the pulling was so strong that it made his ears and nose itch.

Why was it that magic never felt good when he found it? He cleared his throat. Perhaps he was coming down with a cold, he thought with an urge to laugh. What emerged was a shriek of pain. Something had stabbed him in the back.

"This is the edge of the Borderlands," yelled Scythia, pushing the blunted point above her axe into his shoulder with such force that he lost his balance and tumbled from his horse, flailing wildly to avoid knocking into the stone marker.

"You asked me to bring you proof," he whimpered, untangling his limbs and rolling away from the dancing hooves of his horse.

"We could easily be picked up by an Imperial troop and slaughtered this far south. Is that the kind of proof you wanted to give us? An ambush? Who sent you!"

The pulling sensation stopped entirely. It was so sudden that Luther gasped. Nothing? No magic.

He looked around in shock. Where had it gone? He was such a failure that even a thread of magic was easy to lose. If it was even there to begin with, and not just a vain hope of escape.

They all turned at the sound of galloping hooves. There was a horse approaching from the southern road. Not just any horse, Luther realized, squinting. An Imperial white. The horse was one of the fastest in the Imperium and ridden by messengers with urgent business on behalf of the Empress.

Luther reached out a hand to wave, but found he had no voice to call out. Scythia walked by him and waved her axe to warn them away. They kept coming.

The rider was a woman, and she called out, winded. "Leave now, if you value your lives!"

Scythia only laughed. "This is your ambush?"

Luther's hand grabbed Scythia's axe and wrenched it from her grasp before he knew what he was doing. He wanted to drop it, to cry out, but he could do nothing. His body refused to follow any of his thoughts no matter how hard he tried to move again or speak.

"Luther?" said Bregt.

It was like a dream, seeing images, people, sensations, all slowing down. Luther floated above it all, watching his body as it drove Scythia's axe into her head. Luther screamed, but no one heard him.

THE PRAELOR TOOK A DEEP BREATH. There was pain in this body, in its chest, but that would pass. The flame of youth burned so brightly that he hardly noticed anything except sheer pleasure at being alive again.

With a boot, he rolled over the lifeless body of the Dunmiri woman. These were a strong people. They would make excellent slaves.

A white horse reared and kicked the man charging forward before he could finish drawing his sword, sending him to the ground in a lifeless heap. When they saw both their leaders defeated, the other Dunmiri warriors fled from the man with cries, *"Boderi!"*

Dismounting, Lady Jade ran to his side. Her eyes searched his face. With a soft cry, she fell to her knees and bowed her head. "My Lord Praelor."

"You traveled well, I hope," he said, helping her back to her feet.

"How do you feel, are you in need of a healer?" she asked, reaching for a pack on the horse.

She turned back to look at him, eyes alight with wonder.

He wound his fingers around a lock of her loosened hair. "Truly, I have never felt so alive. You have proven your loyalty to me, Jade."

Her eyes fell. "I am your servant, Praelor."

"And for your reward, you will stay by my side and share in my power as a beacon of Imperial power, returned in all *His* glory."

She took his hand and kissed it. "Blessed Be. What shall I call you, Praelor?"

"Praelor Ferris, for now. It makes the transition easier to remember whose body I have claimed. There is much we need to discuss, but until then…" He walked over to examine the fallen man. He knew him once. Bregt. Yes, that was his name. "Can you revive him?"

She held a hand in front of the man's mouth, felt his chest and nodded. Pulling open a bag, she took out a dark lump and made the Dunmiri swallow it.

The Praelor could smell the sweat and fear on Bregt as he stirred. He grabbed him by his fleece tunic to pull him close, enjoying the look of dismay from the younger man. No, not younger. Not any longer.

Bregt struggled to free himself. "Your eyes. Luther, what are you?"

The Praelor gripped Bregt by the back of the neck and felt muscle and bone, the man's breath hot on his face. Such a frail creature. So easily broken.

"You wanted proof, Bregt? There is none better than I," he said, enjoying the essence of new magic and strength flowing through his veins in ecstasy. "Luther was my servant. Bound to me in blood and at my whim, he is gone. Nothing."

"That is not possible."

He let Bregt fall to the ground. Then he stood with ease. He could walk again, could run on a whim, could fight a dozen men with this new strength he possessed. But all that paled when he stopped to breathe, filling his lungs completely and without any pain.

He laughed. The sweet freedom of breathing. To not fight for every last word; words which came so easily that they poured from him in a voice that was strange and unfamiliar to hear.

"I should be angry with Luther for trying to warn you. Foolish boy, to think that he could dare defy me. Leave the Imperium? Impossible. His punishment will be enduring, that I can promise."

Bregt leaned forward and groaned. "Kill me, or tell me what you want so I might die in peace."

"Luther quite liked you, you know. Not that you would have returned his feelings, wretched creature that he was. I will allow you to live, for I need you to bring a message from me to this council of yours."

"A message?"

"Yes. Tell them what you have seen this day. The Dunmiri will bow to us, or the Imperium will unleash a weapon called magic that none can withstand upon your people."

He took a long, deep breath. "The *boderi* are real. Reborn. And they will show no mercy."

ALSO BY JORDAN R. MURRAY

The Emperor's Horn

ABOUT THE AUTHOR

Jordan R. Murray is often found gazing into the distance with a mug of tea in her hands. She spends as much time as she can outdoors, hears music where none is playing, and loves the taste of salt on the wind.

Her inquisitive mind led her to devour books of fantasy and science fiction as soon as she learned to read. Now she crafts her own worlds to explore. Murray and her husband live in Massachusetts with a dog and cat who haven't tried to kill one another… lately

Visit JordanRMurray.com

www.ingramcontent.com/pod-product-compliance
Lightning Source LLC
Chambersburg PA
CBHW021216250626
47155CB00008B/2827